IN THREE DAYS

IN THREE DAYS

ROGER COLLEY

IN THREE DAYS

iUniverse books may be ordered through booksellers or by contacting:

iUniverse
1663 Liberty Drive
Bloomington, IN 47403
www.iuniverse.com
1-800-Authors (1-800-288-4677)

This is a work of fiction. All of the characters, names, incidents,
organizations, and dialogue in this novel are either the products
of the author's imagination or are used fictitiously.

Because of the dynamic nature of the Internet, any web addresses or
links contained in this book may have changed since publication and
may no longer be valid. The views expressed in this work are solely those
of the author and do not necessarily reflect the views of the publisher,
and the publisher hereby disclaims any responsibility for them.

Any people depicted in stock imagery provided by Thinkstock are
models, and such images are being used for illustrative purposes only.
Certain stock imagery © Thinkstock.

ISBN: 978-1-4917-5367-5 (sc)
ISBN: 978-1-4917-5368-2 (e)

Library of Congress Control Number: 2014920382

Print information available on the last page.

iUniverse rev. date: 02/11/2015

DOWNTOWN DENVER

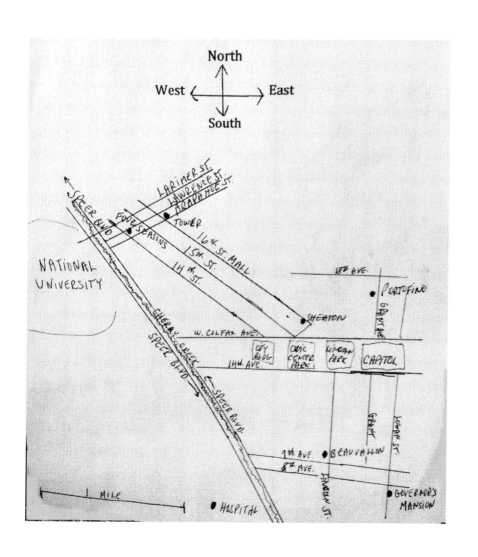

NATIONAL UNIVERSITY

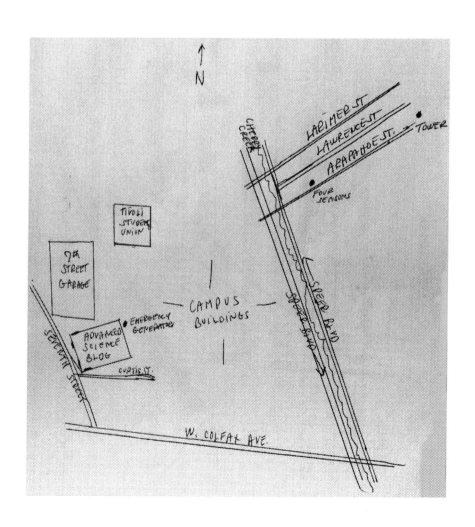

FACTS

E lectromagnetic pulse bombs [EMP's] have been developed and tested by the United States and Russian militaries, as far back as the 1960's. It is common knowledge the United States military today, unfortunately, still has fear of the nation's **defenselessness** against such a bomb being exploded high over the center of the country knocking out both the United States electrical grid and our satellite communications. A potential major catastrophe for America..

The Ebola virus is real, currently primarily confined to Africa, killing on average 70% of those infected, sometimes as high as 90%. While horrific within certain African nations, it has not spread to worldwide pandemic proportions due to its current inability to spread within human populations outside of direct contact with bodily fluids of those infected. The virus has not mutated so that it can spread airborne, like a cold virus or influenza—yet! The human body does not satisfactorily produce antibodies against it as it does to destroy other viral infections. There are currently no approved vaccines or anti-viral treatments to combat it. The potential for a serious outbreak in America is of major concern to the public and the government is working diligently in the early stages to develop anti-viral drugs and vaccines against the Ebola virus threat.

Streets, places and structures named in Downtown Denver are real, other than the Advanced Science Building at the "National University".

PROLOGUE

What is this? It's so black, covering the entire sky. It can't be a fire. It looks like … but it's not a thunderstorm—no rain, no thunder, no lightning. Looks more like a dark fog rolling in, but these ashes? I feel like I'm being smothered in a blanket.

I held my one-year old son Alex in my arms, the child staring blankly at the darkening sky now showering down some mysterious black dust upon us. I could sense the early morning sun to my rear disappearing. I tightened my hold on my young son. I moved back inside off the balcony of our 22nd floor apartment at the former Four Seasons Hotel in downtown Denver. This was our temporary home at the corner of 14th Street and Lawrence Street with its unobstructed view to the southwest, right over the sprawling campus of the National University, the former home of the University of Colorado Denver. I shut the sliding glass door. I felt my heart thumping.

This can't be. Woke up this morning somehow distraught that this was September 11th. September 11, 2021 … 9/11, 9/11, always on my mind. But it's twenty years later—can't be. Must be an explanation. But no odor—can't be a fire from the western foothills or an industrial fire—too uniform across the entire sky. It's not smoke. Smoke would be billowing. Too dark for fog. Fog is gray. It's black like an approaching thunderstorm, but no rain or thunder and lightning. And this black dust coming down … I have to figure this out.

I called to my wife, who was still testing lights, the radio, the TV, to see if the power had come back on. "Rose, Rose ... hurry—wash this black stuff off Alex's face, and out of my hair." I was thinking the worst, like *evil* that's always waiting around the corner.

My thoughts were racing a mile a minute. Rose and I have been through so much the last ten years. My invention at college—just bench top but neat. A little boiler desalinating ocean water using wind and solar power. I hadn't believed I could massively scale it up and push all that water to Colorado from Los Angeles.

Yeah, the abrupt warming threw our country into turmoil. I know the idea to move everyone to Colorado had been brilliant, but the artificial society here couldn't last long. No freedom. A failed utopia. Too many human frailties. I knew it all had to soon fall apart politically and socially. Thank goodness the climate shifted back. Rose was fantastic with her perseverance in discovering what was happening.... Now, just when things were getting good again and most citizens have moved back to their original homes, we get this new mystery. The poor president—still paralyzed by his inability to take action. If it weren't for VP Ali taking charge, we'd still be in a real mess politically and socially.

What do I do? The university labs. Maybe ... right. I should make a dash with Rose and Alex over there and try to figure this thing out. I don't like this.

DAY ONE
ASSASSINS

CHAPTER 1

Amagan, his name meaning 'gift' in Afghan, had been waiting patiently inside the unlocked gate in front of the mansion since before dawn. He had made sure he was out of view, discreetly placing himself behind some full-grown shrubbery near the entrance to the building. It was chilly but not cold in the mile-high morning air. In September, Denver enjoys an average morning low of 48°and a very comfortable average afternoon high of 77°, and it was quite serene and comfortable at the start of this morning, September 11, 2021. On a clear day like this one, it is an idyllic setting with the high golden-domed state Capitol framed against the western 14,000 foot Rocky Mountain peaks, the foothills turning golden in the Aspen trees' autumn beauty.

I'm here—this is it, he murmured to himself, his young face locked solid with a look of full determination.

Crouching behind the shrubbery only 30 feet from the front door, he looked intently at his wristwatch as the time approached 8 o'clock. He heard the boom far away and felt the sudden shock under his feet. He waited just a few more minutes as he looked to the west to sight the black dust rolling in. He felt the excitement. It seemed to him like an ominous dark fog about to snuff everything out in its way. *It's coming in—it's time.* He stood up and rapidly approached the front door—his trustworthy AK-47 rifle held securely behind his back and under his unbuttoned coat. It was long and drab, but it served its purpose well. He knew there was no sentry on duty before visiting hours so he simply rang the doorbell. With the once-popular president having been virtually ignored politically the last three years, he hoped a staff member would casually just open the door.

"Yes. Can I help you?" The elderly, informally dressed housekeeper asked politely.

"Yes you can," as a fully-confident Amagan hurriedly walked in past the poor man, pushed the door closed, then quickly swung the butt of his assault weapon around, striking the helpless man as hard as he could on the side of his head. He fell quickly to the floor. Amagan struck another blow to the head of the defenseless man now sprawled out cold, or probably dead, on the hardwood floor.

Officially known as the state of Colorado's 'Governor's Residence at the Boettcher Mansion', the beautiful Georgian architecturally-designed building occupied a half a square block at the corner of Logan Street and East 8th Avenue. Built on a one-acre plot in 1908, the ornate red brick mansion was gifted to the state of Colorado in 1959 by the estate of Claude Boettcher, a wealthy financier of some prominence earlier in the 20th century. It then became the official residence site for Colorado governors, nicely situated six short blocks south of the Capitol.

The Colorado governor elected back in 2010 was still waiting for the President of the United States, one Paul Jennings, as well as the entire United States Congress, to move back to Washington before reoccupying the mansion. President Jennings had been occupying the mansion since the year 2014 when the abrupt climate crisis had enveloped America, and he, by his Declaration of National Emergency, ordered everyone in the ravaged nation to move to much less climate-affected eastern Colorado.

President Jennings' home staff was simply comprised of the six persons who resided there with him—one cook, one housekeeper, two administrative assistants, and two secret service agents. The president's wife had died many years earlier from a rapidly metastasizing ovarian cancer. The six staff slept in three bedrooms towards the rear of the second floor while the president enjoyed a large bedroom suite on the same floor, the front of the home. In addition to the comfortably ornate living, dining and kitchen areas on the first floor, the rear of the first floor offered spacious office areas. The latter, little used.

Ever since the nation's dramatic climate reversal in 2018, combined with the scandal surrounding the president's chief of staff and by the fall of the two's benevolent but autocratic system of government, the once-beloved president had been paralyzed in his decision-making. The workings of the executive branch were now clearly in the hands of his trusted and competent vice president, Alexis Graham, quartered four short blocks away. Only the president, vice-president, Congress, and the Supreme Court remained in Denver while the nation's citizens were getting resettled back into their original homes.

Amagan knew the layout of the house perfectly. He had been there a week before as a visitor posing as a tourist on an historic house tour. It was now getting darker inside the mansion as all electric power was now cut off. With a quick glance through the large living room windows, Amagan noticed the sky outside was turning increasingly dark, as planned. He had to move swiftly. He ignored whether another staff member might be in the kitchen and sprinted hurriedly up the steps towards the rear. Acting before it was too dark to see, he burst into each of the back three bedrooms. The first two were empty— staff! *Must be in the kitchen, unarmed.* The third and last quartered the two security agents. They must be quite bored, he thought to himself—protecting an unengaged president, and he knew they would not be early risers, especially on a Saturday.

His heartbeat suddenly began to race, even faster than when he was running up the steps. He could feel it beating hard against his chest. His fingers were sweating as he re-gripped his weapon more securely in both hands. His mind flashed: *this is what I trained for—go!* One agent was sitting on the side of his bed putting his shoes on. The other could barely be seen through an open door, standing in the bathroom. Amagan lifted and aimed his powerful rifle at the agent on the edge of the bed and without pause pulled the trigger—five times in rapid succession. The thuds and blood splashes sent the agent flying sideways towards the floor, his shoe flying in the air. The other agent turned around to face the open bathroom door, a look of complete shock on his face. No weapon within reach. He was doomed. Four more shots quickly found their mark.

Amagan hustled down the hall towards the president's quarters. The president had heard the strange pounding noise of rapid gunfire, but could not imagine what it was. He sat up and turned to the side of his bed, his feet now on the floor. He had just arisen from a deep ten-hour sleep in his king-sized bed, comfortable in his loose-fitting white pajamas—until a moment ago. As his heard his bedroom door open, he turned and looked blankly at the intruder, Amagan, who was holding the deadly rifle behind his back. Despite his heavy accent, the assassin first wanted to deliver a clear message before putting the president's life to an end. He moved in closer. The president sat frozen, mouth and eyes wide open with a look of complete surprise.

"At last, I confront you face-to-face…. Mr. President of the mighty United States, you and your nation are doomed. It is the end of America…. While you have isolated yourselves these last ten years, your centuries of atrocities are now at an end…. You will all soon die of our powerful weapon now creeping into all your homes… But to be sure, it is my mission—you are the first to go. The world will now have peace. No more violence…. Your last words Mr. President? Speak … you … of the evil, powerful United States of America."

The president sat on the edge of his bed, still speechless, confused. *What in the world is this about? Who is this? What is he talking about?* But then in the very faint light from his large bedroom windows, he saw this strange man up close—dark skin, black beard, long dark hair, shabby clothes—swing the rifle from behind his back and point it directly at him. "What? What! " he cried. For what must have seemed a very, very brief moment, a millisecond, he felt a warm blow to his chest, a sharp pain, and then … nothing, his white pajamas rapidly turning red.

IN THREE DAYS

His mission was accomplished. The President of the United States was dead. Amagan walked slowly down the hall to the steps, then calmly down. He felt cooler and weaker now, the adrenaline wearing off. He felt a sense of pride—he did his job perfectly, as instructed. *I am the "gift"* he reminded himself. He continued right towards and out the front door, the fallen housekeeper still sprawled out motionless on the floor—too bad for him he thought. All was quiet. He suspected the remaining staff members were hiding in the near dark after hearing the gunshots above. No matter. They will all soon die from the miraculous virus now spreading out in the black dust. But no problem for him—he had the vaccine. He could walk boldly right into the dark fog rapidly enveloping the outside air, the black dust.

He was immune, or so he thought.

CHAPTER 2

About a mile away to the northwest, still in downtown Denver, waited a second assassin. He knew he was exactly where he should be—in the right place at the right time—crouched behind a concrete pillar, not more than 30 feet to the blue Chevy Volt parked next to the door leading to the apartment floors above. The parking garage of the former Four Seasons Hotel overlooking the National University in Denver was now nearly completely dark, save for a battery-powered emergency floodlight dimly glaring off the long line of parked electric cars, each with a recharging line leading from its plug-in slot to the nearby 240 volt power station. The AK-47, no longer concealed, was held nervously but firmly in his hands. Babur's mission was clear—kill Michael Reynolds.

In the top floor apartment, the television set had gone blank and quiet, the kitchen light suddenly off, Michael's satellite mobile phone screen showing no connection. Rose looked over to their son—not at his young age, no, not one year old Alex upstairs in their top floor apartment, comfortably staring at his mother from his high chair, could ever begin to fathom the chaos now beginning to unfold around him and his parents. "You're right, Michael. Something's strange. It's not natural," Rose murmured quietly. "When you brought him from the balcony there was a fine black dust on the two of you. No odor—no smear. Not like fine ashes from a fire. Forest fire ash would be fine and gray. With this black dust it would seem to be some kind of an industrial fire, but it's not billowing out there—it's too even, too spread out—it's everywhere…. Not a thunderstorm—no thunder, lightning or rain. It can't be fog either—it's not wet, and fog is gray not black and wouldn't carry a dusting like this … and what would knock out our power too?

"Same thing I've been thinking," Michael affirmed quietly.

Trying to pry the two of them into a more optimistic mode, Rose smiled and spoke up briskly. "You want to get to the labs, don't you? Okay—he's clean now. I'm ready. Let's go. I'm taking the dampened towels with this dust on them."

"You carry Alex. I have the flashlight. If the elevator is not working, we'll go down the back steps to the car. I'm sure it took the overnight charge," Michael nodded glumly. "It's incredibly dark outside, but this just can't last. Let's get to the university."

"We can walk it in ten minutes if—

"No, no," Michael interjected forcefully. "I don't want any more contact with this stuff…whatever it is."

Michael Reynolds, chemical engineer, was never one to take his surroundings lightly, always probing, curious, concerned. And more alarming—this was September 11th.

—∿∿∿—

Babur's hunch came true. The intelligent, inquisitive Michael Reynolds would want to know immediately what this strange black dust was as soon as he detected it. He would know it was not from a fire. He would want to get to the nearby National University's famed biochemistry and microbiology labs, in the new Advanced Science Building—just a few blocks to the southwest. There they can even duplicate what the sophisticated Atlanta-based Centers for Disease Control, the CDC, do in investigating biochemical and microbiological pathogens. It would not take long to identify the composition of this black dust, even if it was a deadly virus combined with its chemical dispersing agent.

Babur thought it could perhaps be an hour before Michael would appear in the garage after the 8 a.m. Denver time E-bomb explosion shut down both the electrical ground grid and the space communications of America. It could even be two or three hours from now at the outside, but all of a sudden, the door from the stairwell to the parking lot was swinging open, and there he was—Michael Reynolds. The time had come. The assault rifle was ready. Even better—there next to him was Rose Haines, the target for the only female assassin assigned to the mission, Fila, who had decided to station herself in the Four Seasons lobby lying in wait for Rose.

All six in the assassin task force had been vaccinated shortly before their arrival to America. They knew there were no treatments and no cure for this strain of virus, but they were told there was a preventative vaccine and that they were safely inoculated. Little did they know it was all a ruse—there was no vaccine, no antidote, for this more virulent, laboratory-modified version of the deadly Ebola virus. They had been deceived into thinking the fatal virus attached to the fine chemical dispersant, the black dust, would be of no harm to them. Their sponsors had failed in that quest to discover a vaccine. In just two days, the very young, the very old, and the immune impaired in America faced sure death, and in just three days this highly contagious pathogen would begin to kill all remaining Americans. Even so, the brain trust in Dire, the co-conspirators Aazim and Antoine, assigned, trained, and dispensed the six assassins to the United States in order that the top power structure of America—the president, the vice president, the speaker of the house, and the president of the highly intellectually-endowed National University along with the brilliant, innovative Michael Reynolds and his spouse, the resourceful, engineer/scientist Rose Haines, would be immediately taken out. Even if it meant losing six of their own. Six against six—fast.

The strategy: give America no chance for a quick military counterpunch. Give America no opportunity to discover an anti-viral in time. The all-out Master Plan seemed none other than brilliant.

CHAPTER 3

In the sophisticated control room located in their reinforced bunker on the tiny island of Dire, two hundred miles off the coast of India, a dazed Antoine stared blankly at the computer screens. Finally in a subdued tone, the Frenchman uttered, almost incoherently: "It's done. It worked. We're getting no communications. None. From nowhere where our people are located around the world. The EMP's have done their job." He sat frozen, staring blankly down at the barren floor.

To the contrary, his partner Aazim, pacing excitedly around and around in circles and smiling, burst out: "Com'on my dear friend! No remorse! This is our first at rejoicing. Receiving no radio communications from all our sources around the world means the major powers of the world will not be able to spread any word by satellite communications ... nor cable, Internet, cell phone. All electrical ground equipment will be damaged beyond immediate repair...." Antoine looked up, his face unable to hide his bewilderment. Aazim continued on, as his little circles became even more rapid. "Our best estimate is that the atmospheric distortions caused by the electromagnetic pulses will disrupt satellite radio communications for at least three days before restoration to a norm. And much longer if the satellites themselves are physically damaged. Now, Antoine, we just wait to learn how our improved anthrax weapons worked around the world … and our super-deadly Ebola virus in the U.S." The tone of his voice was one of glee. "Our goals, our objectives, our years of detailed planning, my dear friend, will all be achieved. We are superhuman!"

Both men, the 45 year old Frenchman and the 58 year old Iranian, spoke nearly perfect English, and that's how they conversed during their thirteen years of friendship. Antoine's voice perked up after listening and looking at Aazim in his frenzy: "Right. You know it used to be just a joke, my friend—that the only way to end violence in the world once and for all … is to kill everybody."

The two turned and looked at each other, in all seriousness now, right into each other's eyes, staring in a sudden stony silence. That statement was one of an uncomfortable wisdom … or madness…. No one could ever do that deed … until now.

CHAPTER 4

The phone line was buzzing loud and non-stop in the small security room down the hall. Vice President Alexis Graham, at breakfast alone in her morning workout clothes, gulped her last sip of coffee, now cold, and moved swiftly. *It's only eight thirty. Our daily telephonic briefings are at nine, so what's the rush?*

"Ali … General Ralston at the Pentagon. You've noticed? Your electricity is out?"

Ali hesitated. She had used no lights or appliances since making her coffee nearly an hour before. She did notice how dark it was getting outside her condo windows and just assumed it must be storm clouds. Holding the phone to her ear, she did notice now that the lights inside her windowless security room were coming from a battery operated backup system. She tried to click on the reading light on her desk, but with no response. Her computer screen, always left on screen saver, was black.

"Ali. Are you there?"

"Yes, general… Yes. I just clicked on my desk lights and tried my computer, but they don't come on. The Denver grid must be—"

"Only the beginning Ali. We have checked nationwide with all our bases on our secure lines. The United States electrical grid is completely shut down—not at just your temporary capital in Denver.

13

All radio communications are dead also. Our first analysis is that a huge electromagnetic pulse explosion, what we call an EMP, somewhere over the middle of the U.S. has upset the entire radio field in our atmosphere. The military has been worried about this for years. Fortunately our entire secured military fiber optic system is working. It is all underground. The energy input into the system of light transmission and our receivers are shielded from shock and solar battery operated. It is our only method of communication now… and you are the only civilian, as our acting commander-in-chief, tied into the system—"

"General, general," Ali interjected cautiously, nervously. "But how, who—"

"Madam vice president. I believe we are at war. We understand the initial 'how'. A rocket launch could send a nuclear device high above us, a couple hundred miles or more, and detonate it. When exploded it sets off a strong pulse of gamma rays which knock electrons off the atmosphere's nitrogen and oxygen molecules…. Sorry, that's getting technical, but that effect then spreads out and changes the earth's electromagnetic field—the basis of all radio, cell, and satellite communications. It could take days for it to be naturally restored to its normal state and get our communications back, that is if our satellites are not physically damaged … but the strong voltage shock it causes through the ground grid completely destroys fixed semiconductors, periphery equipment at transformer stations, even explode some of the old transformers that regulate voltage transmission, burn out connectors…. Ma'am, it's catastrophic!

"We don't know 'who', Ali, but this is an attack on America. I don't know what's next. You and General Armstrong at the Capitol have the only secure fiber optic systems in Denver. No one is answering there. Maybe they don't get in early on a Saturday…. We must get to the president. You must protect him and yourself. I will call back every hour on the hour with updates of what we learn. Have your staff assist. Your battery-operated devices will work until the need for recharging. I don't know if the solar powered rechargers will work or not. Get to the president, and take your security personnel."

Ali sat listening to the general in a state of astonishment. Normally a very strong woman physically, her hand and arm holding the phone suddenly felt weak, her soft answer almost automatic. It seemed in her mind that she could not believe what she was hearing. "Yes general. Yes, I'll contact the president."

Vice president Alexis Graham, the most important person in America ever since the decision-paralyzed president formally delegated his executive powers to her, was living in a spacious top floor penthouse at the luxurious Beauvallon, on Lincoln Street between 9th and 10th Avenues, four blocks south of the Capitol and four short blocks northwest of the Governor's Mansion. The nearby mansion was where the president had been living the last five years during the national climate crisis. She attempted to telephone him on the wired cable line as well as through her cell phone and her satellite phone. The general was right—no response on any of the three lines.

She would have to get dressed rapidly and walk there with Tom, her only secret service protection. How could she think that lurking outside the front entrance door of the sixteen-floor building with his fully loaded AK-47 was the agile Farzam—'worthy' in Afghan?

Yes, he was physically worthy but was troubled in his thinking clearly. In his wait to strike against the vice president, Farzam could not make up his mind whether he should walk up the emergency-lit sixteen floor stairwell, wait in the parking garage below, hide in the ground level lobby with its emergency spotlights now on, or stay outside with his weapon hidden in his trench coat. He had been told by his superiors on Dire where the vice president resides, but the details of his assassination plot were left to him.

Which way would she go? Or go at all?

The poorly educated Farzam was certainly fully and enthusiastically dedicated to his mission—he had proven that to Antoine and Aazim during his selection process—but on his own he was inflexible, mentally undisciplined. He felt nervous, tense, and conspicuous pacing the sidewalk outside with his long black hair, long beard, and long overcoat concealing his AK-47.

What to do?

CHAPTER 5

Saturday mornings were a welcome respite for Jeffrey Wilson, the 62 year- old Congressman from Houston, Texas. He had served in the House of Representatives for 20 years before being elected by House Republicans in 2010 to be its speaker, a position constitutionally named the third in-line to become the nation's chief executive in the event of the deaths or incapacities of the president and the vice president. He awakened slowly that morning of September 11th as he sensed his wife pushing herself out of bed. He glanced at his bedside digital clock. The time was 7:58. He closed his eyes for what he thought was another few minutes, felt a slight inconsequential tremor, opened them again, and glanced over at the clock. It was black—no illuminating digits. His wife reentered the bedroom. "Jeff, the bathroom lights are not working."

"Yeah. The clock went off.... Hmm, what now?" he sighed.

Back in 2012 when Congress approved the president's Declaration of National Emergency, the powers of Congress were temporarily suspended, but conditioned upon each congressperson retaining his or her seat and status when the "emergency" status ended. Of course there was no end to the temporary Declaration until the climate reversal of 2018, at which time the functions of the Supreme Court and the Congress resumed. During the Denver years between the great American population movement to Eastern Colorado, completed by early 2016, and the 2018 climate reversal, congressional members lived a life of luxury. No work—plenty of idle fraternization. They and their families occupied the best suites in the finest downtown Denver hotels—the Ritz Carlton, the Westin, the Four Seasons, the Marriott, the Hyatt Regency, the Grand Hyatt, the Warwick, the Sheraton, the Hotel Teatro—all short distances to the stately grounds and lush parks leading to the grand state Capitol, the temporary home of the again-functioning U.S. Congress. They had also spread themselves among the best penthouse suites in the finest downtown apartment buildings. They were all still there. Vice President Graham had declared that the federal government should stay in Denver until all Americans could be settled back into their original homes.

For Jeffrey, his wife, and key staff, life was good occupying the stately George Schleier Mansion, a reddish-colored sandstone built in the late 1880's of German design. It was located at the corner of Grant Street and 17th Avenue, only two blocks north of the state capitol building where the Congress had reconvened in late 2018.

"Try the kitchen, dear," Jeffrey murmured.

Moments later, she returned, solemnly replying: "I did. Everything is off, even the house phone … so I tried my cell phone. Nothing … and no Internet connection either."

"Oh, man!" Jeffrey blurted out impatiently. He reached out to his night table and turned on his satellite phone—no response there either. "Let me get dressed. I'll go outside and see what's going on. It's getting darker in here. Check on the rest of the house and the staff. Odd that until now all our electrical and communication systems in Denver have always been flawless."

Seconds later, her voice quivering, she added: "I checked. It's the whole house, Jeffrey. And everyone's mobile phones too. Jonathan said he heard and felt a little rumble a couple of minutes ago. Maybe an earthquake and power outage."

As were the other five elsewhere, Jeffrey Wilson was unaware that he was in line under a Master Plan to receive an assassin's bullets early that morning, he from the AK-47 of Jaweed, meaning 'eternal' in Afghan. Unlike the others, Jaweed, the youngest of the task force, was by far an overly ambitious accomplice. Assigned only to kill the speaker of the house in order to prevent him from taking charge of the American military in case both Armagan and Farzam were immediately successful in their assassinations of the president and vice president, Jaweed had instead decided just before dawn to wait until he could enter the Capitol, where Wilson would surely go in short order. There he would direct his AK-47 rounds not only towards the speaker but also towards all the members of Congress who might have rushed to the Capitol to call an emergency session and maybe even a declaration of war.

Jaweed never stopped to think how Congress could possibly know whom to declare war against unless the communications disruption had failed and they had discovered the identity of their adversary. The Master Plan wanted the speaker taken out in the event communications were not destroyed as planned. But it was obvious from the first moment that both electric power and satellite communications were indeed cut. He only had to look at storefronts and his satellite mobile phone to know that. This was all a bit confusing to Jaweed, but he was going to take as many out as he could no matter what.

Lack of discipline among the disciplined. Jaweed—strong, ambitious, overreaching, perhaps a bit overzealous. It would have been very simple to wait for Speaker of the House Jeffrey Wilson to walk out of his stately home and become an easy target, as he did at 8:20 a.m.

But Jaweed was already several blocks away, approaching the Capitol.

CHAPTER 6

As a fourteen year old growing up in a small village outside the city of Kandahar, named the same for a province in the southern part of the Islamic Republic of Afghanistan, Babur suddenly learned that his maturing life was to become one of constant struggle and conflict. No longer the fun and games of childhood. That year was 2008. The Americans had helped finance the *mujahideen* forces in the 1980's to drive the Russian occupiers out of the country, but the ensuing vacuum allowed the extremist Taliban faction to take control of the national government in the 1990's, their capital established in Kandahar. After the 9/11 attack on America in 2001, United States forces intervened directly into Afghanistan with their military, proceeded to set back the Taliban, and helped establish a new republic centered in the northeastern capital city of Kabul. All that history meant nothing to Babur. What young Afghan boys in early 2008 would care about Alexander the Great—the one who had laid out the city of Kandahar almost 2500 years ago, or that the area was a famous trade center between the Middle East and Asia for centuries, or the recent Taliban re-insurgency, or the occasional central government troops or Americans walking through his village. No, no concern, not until the summer of that fateful year 2008 when his father was attending a meeting at the home of his village's tribal leader.

Babur did not really know or care what his father's or the village tribal leader's politics were until the details of the explosion were revealed to him by his mother and when he saw the terrible damage with his own eyes. The factional loyalties of the village leaders, which he learned included his father, were torn among the still powerful Taliban in Kandahar, the provincial government appointed by the central government in Kabul, the Americans trying to train central government troops as well as themselves to fight the Taliban, and the opposing economics of growing crops for the worldwide drug trade versus cultivating less profitable conventional crops. He learned life in his village was all a series of seesaws, of constant conflicts.

As a result of the explosion, Babur learned for the first time about the rise of the Islamic fundamentalist political movement, the Taliban, dedicated to establishing theological sharia law, founded and taught in religious schools in Pakistan. He learned of the invasion of the Russians and their defeat and withdrawal in 1992, the fighting of the Taliban and their victory against Afghan opposition forces by 1995, the influx of the extremist al-Qaeda faction, the invasion by the Americans in 2003 to drive out al-Qaeda and to fight the Taliban, and now the American frustration with the difficulty of establishing democracy for the Afghan nation.

The bomb killed everyone in the home on that evening. No one ever knew or at least disclosed which faction was responsible. Babur surveyed the ruins, viewed the mangled bodies and stared at his father's lifeless, charred face. He was the oldest of four children, and his mother was burdened with an ever–worsening crippling disease— probably undiagnosed multiple sclerosis. With no family income or savings, Babur had no choice but to work, many times up to fourteen hours a day in any odd job he could find in the village and fields, listening and learning about his country in turmoil. It became an easy decision for him after accidently overhearing a visitor to the village quietly speak about an island near India, a place that was becoming a haven for peace-minded young people to emigrate.

Once there in Dire, he acclimated very easily to the peaceful aura of life on the tranquil island. He was feeling finally true to the meaning of his name in English—"happiness". But his outstanding mental and physical prowess soon caught the awareness and attention of the island's two very astute leaders. Babur showed a strong desire to impress and to succeed at whatever the task. It was not long before the Master Plan was revealed to him in strict secrecy, and at first it seemed repulsive. Slowly, in time, it finally began to make sense. Sure, escape and live a life of tranquility on an isolated small island, or conversely rise to a more noble purpose for the sake of all of mankind—rid the world of mass weapons and violence, once and for all. After all, to have meaning, one's life should have a purpose. The choice became obvious. By 2020, Babur found himself comfortably among a tight knit group of very special people, including other Afghans like Fila, Jaweed, Amagan, Asa, and Farzam. And of course he befell the charm and persuasion of his leaders, the suave Frenchman Antoine and the irrepressible Iranian Aazim.

His metamorphosis was complete—by September 2021, Babur would kill to prevent further killing.

CHAPTER 7

For a brief moment, Babur couldn't believe his good fortune. *Yes, it's them for sure. Already. Both of them. Don't pause. Shoot.* Black pants and black sweatshirt under his long olive coat, his dark whiskers half-shaven, the emergency floodlight eerily reflecting off both his long black hair and the metal barrel of the AK-47—the latter now pointing directly at Michael—Babur knew he could not miss his target. Michael, seeing him now face-to-face only 15 feet apart, instinctively lurched back with startled eyes wide open, raising his hands in front of Rose and his child to protect them. Determined as never before in his deadly mission, Babur pulled the trigger of his rifle … again and again. His face snarled as the gun would not fire. *It's jammed!* Lowering it slightly, Babur looked down at it in panic, and kept frantically pulling the trigger. Michael reacted quickly, pulling the electric-charging cord out of the side of his car, the first in line from the stairwell door, opened the unlocked driver's side two doors, and pushed the near frozen Rose, who was squeezing Alex ever tighter, both into the back seat. Punching the electric starter button as he managed himself inside, he started the car without hesitation, and pulled away silently and slowly.

No sound, and not much speed in these little electric cars. The Chevy Volt had not changed much since its introduction back in 2010.

During the climate crisis fossil fuels had been eliminated, requiring the auto to be completely 100% electric compared to what it was then. Its range without recharge had only improved from 38 miles to 75 miles; its enlarged lithium-ion battery using a 240 volt recharger had only improved to 3 hours recharge time from its initial 4 hours.

Babur continued squeezing the trigger of the AK-47, his face growing ever more furious in frantic frustration. *Damn, damn. These cheap AK clones were made in Pakistan at a secondary factory. Damn!* He winced in remembering that these rifles were supposed to be copies of the famous Russian assault rifles that were designed to withstand all kinds of adverse conditions and be the most reliable military rifle in the world. *So much for that.* Turning and running down the garage towards the exit, he jumped onto his electric powered cycle parked just inside the door, started it, and turned his head, struggling to see Michael's car pulling out into the dark fog left onto Lawrence Street towards the nearby university campus.

"What the devil! His gun didn't fire, but now he's following us! Michael exclaimed.

"What is he trying to do? Rose's voice rising in near hysteria. "Jesus—he was trying to *shoot* us! It didn't work, but Michael, is this some kind of a bad joke? Not a real gun?"

"No, no! Rose, the date, the power failure, the black dust—it's more. I saw the frustration in his face. He is following us on a cycle. I can see his headlight right behind us. I can't go any faster. It's too dark. If this guy is trying to shoot *us*, well who else? … *September 11th*…. We have to get to Ali at the Beauvallon. … No. If I can lose him, I'll try to drop you and the baby off at the lab first. What the hell?" Michael's thoughts came out of his vocal chords, confused, rambling.

But Babur's electric cycle was faster than Michael's Chevy Volt. Despite the near darkness, Michael could see that this maniac was now pointing a pistol in his right hand while steering with his left, gaining ground and now about to pull along side.

"I have to shake him. I have to …" At this point, Michael had already turned right, west onto Speer Boulevard from Lawrence and was

making a left turn onto Larimer Street to cross the bridge over Cherry Creek and enter the sprawling university grounds, the former University of Colorado at Denver—the largest collegiate campus in Colorado, now the National University. Speer Boulevard is a double-lane highway, well separated in both directions by Cherry Creek, bike paths and grassy knolls. Michael maneuvered another sharp turn left, making a 180° turn back onto Speer going east, but Babur coordinated his turn perfectly and was now even with the car's left side. The pistol fired, and Michael heard a glancing 'ping' against his roof, right above his head. Before Babur could fire his pistol again, Michael turned his wheel sharply left at the corner of Speer and Lawrence—instantly crushing the adjacent cycle into the side concrete wall on Lawrence Street separating the boulevard lanes, with Babur ricocheting off the wall high into the air and landing on his head, suddenly sprawled face down on the concrete street.

Quickly braking his car, Michael rushed out, making sure there were no weapons in the assailant's hands, and turned the assailant over. Babur was bleeding profusely from the nose and the side of his head, which was clearly crushed by the impact of him hitting the street. His eyes were wide open, still breathing, but he didn't move; eyes staring into Michael's. A sorrowful groan, and then in a weak voice he uttered: "I have failed, Michael Reynolds. I have failed…." Crying in anguish, he continued. "No matter … you and others of power will die in no time anyway. You will die in misery in three days. Surely this black magic in the air, the Savior Dust, will take you down … peace to the world."

"Who are you? What the hell are you doing?" Michael demanded harshly. "What are you talking about? What is this black dust? " With that, Babur's eyes, remaining open, unblinking, suddenly groaned again and his mouth dropped open—gone, not a breath. Babur, 'happiness', dies with his mission unfilled. "Rose, stay in the car! Don't get out in this stuff. I don't know what it is, but it's not good." Michael glanced around. The dark fog was beginning to slightly subside, but still, no other cars or pedestrians were about. It was Saturday morning, he remembered. He searched through Babur's pockets and pulled out a passport—Afghanistan. It showed a picture of this assailant and his name, Babur Massoud. Nothing else in his pockets other than what looked like about $300 U.S. dollars in his wallet. The pistol was nearby on the street. Michael picked it up and placed it in his belt. *It's real, and it's loaded. This is no joke turned accidentally disastrous.*

The failed rifle was nowhere in sight. Dragging the body behind the car, Michael opened the small trunk, picked the lean man up around the waist, and stuffed his lifeless body into the back compartment. He closed the lid and jumped back into the driver's seat of the car. Turning to a still terrified Rose in the back seat, her body stone still, a look of astonishment, speechless, she looked into his eyes begging for an answer from Michael. "I don't know, Rose, I don't know. All he has is an Afghan passport and a wallet with some money. He's dead. We'll take him with us … I'm going to drop you at the Biochem/MB lab. Be sure to cover Alex's head. Don't expose him any more to this dust.… From this guy's, Babur is his name, dying chatter, it sounded like he wanted to assassinate us and others he says 'are in power'. He failed to kill us but uttered something like 'this dust will be fatal to us anyway', 'in three days'. He called it 'Savior Dust'.… Get up to the MB lab with Alex and start analyzing what's on us before their emergency generators fail. I hope Frost and Dean will show up soon. We need them." He handed one of his damp towels back to Ali after wiping his head and arms. "I'll join you soon. I'm going to Ali's. I know that she has the only secure fiber optics communication … I'll be back."

"Be careful, Michael. Be careful," Rose's voice softened as she pondered this new horrific reality of terrorism. *"Not again. The climate catastrophe. Now this. What's it all about?"*

—⟊⟊—

With the chase ended, Michael turned around from facing Rose, regained control of his side-damaged Volt, and proceeded southeast on Speer Boulevard to West Colfax Avenue, turned right, and went around the back into the university through 7th Street to the new Advanced Science Building—home of the Biochemistry/Advanced

Microbiological laboratories, built in 2015 on a former parking lot right next to the 7th Street garage.

Michael stopped the Volt as close as he could to the doors of the front entrance to the lab building; then in turning to her he calmed his voice. "Rose, does your mobile phone work yet? Try it."

"No, I *have* been trying," a dejected Rose responded.

"Let me try mine again…. No, nothing. How did they knock the power out? Both land and sky."

"Wait," said Michael…. "Okay, I can see no one is here. You're okay. Go!" As Rose and the baby exited through the back passenger seat, with Rose covering Alex's head with her light vest jacket, she paused. The two stared briefly at each other through the car window. Both frowning, each failed in parting to show some signal of hope. Michael drove away slowly in the dark mist which had enveloped them earlier but was now continuing to very gradually dissipate. He proceeded back onto Speer Boulevard, turned right and drove the quarter mile down to East 9th Street, a left over to Broadway and parked just short of the indoor garage of the Beauvallon. Unsure of whether another assailant could be lurking nearby seeking a similar fate for the vice president, "…*others in power…*" Michael pondered the best way to get to Ali's 16th floor apartment. He knew the stairwell to the elevators was kept locked for her security, but because of his close relationship with the vice president, he had the code. He grabbed his flashlight and the passport he had retrieved from the strange man, Babur, now crumpled up dead in the rear compartment of his car, opened his front car door cautiously and quietly tried to sense in the near darkness whether anyone else was around. Moving in through the open garage door and hearing nothing, he shined his flashlight on the security box by the stairwell entrance, entered the code, and opened the door.

So far so good.

CHAPTER 8

The look on the face of Speaker Jeffrey Wilson was one of extreme consternation as he stepped outside into the strange fog. It was not wet and gray like a normal fog, but neither was it like a black smelly ash from a fire, nor the angry black clouds of an approaching thunderstorm. *"Strange ... What is this?"* He noticed a fine black dust on his shirtsleeves. He stepped back under the portico entrance of the Schleier Mansion and brushed it off, ignoring what might be on his face and in his thinning hair. In momentary wonderment, he slowly pulled his mobile phone from his pocket and looked closely for connection bars. Still none. He pondered whether he should just walk the two short blocks south to the Capitol. *Surely there they would know what's going on. But maybe I should wait until this fog lifts.* He reentered his home, safe and secure from the AK-47 of Jaweed ... for now.

"Listen, dear. I'm going over to the Capitol and see what's going on ... as soon as this strange fog outside lifts. It's getting so dark out." Puzzled, his wife looked him in the eye, noticed this sort of black dust on his face and hair and began to wipe it off, observing how light and fine it was. It seemed to float through the air and be gone. No black smear. Neither noticed they had also been ingesting it.

The fatal virus was already spreading through the house.

CHAPTER 9

The grand plot, called the "Master Plan" by the zealous leaders Aazim and Antoine, was formulated in Dire and had been nearly ten years in the making. To the very last minute, in light of the unimaginable scope of the powerful weapons these few people were about to release against the entire world, Antoine never ceased to show his worry. "I know, I know, it's all a brilliant scheme and a technical wonder, unbelievable, but what if the pathogens come back here?"

"My friend, a thousand times I have told you," Aazim would reply confidently. "We have underground bunkers full of food and water for three years, just in case. Don't worry. We are safe … as long as America is taken care of."

It was well known that the Ebola virus, primarily a lethal health problem restricted first to the Congo area of Africa where it was discovered in 1976 and then to three other small countries in West Africa, was of the deadliest order, usually killing on average 70% of those infected. At times up to 90%. For some unknown reason, the human body could not fully utilize its own immune response system to produce antibodies against it, as it does against other viruses. Fortunately, because of its limitation in being transmitted, it never spread enough to have become a source of a widespread pandemic, only several thousand infected, but the disease was always a major concern to micro- biologists and health authorities everywhere. It was very difficult and expensive to develop reliable anti-virals and vaccines to fight it. The crack scientific team lured to Dire with the promise of wealth and fame, laboring in its underground state-of-the-art micro-biological laboratory, had diligently and patiently found the way to achieve a 100% fatality rate among a variety of infected lab animals.

Even more ingenious, they were able to further genetically-modify the virus so that it could be transmissible human to human through the air instead of only by touching infected human fluids, such as saliva, blood, urine or semen. Most importantly, they discovered a way to spread the virus very rapidly by attaching it to a unique chemical dispersant and keeping it alive for weeks. It wouldn't be necessary to wait until it spread only by face-to-face contact or touch. The chemical dispersant, in the form of a very fine black dust, was extremely light and could readily spread through moving air, even squeeze through door and window frames. The dispersant would easily release its attached live virus upon any type of interference, like inhalation or by simply falling onto an object or a person.

For years the bio team in Dire also worked on finding an effective vaccine against this more vigorous version of the Ebola pathogen but was continuously disappointed by their failure to come even close. It was incredibly virulent, and no attenuated versions were discovered that could provide immune protection, like vaccines against other pathogens do. Nor could they discover any anti-viral agents that a human could ingest once infected. Such a state was a concern to those scientists but especially to Antoine. Although unlikely, would it be possible that the virus released in America might ever be swept across the oceans by wind streams and become contagious to the entire world, including those on Dire, despite their bunkers? So up to the last moment before the 9/11 attack, the team was ordered to work around the clock to discover an antidote, but their efforts continued to fail.

Just as the six assassins were deceived into thinking that they were safe, the unsuspecting other 1000 Dirists sent to America in mid -2021 to release the black dust on September 11th also thought they had been vaccinated.

Poor souls—striving for everlasting peace. Life is not fair. Deception is a cruel game.

CHAPTER 10

Michael was surprised to learn that inside the security door in the Beauvallon garage there was no battery-powered emergency light in the stairwell, at least not operating. The stairwell was pitch black. Flashlight in hand, he rapidly ran up the first six steps, slowed to a jog up the next five steps, and breathing heavily walked as fast as he could up the last five to the 16th floor penthouse. He found the floor's security lock and again punched in the code. The doorway opened into the middle of a darkened hallway across from the elevator, closed apartment doors showing near both ends as he scanned his flashlight.

He and Rose had been here many times—ever since the end of the climate crisis and the trapping and arrest of the president's chief-of-staff on kidnapping charges. The three had become the most intimate of friends. One penthouse on the top floor quartered Ali's two security guards and her chief-of staff, John Evans. John and one security agent were in the mountains for the weekend, and the other, Tom Edison, had already been alerted by Ali and was preparing to walk with her to the president's residence.

The other penthouse, spacious and with well-appointed curtains and furnishings, was hers alone. Her personal secretary, her housekeeper and her cook lived together on the floor below in a nicely decorated three bedroom apartment. A perfectly comfortable arrangement for all, but Michael wondered why that even here at this level of responsibility there were no emergency lights installed in the hallway. *This was the most important person in the entire United States!* He found and turned his light on the middle of her wood-paneled door, emblazoned with large bronze letters: 'Alexis Graham Vice President United States of America'. He knocked forcefully, and after a short delay Ali opened the door. He immediately noticed two emergency lights installed inside were on and he felt relieved because through the spacious windows, Michael could detect that it was still quite dark outside, although not so much as minutes before. Ali's face revealed an expression of dismay.

"Ali—"

"Michael, I am so glad you're here. We have a disaster on our hands."

"I know. I—"

"General Ralston just called me on our secure fiber optics line from the Pentagon. He thinks a very powerful electro- magnetic pulse bomb must've gone off over the middle of the United States. All radio communications are out. Ground electrical transformers and connections are destroyed. Our satellite communications systems are not working. He thinks America has been attacked, and —"

"I know. Ali ... listen! That explains the electric grid down, cell and satellite phones out, but it's even worse." His voice was hurried, but firm; his tone crisp and clear. "I was just attacked by an assailant. I dropped off Rose and Alex at the university labs ... You've seen the black mist outside. It's not fog or a fire or a storm. It's a black dust, a dust carrying something—something toxic, or pathogenic—"

"Michael. What? You've been attacked? Who? Toxic! Pathogens? But you're here. What happened? Slow down." The vice president's tone was first one of an increasing stern disbelief, her head shaking negatively with her eyes rolling upwards. A deep sigh. *Impossible!* Within seconds her look changed, her facial expression turning grim with fearful mental images growing of a horrible unknown. "Okay, Michael, go, go, go on," she stuttered impatiently.

"After we lost electricity in our apartment and noticed no connections on our cell and satellite phones and feeling this strange black dust on us on our balcony ... I knew it was not fog or a storm, and I knew it was not ashes from a fire. All along, Ali, I have had a strange feeling. It's September 11. Twentieth anniversary. Our intelligence about those against America overseas has been sorely missing. Our defenses are down. This guy... we went down the exit steps to the garage for our car. We did not want to expose ourselves anymore to this dust by walking to the university. We wanted to get to the Biochemistry/MB labs to analyze the dust, but in the garage, an Afghan, named Babur pointed a rifle at us! ... Ali—my God, he was squeezing the trigger, but somehow, it did not go off! We got in our car and drove out, but he followed us on a cycle ... pointed a pistol at us. He shot and I heard a ping off the roof above my head. It was pretty dark out. I knew then this could not be a prank. I was lucky. I was able to swerve into him and knock him off his cycle before he fired again. He had no helmet. His head hit the street hard. He died ... he is downstairs in the back compartment of my car ... dead."

Michael paused to catch his breath again. Excited, he wanted to go on, but Ali's eyes widened and her mouth dropped as she stared in disbelief. "My goodness! He was trying to shoot you?"

"Worse! Not just me. I got out of the car, and before he died he uttered to me that he was on a mission to kill, quote ... 'those in power' ... but it gets even worse than that. His last words were that it did not matter that he failed in killing me because we would all die from this thing that's in the air. This black dust.... Ali we have to find out what it is. And you have to protect yourself."

Ali now stood more erect, her facial expression transformed from fear and disbelief to one of determination. "Michael, we have to call General Ralston and let him know what's going on. He asked that I warn the president that someone is attacking America and about the electro-magnetic pulse that knocked out our power. I was just about to walk to his home with Tom when you knocked."

"No, no. Look, I'm already exposed to this stuff. And you may be a target too. There may be more of them. Stay here, stay in. Don't open any windows or balcony doors. If it's something toxic or pathogenic, we don't know what it is yet or how it might spread other than by the mist. I'll go to the president."

Grasping her elbow, he led her up to the full glass of the balcony doors. The large balcony of the top floor penthouse faced southwest towards the nearby sprawling campus of the National University, always clearly in sight, but now invisible through a fog of who knows what. "Look outside, Ali. It was even darker before."

"And I thought it was just a brewing thunderstorm," Ali replied softly, pondering the options.

"I'll go to the president's residence, Madam Vice President, not you. Please—bring Tom in here, armed, and don't open the door for anyone unless you know who it is. I suspect there could be more assailants out there. Be safe, Ali, and tell General Ralston about the dust."

Little did Michael realize that the fine chemical which had showered upon him contained a virus that infects through the nasal passages and into the lungs, and was already working its way deeper, and that it had already been partially dispersed into the air of the apartment of the vice-president. Few windows and doors are perfectly airtight. Along with his breathing into her face, she was already fully exposed.

CHAPTER 11

Asa, 'healer' in Afghan, was the only one of the six who could not resist the vices and luxuries of America—those very symbols his parents in his native country detested, like alcohol, nudity, and gambling. But the strict, religious days of his youth were over. Those who migrated to Dire from Afghanistan and Pakistan were much more secular than Asa's Islamic parents. Since the end of the climate crisis in 2018, tourists were again welcome to visit the United States. Many of the major airports had reopened. It was easy for Asa to make the journey. He stood in awe admiring the beauty of the city of San Francisco.

Each of the six assassins had arrived in San Francisco on different dates during the early summer months of 2021. Six AK-47 rifles for these assailants had been crated and shipped separately from Islamabad, Pakistan, without inspections upon leaving or arrival. Each of the six Dirists had been instructed to pick up this most mass-produced rifle in the world at different times at the office of the shipping agent at a designated San Francisco wharf. The AK initials meant Automatic Kalashnikov, after Mikhail Kalashnikov, the Russian who developed the assault weapon as the official Russian army military rifle in 1949. It was inexpensive and easy to produce and maintain. Its cartridge held thirty rounds of ammunition. It was incredibly reliable, even in bad weather. Over time, some 75 million of these semi-automatic/fully automatic rifles were produced, and by the 1990's, the AK-47 had been widely dispersed through the Islamic world in Afghanistan and Pakistan. It had become the most famous, most notorious weapon in the world.

Also included in the crates alongside the rifles were six pistols and plenty of ammunition for both weapons. The pistols were the Russian classic—the semi-automatic issued the Russian military from 1951 to 1991, the favorite in all the James Bond movies, the spring-loaded, 8 bullets per magazine clip, the simple and easy to use .380 caliber Makarov.

The small crates also contained some insignificant pottery, as so described on the 'contents' label. All six 'tourists' had been issued international driver's licenses and $10,000 U.S. cash. Using professionally faked credit cards, they were instructed to rent their electric vehicles from six different rental agencies, to leave San Francisco on different dates, and slowly drive to Denver by late August. Even though national security and foreign intelligence had become inconsequential in America with the U.S. National Security Agency and the Central Intelligence Agency, both in effect defunct, the assailants' instructions were to arouse no unwanted suspicions about Afghan/Pakistani visitors. Antoine and Aazim never were able to convince the Afghans to neatly trim their long black hair and beards. That was one part of their Afghanistan culture with which they wished to stay loyal.

Only Asa among the six had the inclination to divert to Las Vegas for six days, and he alone of the six found out what a personal joy those late nights can be. Perhaps it was a latent rebellion from his strict upbringing. Upon arriving in Colorado, all but Asa booked in at the lesser hotels in downtown Denver—the Hilton Residence Inn, the Embassy suites, the Courtyard by Marriott. No need to attract attention to the men with their long dark hair and beards and dark skins in a concentrated area where the well-heeled elite American politicians and their prima donna staffs were quartered in the higher end hotels.

But Asa could not resist. On September 3rd, he checked in to the Arizona red sandstone masterpiece that had been completed way back in 1892, the Brown Palace Hotel on the corner of Broadway and Seventeenth Street. Part of the elegance of old Denver—the interior Victorian architecture with exterior Italian renaissance design was revealed in the magnificence of the inside six floors of balconies leading up to a stained glass skylight in the middle of the high ceiling. The dining rooms were luxurious. Asa was not aware that the top military brass assigned to America's temporary capital resided on the private top two floors. The highest-ranking general, Brigadier General Armstrong, enjoyed the best suite in the hotel on the top floor. The general's military office was located in the executive office wing on the first floor of the Capitol building, two blocks to the southeast. Other than Vice-President Graham's penthouse office at the Beauvallon, this military headquarters was the only Denver location for the federal government's secure fiber optic communication system.

Security for politicians and the military brass had been almost completely lacking during the last ten years as the pressing issues of climate, economics, and politics dominated the nation's agenda. No one had yet arrived at the Capitol's military office on that early Saturday morning September 11th. The secure line buzzed and buzzed unanswered, General Ralston on the other end at the Pentagon impatiently perturbed. Denver right now was the temporary capital of the mighty United States of America, and it was hard to imagine that this special phone was unmanned. At least Ralston had been able to contact the vice president.

Asa may have been momentarily swept away with the "good" life of America, but he remained fully dedicated to his mission and was relentless. He was also deeply in love with Fila, the one female member of the group of six assassins. While he wanted to sample the vices and luxuries of America, he also knew he would never offend or betray his true love.

Now concentrating on his mission, he reviewed his assignment to assassinate the one person thought to be able to possibly coordinate a rapid response to the virus—Richard Frost. Frost, through his technical background and oversight of the operations of the famed National University. Even more true if his target could utilize his protégé, the brilliant Rose Haines, and her engineering-minded husband Michael Reynolds. It was thought by the Dirists to be an improbable scenario but theoretically possible—to quickly find a simple antidote to the 'Savior Dust'. Frost had been appointed by an action of Congress in 2019 to the dual positions of President and Dean at the National University. Dean of the Bio-Chemical Engineering Laboratory and president of the nation's leading academic university—located contiguous to downtown Denver, less than a mile west of the Capitol building. Richard was magna cum laude Biochemistry at Princeton University and went one on to become the Dean of Engineering and then President of the University of Colorado at Boulder, the beautiful campus just north of Denver tucked away against the foothills of the Rockies.

Asa had observed Frost's daily movements to and from his residence at the luxurious Portofino Tower apartments at 18th and Grant Street. Directly across the street were the National University's president's offices—housed in a modern red brick building at 1800 Grant, just two blocks north of the Capitol. It was unusual that Frost's office would be located almost a mile east of the campus area. Maybe it was because the former University of Colorado had more than one campus and there was already enough construction work during the climate crisis to transform the large Denver campus into solely a national academic center. Asa was unaware of a person named Dr. Jonathan Dean, the famed head of the university's Advanced Microbiological Laboratory, who was just as likely as anyone to find an anti-viral to the magic dust's carrying companion. Somehow Dean seemed to have been missed as a target for assassination.

Asa reckoned that he should keep his rifle concealed in a long duffel bag and pace Grant Street the morning of 9/11, strolling casually between the Portofino's front and rear doors. The front was located directly across the street from the doors leading to the president's offices. His made only one tactical mistake: it was Saturday morning and weekend schedules were different. He hadn't observed Frost's coming and going on weekends.

Both General Armstrong and President Frost regularly enjoyed early Saturday morning jogs, followed by breakfast together afterwards at a downtown hotel. On this Saturday morning, September 11th, the two were up at 6 a.m. as usual and met in front of the Brown Palace at 6:30. All was calm and quiet on this beautiful, clear, early autumn morning in the mile high city.

"Morning. Our usual, Dick?" grinned the general.

"Right on. I really feel especially good this morning. Let's go!" Frost replied amicably.

Dressed in their gray sweat pants and long sleeved sweatshirts, one with 'ARMY' and the other 'NATIONAL' scrolled across their chests, the two 60 year olds began their slow jog, a block down Tremont Place to a right on the 16th Street Mall, a pedestrian street looking the same as it had 10 years before, with only electric buses providing assisted transportation, then northwest on 16th street out to Lawrence, left down past the Four Seasons, and then a left on the bicycle trail along Cherry Creek alongside Speer Boulevard southeast down to 11th Avenue, over to Grant, north on Grant to the Capitol grounds at East 14th Avenue, left through the spacious Civic Center Park, cutting north up to Court Place, and then another block to the Sheraton Denver Downtown Hotel, a great place for breakfast at the 15 Fifty Restaurant—virtually a full circle; they jogged twice around in their nearly one hour long workout. Despite the fact that metropolitan Denver and all of eastern Colorado had been completely transformed during the climate crisis years, downtown Denver was left virtually untouched so that the federal government could quickly move into its larger buildings without construction delays.

Asa had not taken his post in front of the Portofino until 7 a.m., an hour before the scheduled EMP bomb and the black dust release, but a half hour after Frost had left for his morning jog.

The assassins were deadly, but they were not perfect.

As he waited patiently, Asa had time to think and recall. The five men—Amagan, the gift; Farzam, the worthy; Babur, of happiness; Jaweed, the eternal; Asa, the healer—were all selected objectively upon the basis of their physical excellence among hundreds in training for this mission. Subjectively, they were chosen for their displays of supreme dedication to the most worthy cause of ending violence in the world once and for all. They were going to help *save* the world for posterity. And fortunately for them, this venture was not like a radical Islamist suicide mission. They were protected from infection with their inoculation of a vaccine against the Savior Dust—that something very mysterious to them but something pathogenic that would kill all others in contact with it by the end of three days from initial exposure. Asa felt safe.

The sixth assassin was a woman, a woman he had fallen in love with at first sight on the tiny island of Dire. Asa had wished she could have joined him in his romp through Las Vegas and be with him in his luxurious hotel, but he knew that to her, dedication to their mission had to come first. The people welcomed to Dire were secular and not bound to the practice of subjugating women to the home. Fila, in Afghan 'one who loves strength', had certainly earned her appointment. She was steadfast, determined, tough, and the brightest of them all. Asa and all the other potential assailants refused to believe the rumor that some part in her positive selection process was due to the fact that the great leader Aazim was attracted to her outstanding beauty. If that were really true he would have kept her nearby and away from a risky assignment. It did irritate Asa, though, that Aazim seemed to pay special attention to her. Fila's assignment was to annihilate Rose Haines, the brilliant engineer/scientist, nearly as famous as her husband, Michael Reynolds.

Staring at the Portofino while waiting but mentally recalling Fila's strategy, Asa tried picturing just where she was at this very moment. He remembered Fila's hunch was that since the research on Michael

Reynolds revealed him to be extremely inquisitive and impatient, he would probably either quickly drive his car to the advanced laboratory at the university or to his powerful friend's residence, Vice President Graham. He would probably do this after all communications were cut off and the strange black dust rolled in, leaving Rose alone in their apartment with their baby boy. A mother would not want to expose her young child to a strange dust. Fila would wait awhile in the lobby giving time for Michael to leave and then use her flashlight to find her way up the Four Seasons steps alongside the inoperable elevator bank, knock on the apartment door innocently, surprise Rose, and then do her job.

It would be easy, if only Rose Haines would be there.

CHAPTER 12

As Michael was about ready to leave Alexis Graham's apartment to head to President Jenning's residence, he gently grasped the vice president's forearm again, turned her towards him, and gazed into her face with a solemn stare. She glanced up quizzically into his bright blue eyes, his handsome face now reddening, displaying some inexplicable emotion. She had already accepted his warnings about a toxic or pathogenic dust outside and to stay put behind locked doors with her protector, Thomas. Michael had only kissed Ali lightly on the cheek before—many times, coming and going socially, but now he would not let go of her arm or remove his gaze. This time, he had to be sure to make his point.

"Ali, I know we have been through a lot, but this is different, moving his grasp onto her upper arm, his face only inches from hers, staring intently. "If General Ralston is right. If we are under attack … if this guy who tried to kill me is not alone. If this dust is really deadly, we need you here to stay up with General Ralston and be safe. You are our nation's true leader…. Can you remember? Do we have any others on the military's fiber optics network? Defense contractors? The CDC in Atlanta? AT&T? Pharmaceutical companies? Please … find out." Releasing his hand from her arm and retreating a foot, he realized he might be overstepping his bounds by his proximity and sounding so commanding. But Ali felt comforted that Michael was taking charge. He seemed alert, cautious, resolved. His closeness, his intimacy, eased her growing fears. Clearly, he had made his point about the gravity of this sudden tumult and the importance of her role in it.

Regaining her composure, but staying close to him: "Yes, I forgot. Certainly. In General Armstrong's office next to the president's office in the Capitol. And I think it's tied into at least a dozen bases around the country. I'll find out who else."

"Good.... Ali, before I leave call there. Right now. We need help," Michael spoke calmly in tone but looked stern in his determination.

"Follow me," Ali nodded. The two walked briskly down the hallway and into her office. Ali glanced at a notepad that was under the red phone on her desk. She punched in a number and waited impatiently. Nothing but repeated buzzes in her ear. No answer. It was early Saturday morning. The military staff was off—working like civilians.

"They are not there, Michael. No answer."

"Keep trying Ali, and stay in touch with General Ralston in Washington. I'll warn the President and then head to the Biochem/MB lab. If we don't get our mobile phones back on, I'll come back later to check with you. Three loud knocks on the door and please ... ask who is there."

"Michael, be careful, Ali pleaded." It was now her turn to squeeze his arm as she drew close. She hugged him tightly.

"Right. I'll be okay. I promise." And with that he headed to the door thinking how he should exit the building. He opened the door to the hallway cautiously and turned on his flashlight. He had a choice of the way down—the garage stairwell he ascended or the exit steps next to the sole elevator that led to the front lobby. If there was another assailant nearby targeting the vice president, at least he had not yet come up one of the two stairwells.

Michael pondered the options. An assailant could by now be lurking just outside the garage where Michael had parked his Volt and had cautiously entered, or he could be in the lobby, or be outside the front entrance or at one of the side exits. Michael had to guess. He opened the door to the steps leading to the lobby. The emergency lights were on in this stairwell. It was bright. Too bright. He decided instead to go down the dark garage steps but this time without his flashlight on, holding on to the railing all the way down sixteen flights. He held the dead assailant's pistol in his other hand, just in case another Babur appeared. As he slowly opened the garage door when there were no more steps down, he peered towards the exit ramp and was glad to see the sky outside seeming to be brightening—certainly a little brighter now than the sky outside Ali's balcony doors. *Maybe this so-called 'Savior Dust' won't amount to much after all,* he thought to himself almost out loud. Michael was one gifted with great intuition for considering all possibilities, good and bad, but sometimes had to struggle to keep his general spirit of optimism. He was trying hard now to think what he could do other than to warn the president and vice president about what his assailant had said.

He heard or saw no one. Others in the condo building must be sitting by idly, waiting for the power to come back on and for their mobile phones to work again. Besides, early Saturday mornings were always quiet in downtown Denver so it was no surprise that all was so quiet. He could walk the five short blocks to the president's residence, but he would still need his car to get to the lab. He approached the Volt and noticed the dents in the side fender and on the roof above his door. The gunshot followed by the crash flashed through his mind. He felt himself glancing in all directions as he moved forward to get in. *Is this really me?* He imagined it like a television show—a detective series, examining everything, looking everywhere. *Okay, safe. Get in the car—move.* He exited from his spot next to the garage and drove the short five blocks southeast as fast as the Volt would allow. Only a few cars on the streets. No one in a hurry. He parked well past President Jenning's spacious home—the stately building which still had the brass plate outside reading 'Governor's Residence'.

Continuing in his cautious mode, he slowly approached the front entrance peering left and right. He took a second to observe the six

Greek pillars at the top of the five steps welcoming visitors to the front entrance ten feet away. Beautiful. Impressive. He thought he might just be bold enough to try opening the front door—sure enough it was unlocked. He walked into and along the hall way, slowly glancing behind, just to be sure he wasn't being followed. He stopped still in a sudden moment of shock, as in the dim light just inside there huddled a crouched man holding the head and shoulders of another in his arms. The man shuddered in fear, speechless, sensing Michael's shadowy appearance holding a gun in his hand.

"It's okay. I'm a friend …what happened? Where is the president?" Michael said sympathetically, quickly regaining a more confident composure.

The shaken man on his knees looked pleadingly at Michael and weakly blurted out: "I'm the cook…. The housekeeper—here. His head is split open. All this blood. I put an icepack on it, but I think he's dead. My cell phone doesn't work. The president is upstairs, front room. The secret service, in the back … I heard shots—gunfire. It's quiet up there now. I saw no one. It was dark. I'm afraid to move. I'm afraid to go up there. Who are you? Call the police!"

Michael coolly replied: "No, no calls. There are no phones in service. Stay here. I'm going up."

Clearly understanding what the cook's description of hearing shots fired could mean, but not knowing if a singular or multiple assailants might still be in the home, Michael was reluctant to turn on his flashlight as he approached the poorly lit interior space. Slowly, carefully, he found the staircase up. Listening intently, he made his way up, one hand on the railing guiding him and the other on the pistol. No sounds, except the low wail of the president's cook sitting by the front entrance next to the fallen housekeeper. It was almost completely dark on the interior stairs. Michael turned on his flashlight briefly, pistol more firmly in his grip, and noticed the doorway towards the front of the home was wide open. He shut off the light and proceeded toward the open door. Some soft light inside, probably from the room's large windows now that the dark fog outside was partially lifting. Michael stopped and looked in.

He froze—shocked. It was a horrible scene. The president lay on his back sprawled out across his king-sized bed, profuse red stains almost completely covering his otherwise white pajamas.

Michael regained his nerve and moved closer, stopping within five feet of the bed. He had never seen anything like this before in real life; only in distasteful violent movies. Instinctively, he looked around, raising his arm pointing the pistol, and listened in the event the assailant could still be there. Nothing. Complete silence. He approached even closer over the bed. The lifeless president's eyes were open, his face contorted. *Assassinated!*

Feeling almost nauseous witnessing the horror close up, Michael backed up, turned around, and moved through the doorway. *The Secret Service agents!* He shined his light momentarily down the hall, still all quiet, and walked slowly on towards the open door. The scene inside was as terrifying. There was nothing more he could do here and no way to call for help.

The dim reality of what was happening in Denver was settling deep into Michael's mind. This was terror to the nth degree. He shook his head hard, as though to digest this reality and get a hold of himself. *Think.* His feelings of fear were momentary. They passed as Michael strangely, somehow, began to feel a warm surge inside him—a growing sense of determination.

Caution to the wind, Michael ran down the hallway, down the steps, past the grieving cook without saying a word and outside to his car, glancing only to see if anyone was raising a gun at him, debating whether to first tell Ali of the killing of the president, or get quickly over to the lab. What could Ali do? She knows we are under siege. She promised to stay in her locked apartment with her security guard. *Right to the lab where I left Rose and Alex to check on them. Then back to Ali's—she has to become president!*

He noticed more of this black dust on his arms and wiped them clean with his handkerchief. *Have to find out what this 'Savior Dust' is.*

Michael started on his short drive back to the university without incident. The blackish dust had continued to lift. There were few cars on the roads. Driving the little Volt at full speed, he suddenly felt his heart beating faster as he remembered that the outside doors to the Biochemistry/Advanced Microbiological Laboratory Building were always kept unlocked, even on a Saturday morning. Only the doors to the individual laboratories were kept locked to prevent theft of valuable equipment. Rose had the codes to those inner doors, but *the outside doors were unlocked! … I left her to enter by herself when I dropped her off with Alex. What if—?*

Prior to the climate crisis, the huge campus at the west end of the Denver downtown area was shared by three collegiate entities: the large University of Colorado at Denver, the Community College of Denver, and the Metropolitan State College of Denver. All three were converted into the National University in 2015 as the top professors in the country arrived in Denver. Physically, the campus was separated from the downtown high rises by Cherry Creek, running diagonally northwest to southeast and sitting slightly downhill from the downtown plateau. Perfect viewing, a grand panorama, from the penthouses of the Four Seasons and the Beauvallon.

Other than the old pink, Spanish-styled church situated in the center of the campus featuring its twin bell towers, the historic highlight among all the modern red brick academic buildings was the Tivoli Student Union Building. It was once the home of the gigantic brewer of Pilsner beer, the Tivoli-Union Brewing Co. The centered red brick building completed in 1864 with its rising tower was a masterpiece in architectural styling and now served to give the campus its distinct character. It still served as a student union for the National University, the leading engineering and science academic center in the country. Next to the student union, a new Faculty Union building had been built on the adjacent athletic fields—all copper-toned reflective glass, four stories high with a flat roof nearly full of long rows of high tech solar panels. Gazing west past the campus buildings, the foothills and distant peaks of the rising Rocky

Mountains painted a never-tiring picture of spectacular, natural beauty.

After Michael had dropped her off at the lab complex, Rose moved quickly into the science building grasping Alex in her arms, spreading one of her towels over both their heads. The building lobby had been empty. Lighting was fully on, including the stairwell up. Holding Alex securely with one arm, yet still trembling from the shooting and crash episode, Rose carefully touched in the code for entrance into the Advanced Microbiology Laboratory on the second floor. The lights, the security system, and the lab equipment inside could all operate on electricity generated from a battery backup system—designed just in case of the unlikely event of a power failure caused by fire or earthquake. It was important that the electron microscopes, the state-of-the-art computers, the freezers, and the refrigerators continue to operate in a period of temporary downtime. Microorganisms must be viable to be grown and studied. The only problem now was that the battery system would last at full power for only about three days. The batteries were located on the ground level in a generating station just outside the rear of the building. There were no solar panels on the roof of this building to recharge them.

Rose remembered Michel's words: the assailant had said "fatal … in three days". Wild, crazy thoughts went through her mind as she entered the lab and locked the door behind her. *Power fails—how? Is this a toxic chemical? Are we now mortally infected? Are we in a race against time?* After rechecking to make sure the lab door was locked, Rose sat Alex gently down atop a lab bench, his face quiet and body content, his eyes staring right into his mom's. She opened a drawer, pulled out a handful of cotton swabs and carefully began to rub her arms and face, and then the young child's. She dabbed at the towels used to cover their heads as they had entered the building with more of the cotton to collect and isolate this so-called 'Savior Dust'. She pulled out the cloth she had used back in the apartment to clean the dust from Michael and Alex. She then washed Alex's and her own face and hands with water from a lab sink. At last, Rose was comfortable in her element, knowing that she had plenty of chemical samples and an electron microscope right in front of her. For the first time in the last hour, she felt calmed down.

The examination, the search for an answer, had begun.

———✺———

The Volt instrument panel still showed a nearly full electrical charge as Michael pressed on towards the labs. He continued to worry about Rose as he pushed the accelerator to the floor. He sensed his driving visibility continuing to improve even though there was still quite a bit of fine black dust swirling in the light morning breeze…. *Wait!* He remembered that in the rear compartment of the Volt was the dead body of his assailant. *What do I do with it? Rose was there now, the MB Lab. That would be secure. In there.*

West on East 8th Avenue and right on Speer Boulevard. From there, nearly straight a mile to the lab. Left on Colfax and into the campus; the back way up 7th Street. Michael slowed, looked cautiously all ways for anyone suspicious, and pulled right up near the front entrance door of the Advanced Science Building. *Good!* No one was about on an early Saturday morning. Tightening his belt, he tucked the assailant's pistol securely inside it against his body, opened the rear compartment lid, grabbed this strange guy named Babur under his arm pits, pulled hard, and dragged him out of the Volt and into the building, looking everywhere in case another assailant could be on the hunt. *Surreal* was the first thought racing through his mind, until he paused to realize that *he* was to be the dead man, not this heavy weight in his arms. Continuing, he slowly trudged up the steps to the second floor Advanced Microbiology Laboratory. *Thank goodness no one around to explain this to and no other bad guy in sight.*

Rose heard the knocking on the door and viewed Michael's face close to the look-through glass near the top. She moved Alex over into a large drain basin and hustled back to open the secure door. Only the academic elite was permitted into this 'advanced' lab. To her surprise and then dismay, Michael dragged the body of his assailant through the doorway and inside.

"Close it. Lock it," Michael said panting heavily. "Hurry." Rose's calm demeanor left her quickly as she saw this terrorist once again—only now bloodied, dead and limp.

"Michael! Why in the world bring him in here?"

"Rose, from Ali's I went to the President's mansion. He's been shot ... he's dead! It wasn't just me, or you, that they are after. Who are these people? Who killed the president? We need evidence. Identification. Who is behind this ... I learned from Ali—she has the only working communications outside the Capitol building—through the military's underground fiber optic system. The Pentagon believes some type of huge electromagnetic pulse bomb went off and paralyzed the entire country's electric power and communications systems."

Rose's mouth dropped open, her eyes widened, as an astonished look of disbelief gripped her. She remained frozen for a moment until she heard Alex whine in discomfort while trying to crawl out of his lab sink exile. She ran to him, pulled him out and held on tightly as she re-approached Michael, who was now spreading this Babur man out on the floor. Bending to his knees, he started searching through Babur's pockets again, this time much more slowly and carefully. Again nothing but a wallet and a passport, both of which Michael had already stowed in Babur's front jacket pocket. He opened the worn-looking wallet again. The cash was there, but feeling further into the folds where extra money is usually hidden he felt hard objects. He pulled them both out. One was a magnetic room key, but no address or identification showing on the plastic card. The other a slender piece of paper folded over two times. Michael quickly unfolded it, scanned it hurriedly, and looked up into his wife's pleading eyes.

His voice was now quiet; his tone calm and somber. "It's the hit list, the so called 'power' he was uttering about as he died. It's six of us, and six assigned assailant names next to each. Babur was to get me. Amagan to kill President Jennings, Farzam to Ali, Jaweed to Speaker Wilson, Asa to Richard Frost, Fila ... Fila is assigned to your name ... to you, Rose.... They got the president. They missed me, but why are we both on it? Who are we?" Rose stood taller, leaning side to side with a look of amazement on her face, then feeling limp, hugging Alex even tighter with her two arms. She shuddered as she looked at the still face of the dead man lying flat on his back on the lab floor. Michael stood up straight from his bent kneeling position over the stony silent assailant, turning to his wife. "The president, the vice president, the speaker of the House, yeah, the top American political power, but us … and Richard Frost? Why?"

Both stood facing each other, sharing feelings of dismay, the bright-eyed young child Alex oblivious to the events of this last hour.

"They must think we are the ones who can find out what this 'Savior Dust' is and detoxify it, or if it's alive, maybe attenuate it, or kill it," she finally responded evenly and coolly as she turned her attention back to her young son.

Sometimes, pressing a loved one close is a good mechanism for putting a worrisome thought out of mind.

CHAPTER 13

By nine o'clock, Speaker of the House Jeffrey Wilson was growing increasingly impatient, almost mad at the loss of his customary conveniences. He was dressed now in his typical Saturday wardrobe –brown loafers, tan khaki slacks, and a long-sleeved blue cotton dress shirt, open by two buttons at the collar. He glanced again outside the living room window, frustrated still no electrical power nor phone nor computer. Maybe it was time to take the short two-block walk to the Capitol south on Grant Street. The air outside was clearing somewhat now compared to an hour before, and he knew there was a secure fiber optics communication system in General Armstrong's office at the Capitol. He also knew all the chairs of the many House and Senate committees would probably realize that as well. He bet to himself that all of those rascals would be headed there to find out what was going on and want to take charge. *But I'm the man in charge.*

"Okay, dear, I'm leaving now," he called sharply to his wife who was sitting glumly by a large living room window scanning pictures in a magazine. She looked up but did not respond. Jeffrey began his journey, oblivious to his intended fate. Oblivious to the fact that the president's cook, finally realizing he was the last remaining alive at the 'Governor's Residence', had simultaneously begun his walk to the Capitol for help, just six short blocks north of the mansion. Many residents were now beginning to wander out from their downtown apartments and condos, mistakenly, innocently, believing they would catch some word of the power outage and for a while at least escape their darkened abodes. The sun was not yet visible in the cloud of black dust engulfing their downtown residences. Little did they realize the "Savior Dust" had also blanketed the whole city, the whole state, in fact the entire country.

The Colorado State Capitol building appears as a masterpiece in design and setting. Back in time, the land area of high plains lying to the east with the Rocky Mountains rising to the west was designated by Congress first as a Territory, named Colorado, meaning 'colored red' in Spanish. Statehood was granted in 1876, and ten years later construction of a state Capitol building began on a ten-acre site in Denver. Fifteen years and three million dollars later, the gigantic undertaking was completed in1901. Present cost inestimable. Only local construction materials were used—walls of granite, foundations of sandstone, floors of marble, and interior walls of unique rose onyx. The building design was of a Greek cross with its four wings extending from the center, each wing designated for the state's governor, its House, its Senate, and its Supreme Court. The cross was designed to be a hundred yards by a hundred yards.

The highlight—the gold covered dome rising from the center rotunda almost another hundred yards high, its exterior shining brilliantly in the Colorado sunshine. All together the Capitol comprised nearly 700,000 square feet of interior space, but with its huge ornate hallways and central staircase, only 35% of that total served as workspace.

When the feds arrived in Denver during the national climate crisis of 2012 to 2018, all state officials in the Capitol and their duties were suspended. Of course, the same was true for the federal Congress and Supreme Court. During those emergency years, the Capitol building was completely occupied by President Jennings and the heads of his extensive executive agencies. Duties of all three federal branches were restored when the Plan of Return was formulated at the end of the crisis in 2018. During the post-climate crisis years the original functional wings of the cross were restored. But this time not by the state but by the feds—the U.S. House of Representatives, the Senate, and the Supreme Court.

At the end of 2018, state officials moved in with their local compatriots across the adjacent Civic Center Park and squeezed into the massive City & County Building to the west of the park. This arrangement was to be temporary. The feds would move back to Washington D.C. as soon as all the citizens who had been ordered to come to Colorado during the crisis were back home safe and sound, estimated to be by mid-2022.

Jeffrey walked at a fast pace, anxious to beat the others. The entrance doors were all locked at this time of day. Tourists were not admitted until 10 a.m. The Service Entrance was available at all times to the proper officials and staff, and the sole security guard sitting outside the door smiled sleepily at Jeffrey as he approached. "What's going on, sir? Dark out. No power inside."

"That's what I'm here to find out," Jeffrey hurriedly replied, sliding his magnetic card to open the door and hustling over to the dimly lit staircase. Just one emergency ceiling light was on at this basement level. The executive offices were up one flight on the first floor. Both congressional chambers were located on the second level. General Armstrong's office was just down the hall from the president's and the vice president's offices inside the first floor executive wing. It was dead quiet as he proceeded up the steps and onto the first floor, just a few scattered battery-powered emergency lights lighting his way. He felt a sense of surprise as it appeared he might be the first one here. There was not a sound coming from anywhere. He stepped hurriedly into the general's spacious office. Only one person, a uniformed corporal, was there, looking up with a welcome greeting at Jeffrey's entrance in the dim light.

"Mr. Speaker, sir, I am so glad to see you. I arrived a half hour ago, and the only sign of life here is General Ralston constantly calling from the Pentagon. He is very anxious for General Armstrong to arrive. Something about an EMP explosion crippling our communications systems. I didn't know whether to run to his residence at the Brown Palace or stay here by this phone—"

"EMP—means electromagnetic pulse," blurted out Jeffrey. "Damn! We've been working on that for many years…. Are other members of Congress here, or the president, or vice-president?"

"No sir. I've seen no one, but I did not go upstairs where the Congress—"

"Okay, right. I'll take over here, corporal. You go after General Armstrong at his residence. Tell him it's urgent. Did General Ralston tell you anything else? Accidental? Just Denver?"

"No sir. He did not, but his voice sounded very alarmed."

"Probably a botched military exercise with underdeveloped technology," the speaker growled. "We've been through this nonsense before."

The corporal nodded his head sheepishly, quickly rising and departing on his mission to arouse General Armstrong.

Alone now, the speaker fumed as he paced impatiently, never imagining the presence of the nearby assassin—the irrepressible Jaweed. He was hiding in a second floor corner just above the executive offices, close to the congressional chambers, in his mind disobeying his orders but more importantly bravely waiting proudly and patiently for his prey. He had gained entrance to the building through the Service Entrance when the lone guard there had carelessly left the door ajar while wandering off for a visit to the Men's Room.

He smiled to himself, opening his long brown trench coat and admiring his polished AK-47. *My plan is perfect. I cannot fail.*

CHAPTER 14

The small circular island of Dire, only five miles in diameter, was blown out of the ocean as a volcano thousands of years ago. It was once the forced home for thousands of Southeast Asians suffering from a highly contagious, incurable plague. No nation claimed it as its possession. In recent years, only Chinese military intelligence gave notice and gathered information about a movement surreptitiously gathering and moving adherents onto the island. It was unclear whether or not the movement coalesced around a radical ideology or not. From all reports, it did not appear to be a religious calling. The new leaders of the now democratic China believed the calm, beautiful, small island appeared innocuous but worth keeping an eye on the activities of its mysterious residents.

Born and raised in Paris, Antoine spent most of his adult life in Switzerland. Following his wealthy father's footsteps as an influential banker, Antoine became an expert in successfully executing financial deals for international arms traders. In his professional life, he deemed himself a perfect success. Prosperous, well-educated, respected, approachable, firm but fair in all his dealings. In his private life, while a handsome bachelor exuding outward confidence, he felt conflicted inside. Despite his full, wavy hair and beautiful blue eyes, he spent little time with the women attracted to him. During holiday time at his luxurious residence on the French Riviera near the beautiful city of seaside Nice, instead of slowing down and relaxing with friends, he more often preferred to be alone, reflecting upon the fact that all those arms he had traded were actually doing to harm thousands of innocent people. He detested repeatedly seeing scenes of massive bloodshed in his recurring dreams.

In time, he grew increasingly frustrated with the realization that despite the absence of the large devastating world wars of the previous century, humans never seemed to be at peace with one another. It haunted him that the production and flow of assault weapons increased year after year, lucrative for him but causing suffering for so many innocents. His mind imaged Irish Catholics fighting Irish Protestants, Russians fighting Georgians and Ukrainians, Chechens fighting Russians, Arabs fighting Jews, Israel fighting Hamas and Hezbollah, Shiites fighting Sunnis, African tribes fighting African tribes, Chinese fighting Tibetans, Communist Koreans fighting free Koreans, Pakistanis fighting Indians, Afghans fighting Afghans, Islamic radicals fighting all who disagreed, heavily armed guerilla groups everywhere. *Would it ever stop?* He dwelled on that question ... to the point of obsession.

By chance Antoine had met Aazim when the two were working an arms deal for Iran. Aazim was the head of Foreign Intelligence for the strongest declared theocracy in the world—the nation of Iran. His father, a devout Shiite working a lifetime in key government posts, had married a minority Sunni. Their mixed marriage was kept quiet within the powerful Shiite theocracy. With mixed emotions, Aazim was keenly aware of the centuries of bloodshed between the two main sects of Islam. As a product of a mixed marriage, he always secretly harbored reservations about the antagonism among the Arab states—the majority Shiite nations of Iran, Iraq and Syria against the majority Sunni nations like Saudi Arabia, Turkey and Egypt. He became increasingly secular, wishing religion could be kept personal.

In time, Aazim grew increasingly disenchanted with the quests of the legally supreme ayatollahs to one day establish Persia as the governmental center of worldwide Islam by using nuclear blackmail to achieve that goal. Despite public announcements to the contrary, Iran's growing secret arsenal of weapons of mass destruction was truly awesome in size and scope. And to his private lament in his key position of overseeing his nation's foreign intelligence gathering he was right in the middle of what he discerned as a sea of on-going violence. But those bold religious supremacy plans of the Supreme Ayatollah gave Aazim the seed of an even more outrageous idea. He thought the Iranian use of nuclear blackmail would be used for the wrong purpose. He dreamed of what he imagined a more noble goal—weapons blackmail to end massive human violence once and for all.

Through casual email exchanges after their arms deal, the two men of similar persuasion grew closer and closer in revealing their personal frustrations, their growing distaste for violence, their revulsion against corrupt leaders punishing their own peoples, and their consternation with so many competing ideologies and religions continuing to lay the basis for so many mass killings, the constant flow of harmless and innocent refugees. Finally, the two personally met in Paris in June of 2008 to share their mutual dismay. They arrived at a most brilliant solution: Antoine, the international banker dealing in major arms trades, could secretly purchase the most advanced weapons of mass destruction in the world through his vast network of dealers, both legitimate and illegitimate, and pay for them by siphoning billions of dollars from accounts of unsuspecting Swiss bank depositors. It would be easy for him to organize a new bank he would own, open dozens of fictitious accounts which he would control, and pay interest on billions of dollars that he could transfer in as his clients' "investments". A perfect pyramid scheme. A perfect diversion of funds.

On Aazim's part, he could find a secret location and recruit a hundred thousand men and women who shared similar frustrations and would want to live in peace on this remote island. Once there, a select 20% would be inculcated into supporting the motivation of their new leaders—the noble goal of ending violence once and for all. It would not be by a plan of *preaching peace* as so many had before, but by *executing a plan of action*. Yes, 'Peace', that universal laudable goal attainable though a pleasant combination of a wish, a hope and a prayer—noble thoughts of the mind but ineffective in practice. Then how else can universal peace be achieved? How? By actively eliminating the world's major weapons. No nuclear détente here. But how can this be done? How? By a one-sided advantage. By forcing disarmament under the threat of imminent death. A truly noble scheme of blackmail.

Half of the twenty thousand selectees would develop the technology and half would volunteer to venture overseas to execute the plan. The bold scheme would consider using a combination of nuclear, non-nuclear, biological, and chemical weapons. Delivery systems would consider using rockets, drones, and their own people in clandestine roles. With an incredible sense of enthusiasm and perfect execution after that fateful Paris meeting, the two had achieved what seemed a miracle in just 12 years. By 2021, they had secretly populated the little island of Dire with 100,000 devoted 'Dirists'.

The world-class scientists they had recruited had strengthened the deadly anthrax bacterium 100-fold, and in such a light powdery form it would easily float through the air in order to spread rapidly. They perfected a vaccine and an antidote against the genetically-modified pathogen for themselves, and one which would be used as part of the bribe scheme against nearly 100 targeted nations: *"submit to the demands of us Dirists to disarm and live ...or refuse and die"* would be the simple message.

Some 9000 devotees would be placed around the world to deliver the anthrax weapons, and assuming success, to provide instruction for rapid manufacture of the vaccine and the antidote for the submissive nations. Plans were completed showing how to stockpile and subsequently destroy all the surrendered weapons. In order to take charge and let the world capitals know of the seriousness of each nation's predicament, drones would be deployed to deliver high-altitude explosions of non-nuclear electromagnetic pulse bombs. The disruption of air and ground communications by surprise, even for just a few days, and the longer term loss of electricity through physical damage would allow the victim governments to know the power and seriousness of the attackers.

The only worry the two master planners dwelled upon, besides the fact that some of their select followers began to call them the 'Saviors'— a connotation they did not like—was the mighty United States of America. There resided the top scientific and engineering brainpower, the best weapons, the most determined and most inventive peoples in the world, the most likely not to accept the bribe offer to submit their major weapons, and the ones most likely to quickly counter attack. "Forget the bribe. Let's just destroy them, not just their weapons but them," Aazim had declared one day back when America was wrestling with its North American climate catastrophe. He sounded serious.

"'Destroy them'? You mean kill all the people?" Antoine had responded in an incredulous manner.

"Of course—yes, kill them all. Only America has military bases all over the world. Mostly idle these past few years, but when their climate crisis is over they will reactivate them as never before. How can we stop them? They may have secretly developed and hidden WMD's that are better than ours … take them out!" Aazim's eyes lit up.

The two stared long and hard at each other in that moment, until Antoine softly replied: "Your rationale may be right, my friend, but we never thought we would have to go beyond the **threat** of causing massive death, not actually go through with it. To slowly die from the anthrax or to be saved from it by our vaccine and antidote—that choice we thought was clear. They would submit. 'Give up your weapons in exchange for life'. But—"

"Antoine, my dear friend, but you must now know that you *have* to see the wisdom of what I say. Killing Americans is not *your* moral issue. Yes it appears to be the ultimate violence, but it's our means to an end. *Your* moral issue is saving billions of the peoples of the world from future harm. You will someday die in peace, happy with what you have achieved for posterity. We had agreed that this is our noble mission. If there really are all-loving gods, they will be grateful for what we together have done."

Antoine looked at Aazim's glowing face, his friend's wide smile and demeanor brimming full with confidence. The brown-skinned, brown eyed, sleek black haired Persian was gloating. The Frenchman's thoughts raced ahead: our one megaton atomic bomb, 60 times the power of the one the Americans had exploded over Hiroshima back in 1945, the one I purchased from Pakistan, combined with the North Korean intermediate range rocket that was available for purchase—perhaps Aazim could place the nuclear-tipped rocket in northern Mexico. The bomb could be set to go off at a high altitude, maybe 250 miles above Kansas, the American geographical center. A powerful nuclear explosion that high would produce an electromagnetic pulse far more powerful than the combined three dozen non-nuclear electromagnetic pulse bombs delivered by our drones over the major capitals of the world. The entire Unites States communications systems would be out.

And then, far beyond the powerful anthrax bacterium our scientists are developing, that incredibly dangerous new airborne strain of Ebola virus contained in our laboratory vials ... if we could find a way to distribute the virus, like maybe on some airborne chemical dispersant, then yes, Aazim could get his wish. Antoine's mind swirled on, thinking that the only problem would be that we can't seem to develop a vaccine or antidote to it. It would have to do its job quickly, and then the virus itself must die out before it could spread around the world and back to us! *Impossible mission, or maybe we could....*

Antoine's mind then went blank after imagining such an outrageous plan. *Folly?* Shaking his head, smiling, he freed up his mind and turned his attention to the irresistible scene of the orange-red sun setting into the Indian Ocean. The comfortable porch on their little seaside house perched on a hillside on Dire faced southwest. Perfect for enjoying the beauty of nature and putting all other thoughts momentarily aside. Aazim was still smiling, he too enjoying the view in the warm, humid evening air. It was then mid-summer, 2018. Three years to go to the 9/11 attack.

Can we pull it off? Antoine mused to himself as the sun sank into the Indian Ocean.

CHAPTER 15

Breakfast at the Sheraton was long and satisfying for the two post-joggers. The spacious hotel lobby, the interior restaurant with its high ceiling, and the convenient location near the Capitol all added up to rewarding them with a very delightful ambiance. The affable General Armstrong and the academic Richard Frost enjoyed each other's company immensely. Both were astute and could converse in depth about almost any subject. In these relaxing moments on quiet Saturday mornings, they especially liked to talk about the recent renewal of college football and professional sports across America. Colorado was playing away that afternoon in Iowa, so no big local game was on tap that September 11th, 2021.

"Man, after all that jogging and sweating, I think we just put on more weight with that big breakfast than we lost on our last five runs," Richard joked.

"You're right, we're both 60 year old gray hairs, but I think though at our ages it's quite prestigious to look a little portly. We're *big shots*, you know," the General retorted with a chuckle of satisfaction. Richard laughed lightly and took his last sip of coffee.

"Let's get outside and stretch a little bit before heading home to the showers, General." With that, the piped-in music stopped and the lights suddenly went off. The two had felt a slight rumble. Both sat up erect in the near totally dark.

"Earthquake!" Frost was sure.

"I don't know. More like a jet off in the distance breaking the sound barrier," the savvy Army man replied.

But then silence and stillness prevailed, except for the murmurs of the few other customers in the restaurant wondering out loud what was going on. Suddenly, the emergency power system kicked in, the lights came on, and all seemed well again.

"Okay, lights! ... Now come on, Dick," the general continued. "No game today. Relax. I have nothing to do this morning. Let's have some more breakfast and make some bets on tomorrow's pro games. I have the sports page here." The two sat back again and carried on their sporting conversation, unaware that the hotel's emergency generators, not the normal power system, had restored power for the lights and music. Nor did they notice a few minutes later that the outside daylight was fading. The black dust had arrived. With delivery of more coffee and toast, their waiter grimaced and mentioned that an unusual fog, thunderstorm, or dust storm must be brewing outside and that emergency generators were supplying power.

"It is very dark out, gentlemen," the server added. The two joggers casually glanced out through the far windows, but pursued their heated debate over which teams would be victorious in their season openers, taking notes as they went along. An hour fleeted by. It was nine o'clock already; the lights now began to dim as power began to fail as the emergency generator struggled to power the whole hotel.

"That's it! Enough of this flickering." General Armstrong stood up and pulled his mobile satellite phone from the zipped back pocket of his sweatpants. He was always the man in charge and would quickly learn why the main electricity was off for so long and also why it remained so dark outside. Frost's cell phone lay on the table, and he quickly fingered it not to be outdone. No connection bars on either. Neither mobile system was working, neither satellite nor cell.

"Let's go outside and get connected," the general beckoned to

Frost. To their consternation, no connections out there either—even at the quiet front entrance circular driveway of the hotel facing Court Place. The waiter was right. There was what seemed to be a dry and odorless dark fog or smoke outside. Particles—more like a forest fire or dust storm were settling down but black. The gray colored sidewalk cement was now covered in a black something. The tall office buildings rising all about the two men could not be seen through the mist. *Mysterious,* thought the biochemical engineer Frost.

"Look, I'm always in the know, but this…" the general said haltingly. "Neither of our phones works. Could be a microwave disturbance? Looks like electricity is still off all around us. Unusual, Dick, this funny mist. It has black soot like from an oil or electrical fire, but I don't see or smell anything. Those fires are usually isolated and billowing—this thing is everywhere. My office in the Capitol has a secure fiber optics communication system. It's only a block away. I'll find out. Want to come?"

"Well, I certainly have the time, so let's go. And General … the traffic lights are out too, so it's not just a Sheraton outage. Never happened before in Denver since I've been here. You know, it sort of reminds me like 9/11 when Lower Manhattan completely disappeared in a cloud of dust. Except that dust was gray and this is black. Would look like tires burning with all that black smoke, but I don't smell a thing either. You know, burnt ashes from a forest fire could be black not just gray so maybe the wind just happened to center them here. Yeah, the ash mist could be gray and light but the fallout could be heavier and black." Frost half smiled even though he noticed the black dust settling on his arms and shirt; he was momentarily content with all his additional observations and possibilities, oblivious to the other possibility that this could be anything toxic.

The two walked swiftly down 15th Street from Court Place a short way to the dimly-lit Capitol grounds, first entering into Civic Center Park bordered by its classic Greek columns, eastward a 100 yards into Lincoln Park with its red-toned obelisk honoring Colorado war veterans, another 100 yards and up the steps past the huge Civil War statue on the west side of the Capitol building. Before circulating around to the east side entrance, they both paused in the near darkness and looked skyward to the west, Frost commenting first, obviously with mounting confusion. "We had a perfect sunrise this morning. We can usually see the high Rockies from here. *Now look*; this fog has not lifted much. I can barely see one hundred yards…. but we agree it's not fog. It's not a wet mist and not gray. We're not in a dark storm cloud. We both are still collecting like a fine black dust all over us. It's on your face and hair, General. Seems like a fuel explosion fire somewhere … but like we said it's so even and spread out everywhere." The two men stood like the surrounding statues for a moment—just peering and wondering.

"It's on your arms and shirt too, Dick. Let's get inside to my office." It was 9:15. Speaker Wilson had arrived just moments before and was impatiently pacing General Armstrong's first floor office after sending the lone corporal scurrying after General Armstrong at the Brown Palace Hotel.

Upstairs, still hiding in the shadows of the emergency spotlights, Jaweed felt amused with himself. He believed in his mind that he was becoming cleverer by the minute. And he felt absolutely no nervousness at all, despite the anticipation of what he was about to perform. For his cause, it would be a great deed to take out as many in the United States Congress as possible, even though his only assigned target was the third in line—the Speaker of the House, whose photograph Jaweed had studied many times. He would wait until crowds of them, out of curiosity, would eventually gather in the House chamber. *After all, I am a trained killer. After this, there will be no more U.S. Congress.* How complex human nature can manifest itself—one day seeking peace and another seeking violence.

Knowing it would be increasingly difficult to avoid being noticed in his not so secluded hiding place, he became aware of a solitary maintenance worker slowly making his way in the dim light. He thought quickly. Pulling his six-inch hunting knife from its holster attached to his leg, Jaweed quietly approached the slow-moving man from behind and in a flash efficiently slit the man's jugular, holding the man's loose shirt high to slow the gushing blood. He dragged the body into a nearby office and into a closet. He knew he could have initially hidden himself there as well, but then he wouldn't know what was going on in the chamber. After placing his long coat on the floor, he quickly took off his own pants and shirt and put on the worker's, shirttails out, using his own undershirt as a bandana around his neck to hide the blood stains on the worker's collar and shirt top. He tucked his pistol inside his belt buckle, obstructed from view by his overhanging shirt. He returned to the scene of his deadly deed and placed his AK-47 from his shoulder into an empty black plastic trash bag that was hanging on the side of the worker's mobile cart. He placed the gun inside the cart, barrel down, unable to be seen to any potential observer.

He paused to remember how he had excelled in firing the AK-47 during his training. He smiled to himself; his mind flashed. *I, Jaweed, was the best! Now, in the Capitol of the United States of America I am ready to attack!*

On the first floor, directly below the plotting of the over-zealous Jaweed, Speaker Jeffrey Wilson sighed with relief as General Armstrong and Richard Frost entered the executive office wing, both expressing surprise to find Wilson there alone. Wilson was standing by the general's large oval desk on which sat the red telephone console, the terminal point of the secure fiber optic line. It seemed peculiar that there were no emergency lights mounted inside the general's office, but light coming in through the windows was now just bright enough for immediate cognizance.

"Mr. Speaker–"

"General. We have a major problem. You know the power is out.

All communications down but this." Wilson pointed to the phone on General Armstrong's desk. "Call General Ralston at the Pentagon. He told your corporal who I sent looking for you something about an EMP explosion knocking out the grid." The general and Richard Frost were speechless as looks of bewilderment crossed their startled faces. "You military guys have been playing with this technology for decades," Wilson continued. "What the hell did you do now?"

Without a retort, an annoyed, perhaps militarily embarrassed, General Armstrong reached over for the secure phone on his desk, his eyes narrowing. Frost, still speechless, sat down on the edge of the closest chair and observed. Wilson stood sternly by the desk, still showing his annoyance. To Frost, the speaker appeared mad as blazes at the general.

Armstrong quickly punched in the call code. Waiting for General Ralston to answer, his only thought was that after all China and Russia must have such EMP technology too, but there is no way since the end of the Cold War 30 years ago they would ever attack us. No, it must be our own guys causing another military accident fooling with experimental technology. The general thought Wilson must be thinking to himself: *They have to be reigned in!*

"No, no, no! I have checked through our secure fiber optics military system calling out to all our bases. It was not our guys causing this. It was not an accident," General Ralston repeated loud and clearly to General Armstrong. "This is an attack. It's nationwide. It had to be detonated high above mid-America by a powerful atomic bomb.... Damn it! I don't know who did it. The commercial electrical grid on the ground is burned out, everywhere. Microwave cell towers have burned out connectors. Our satellite communications systems are scrambled … listen, I have alerted the vice-president. She has the only civilian fiber optic connection. I told her to tell the president. You follow up. Get them both over there to your office. Get the Congress in session there. We need a declaration of war … are you there Armstrong?'

After a long pause, General Armstrong meekly replied: "A declaration of war? … War against who?"

CHAPTER 16

It was now 10 a.m. in the lab. Michael, pacing the hard tile floor, was deep in thought. America had been through a lot the last ten years, but this was different. We could struggle as a nation, he thought, and yet we were able to cope with an abrupt, devastating climate change, with domestic turmoil, with political upheaval, with social unrest. But now—an enemy boldly trying to annihilate us? They take down our communications systems; they spread perhaps a poison, or deadly bacterium or virus; they have six assassins murdering our leaders? *I'm all about developing technology. I have no training for this. What the hell do I do?*

Finally coming to a halt, placing both palms on the bench top, he leaned in and said to his wife without looking at her. "Rose. We need a plan. I'm guessing Dick Frost will head over here if he can't figure out what this black dust is. Meanwhile … make Alex comfortable. Keep the door to the hallway locked. Start the immunoassays to see if this stuff is really toxic or pathogenic like this guy said … I'll go back to Ali's and let her know about the president and that she too is marked for assassination. I told her not to leave her apartment and keep the door locked. You keep this guy Babur's pistol. It's loaded. We need help, Rose. We have no FBI anymore, only a small military contingent and the local police. Ali will have to get through to them...." Michael paused, momentarily lost in thought, uncertain as to whether or not he said everything he wanted to say to Rose.

"Okay, okay. That's a start. I'll be fine here." By now Rose seemed as though she had pulled it all together. "Our computers and lab equipment will run full power for at least 48 hours on our backup generator, maybe longer. Our reference library on toxic chemicals and microscopic pathogens is right here behind those panels.... Maybe this dust is all a ruse to scare us. They just want to shoot Americans they don't like. Terrorists. Michael, you go. Have confidence. You can help her. Ali has strength. Just be careful." Sounded like a *brava* statement from Rose, but Michael could sense that reserved underneath her strong words was a desperate sinking feeling consuming both of them—that this was like a nightmare with no good ending.

They hugged one another firmly, and then Michael was gone. As far as he could tell, the lab building was still empty, but once outside in the steadily lifting fog he discerned a number of students wandering the campus walkways, probably wondering why all electric power was out and their mobile phones were not connecting. He looked intently at the females for signs of suspicion fearing one could be this "Fila" seeking out Rose. All looked simply bewildered. No long coats, like Babur, possibly concealing a rifle. Once settled back into the Volt, he drove back out West Colfax and down the half mile on Speer Boulevard, again to the Beauvallon where he prayed Ali had listened and stayed put.

This time on his trip to the vice-president's residence he now knew that an assassin named Farzam was assigned to kill the vice-president. He hoped that the attempt had not yet been made, or that it had failed, or that Tom had been able to protect Ali, or what? He cautiously proceeded to the dark garage again. After parking and cautiously exiting the Volt, he shined his flashlight every which direction in the garage. No one. Punch in the codes. Up the stairs again to the top floor. The door to Ali's penthouse was locked as agreed. Three knocks and "Ali, it's Michael."

"Come in, Michael," Ali whispered as she opened the door, holding the secure phone to her ear. Tom stood behind her, nodding, then softly saying to Michael. "It's General Ralston from the Pentagon talking with Ali, General Armstrong, and Speaker Wilson on the secure line. They are trying to contact President Jennings too and have everyone meet at the Capitol." With that news, Michael raised his arms abruptly to interrupt the conversation.

"Stop! The president is dead. I came to tell you. I was there. Murdered. The Speaker is on the list and—"

"What?" Ali dropped her hand holding the phone, looking at Michael in astonishment. "Someone was after you. Before, you had said 'those in power'. My god Michael—the president, the speaker … me?"

"Yes you too, Ali. You have to stay here. Do not go to the Capitol. Do not go out."

Raising the phone again, her voice trembling: "Gentlemen. Michael Reynolds is here. He had an attempt on his life. They got the president. He is dead. Get security over there. Speaker Wilson may be next.… Who else Michael, who else?"

Six. Six assassins, six targets. The president, vice-president, the speaker, Richard Frost, me, and Rose. The "power" … and those who might be able to find out what this black dust is."

Speaking up, Ali repeated Michael's exact words into the phone. Then without pause Michael continued: "I have to find Richard Frost. He may be home. He may be heading to the university. I have to warn him."

"No, Michael. Dick is there … at the Capitol in General Armstrong's office. Gentlemen, again—get security. Lock down the building. Check the president's mansion. We *are* under siege … no, I won't come. Michael's right. I'll stay here… Yes, yes, I hear you …but you'll figure a way to get me sworn in here."

Michael's thoughts flashed. *What* security could the vice president be calling for? Since after the chaos of the climate crisis years, Denver was so calm that there were only three security guards at the Capitol at a time. The only military personnel there were General Armstrong and his small, unarmed staff. A 50-person Army and Marine garrison on call, along with a small number of city and county emergency response police, were located at the stately City and County Courthouse building three blocks away to the west of the Capitol, directly across Lincoln Park and Civic Center Park.

At that moment, the corporal who had been sent to the Brown Palace to rouse General Armstrong reentered the general's office out of breath. He was immediately given his new assignment by the general. All of the other military staff members assigned to the Capitol were given weekends off. "Corporal Edmonds, find building security. Have them lock down all the doors—not to be reopened except for military and police and identified members of Congress or Supreme Court. Hustle across the parks to the courthouse and bring back all the Army, Marines and police officers you can find there. With their full arms. Oh, except five. Send five to the Beauvallon to guard all entrances for protection of the vice president. Hurry!" Ali had put her phone on speaker so that Michael and Tom could hear that full command.

Michael now compounded the bad news as he announced loudly so that all could hear. "If Ali has not already informed you, the black dust falling throughout the city may contain a deadly toxin or pathogen, the statement my assailant claimed before he died that it would take us down in three days' time." A momentary silence ensued before General Ralston in Washington responded: "My god, it's everywhere here too, this black dust ... and at all the bases I have spoken with around the country. Everyone first thought it must be ashes from a fire, but it's not."

"General, we have it isolated at our labs at the National University," Michael continued. "We're studying it now. Let's pray it's no more than an innocuous chemical or a normal influenza bug attached to some kind of dispersant. It's not burning my skin or causing a breathing difficulty so it's probably not a chemical weapon.... Richard, we need your help there."

—❀—

It was half past 10 a.m. By now at least 50 members of Congress had wandered into the Capitol building and congregated in the second floor House of Representatives Chamber, alarmingly curious as to why the power had been out so long and what in the world was going on with this black dust everywhere. Some had cell phones; some had direct satellite phones. Neither system was working. Growing more concerned by the minute, knowing he was dead wrong about our own military accidently knocking out power and communications and then learning that he himself was a target, Speaker Wilson had to be sure that all entrance doors into the Capitol were secure and that military help was coming. He hurriedly paced to the bottom floor doors checking the lock on the semi-darkened southern basement entrance, then up the steps to the first floor east entrance, west entrance, and then to the main entrance on the north side. All were locked. The three armed security guards scurried about, confused as to what was going on and what they should do other than await military and police, unaware of Wilson's double checking.

The Speaker had a hunch other congressional members would have shown up by now, so decided to check their second floor chambers. Nearly out of breath, he slowed to a more moderate walk in the dim light, past the famous murals on the first floor rotunda walls, and paced up the ornate marble steps to the second floor. Hearing loud voices, he entered the House chamber, stopped abruptly and stood erect, gazing at the dozens of representatives and senators standing in the aisles, faces only slightly illuminated by the emergency lighting behind the chamber lectern and some dim light coming through the large windows behind.

"Jeff! What's going on?" All eyes turned to the Speaker. Jeffrey Wilson, who had never in his life had any direct dealings with violence. He felt his chest growing heavy, a lump in his throat.

Silently striding to the middle of the giant room so that he could gather them all around him, Speaker Wilson was trying desperately to come up with the right words to explain ... *attacked* ... *toxin* ... *pathogen*. It was a pathetic picture as he was completely unaware of

73

the maintenance man who had followed him through the chamber door. Jaweed had studied plenty of photos of his target. There was no mistake—this was his man. And gloriously to his purpose, there encircling his prey was a horde of those warmongers from days past. The time had come; it was worth his wait. Standing just inside the elevated entrance, Jaweed pulled the AK-47 from its hidden space inside the cart, turned it towards the crowd, raised the weapon, and opened fire—continuously holding the trigger on full automatic—right at the speaker. Even in the dim light, he could see the flow of blood spurting from Wilson's neck and head; he had hit his target, but he just kept on firing, weaving the automatic-firing rifle up and down, back and forth, shooting at the entire gathered group. All thirty rounds; another magazine; and then a third. Ninety bullets in all. As the screaming congressmen went down hit or hiding, Jaweed felt within himself a tremendous sense of power, of domination, something he had never experienced before. His three magazine clips now emptied, his targets' cries and shouts subsiding, his thoughts turned to wondering how many he had shot, but ... *enough*. Despite the horror he had just inflicted, he felt no remorse. *I am a killer for everlasting peace!* A wide smile parted his cheeks as he viewed the scene of horror and panic.

That's it! Done! He turned and ran out of the chamber entrance door, stopped to retrieve and put on his coat, then down the rotunda steps to the main entrance, tucking the AK-47 between his coat and the long maintenance shirt that he was still wearing, unlocked the inside bolt to the door, and out before noticing one of the Capitol security guards trying to catch up to him as the door was closing. He knew it was only nine blocks northwest up the 16th Street Mall to the tower where all the Dirists were to meet after completing their assignments.

The tower building, located at the street corner of 16th and Arapahoe, was built a hundred years ago to house the largest department store in Denver. The peak of the clock tower centered over the building was noted as the top of the tallest building of the time outside of New York City. As Jaweed hurried from the Capitol towards this meeting spot, he looked to his left in the mist and noted a large contingent of armed uniformed men walking briskly across Civic Center Park and into Lincoln Park contiguous to the Capitol. What to do? Reload? Take on the advancing force? *No, that would be suicide. I only have one more clip. I luckily have the vaccine, and they are doomed anyway.*

He ran out of their sight as quickly as he could, up Broadway a short sprint to the 16th Street Mall, past curious streetwalkers and towards the tower. The Mall is actually a pedestrian shopping street just southwest of Denver's tall downtown office skyscrapers. The nine blocks before the tower are filled with lower built hotels, shops, and restaurants that make the high rise Venetian tower a standout. Jaweed felt exalted. He couldn't wait to climb the darkened steps to his comrades to brag about what he had just accomplished. Amagan was already there, his assignment complete. Jaweed burst into the small room below the clock, panting heavily but joyous. Seeing Amagan standing erect, rifle up then relaxing his arms, Jaweed dropped his AK-47 to the floor and hugged his friend tightly with both arms. "Amagan! I did it! Not only did I get the Speaker of the House, but dozens more in Congress. I am so happy! And you? Success?"

"Yes, yes, my friend. The President of the United States is dead," Amagan answered calmly, his eyes turning down. "Before he died, I told him it was his end and the end of the United States. It was not ..." Amagan paused and did not return the look of Jaweed's joy as he stepped back. He felt it was a gruesome act, necessary, but devoid of the obvious happiness Jaweed just experienced. This is the conflicting nature of our human way, sometimes cruel in seeking advantage, sometimes compassionate in the suffering of others.

"Amagan, you have done your job well. Do not have regrets ... where are the others?"

"I don't know. We wait."

CHAPTER 17

He had been pacing the sidewalk across the street for four hours—
from 7 in the morning to 11, growing increasingly weary. All
was happening on time—for that fact he was glad about. The boom,
the loss of power, the Savior Dust rolling in, the darkness, the slight
lifting. But now he was growing increasingly impatient waiting for
Richard Frost to exit the upscale Portofino Tower apartments across
from the National University's executive office on Grant Street. Asa
had reasoned that curiosity alone would draw his assigned target out
of his home, and then Frost would either walk to the Capitol three
blocks south or drive to the university campus some dozen blocks to
the west. Either way the famed biochemist had to exit the front door of
the apartment to walk down Grant or across the street to the parking
lot below his office where he parked his car.

Time's up—I need to move right now. Tightening his long coat around
him to hide his AK-47, Asa walked briskly from the outside pillars of
the office building directly across the street from the Portofino and
through the unlocked main entrance of the apartment building. With
no one in the small lobby, he quickly found the stairwell door in the
dim light of the one emergency light that was on in the lobby ceiling.
Moving slowly up the darkened stairs one floor to Frost's second floor

apartment facing Grant Street, he knew exactly where he was going. He recalled the apartment number from his pre-planning routine and soon found it in the glow from the second floor emergency lighting. After knocking forcefully, the door seemed to open in no time as Frost's wife probably thought her husband was finally returning from his Saturday morning jog with General Armstrong and had forgotten his key. Not the first time. With the glare of several candles lit behind her, Asa could not see her face clearly or her expression of surprise then horror as he quickly grabbed her neck with his left hand and her shoulders with his right arm, spun her around harshly and demanded in a firm, clear voice: "Where is he? Where is your husband Richard Frost?"

Unable to release herself from his firm grip, she gasped. "I don't know. Please –"

"Is he here?" Where is he?" Asa repeated, exasperated, tugging her neck and shoulders more firmly.

"You're hurting me. Who are you? Please." Asa loosened his grip on her neck slightly. With Asa behind her pulling her shoulders closer, from behind she could not see the face of this young, long-bearded, long black-haired attacker. Her voice trembled. "He leaves early Saturday morning to work out with General Armstrong. He's usually home by nine. Maybe, the power failure, my phone doesn't work…maybe he walked to the Capitol, or maybe to the university to see what's going on … who are you? A student? What do you want with him? Let go of me."

Asa had no choice. He tightened his grip even firmer with both hands. She struggled, but he was much bigger and stronger. She was doomed. His mind raced. She must be silenced lest she get freed and somehow warn someone of his intent to find Frost. With his AK-47 strapped to his shoulder under his coat, his pistol in his right coat pocket, and his left hand around the throat of this slightly built, middle-aged woman, he felt her struggling even harder to break his grasp. Asa made his decision. He tightened his grip on her upper arms and shoulders with his strong right arm, dropped his left hand from her neck, and without pause, reached into the right breast pocket of his jacket, pulled and clicked open his switchblade knife, ramming it hard into the woman's belly, just below her ribs. As she gasped and fell towards the floor, he guided her onto her back. Her eyes were wide open in fear; her mouth open gasping for air, her body shaking. He leaned down and to end her agony he neatly slit her throat, ear to ear, taking care to not let her blood reach him. She went still and silent…. No regrets. *All part of my training to save the world.*

As he left the building, Asa thought he should reconfirm whether Frost was nearby or not, crossing the street to the university parking area to see whether Frost's car was still there. It was. He glanced around. No one could be seen anywhere near the entrance to the office building. Adrenaline still flowing fully from his experience at the Portofino, he entered the entrance door and scrambled as quickly as he could go—up the emergency-lit stairwell eight stories to university' executive offices on the top floor. Strange that on this Saturday morning all the office doors were unlocked, yet no one was there. *Must be*—Frost must have taken the short walk to the Capitol after the morning run that his wife had described to find out what's going on about the power outage and the black dust. Asa ran back down the steps and started to walk swiftly in the same direction, brighter out now but still a black dust blowing in the breeze.

CHAPTER 18

Standing in General Armstrong's office, it was impossible for Richard Frost not to hear Michael's excited voice on the general's speaker phone describing the attempt on his life, the names of the six assassination targets, including his own, and a possible deadly toxin, bacteria or virus riding on a chemical dispersant. "Incredulous", he whispered out loud to no one, his head shaking. General Armstrong, not hearing or seeing him, was lost in his own thoughts of disbelief. Then Frost heard the rapid-fire shots and faint cries coming from above. Speaker Wilson had gone upstairs! *What do I do?* His panicked thoughts flowed incongruently, in pure confusion, trying to make sense of the unfolding chaos. *I'm* a target. If they looked for me at home and I'm not there, they might come *here*, to the seat of power. And my God, Wilson upstairs—the shots! Or would they go to the university thinking I would seek answers in my lab to this strange black soot in the air? But at home—Michelle. My wife. *Oh God, is she safe there?*

He sat back down slowly, paralyzed by his indecision.

"Vice-president Graham, General Ralston, I'll call you back. Speaker Wilson has left my office. There's a commotion upstairs." Ending the call, General Armstrong hurried out of his office past the stunned Richard Frost who was staring blankly ahead in the dim light. Thankfully, within moments, two uniformed Marines appeared, probably to check on the general. By now Frost had made his decision— first, hurry home, check on Michelle, and then drive to his biochem lab, making sure to avoid anyone suspicious on the way.

"Officers! I'm President Frost from the National University. There is a sinister plot underway, and I am one of the targets. Please ... come with me," he demanded in a halting voice. Frost moved towards the door. The three walked into the hallway now filled with military and police who had heeded the call for help. Richard paused momentarily, guessing what might have happened above with Speaker Wilson a target. Everyone looked confused, except those moving up to the second floor chamber expecting to view the carnage. They would soon be in shock at the sight. Frost nodded to the two young Marines to follow him, and the three hurriedly moved out the main entrance and began their walk up Grant Street, Frost pulling his jogging cap down over his forehead and the collar of his jacket up. By this time, there were plenty of people milling about in the streets and sidewalks trying to find out why their power was out and what this dissipating but ubiquitous dark mist and black dust were all about. No one had noticed Asa with his AK47 hidden under his long jacket standing outside the Capitol building at the Congressional side entrance pondering his next move, unaware that Richard Frost had already slipped past him through another door.

Compared to the many residents slowly milling about in dazed confusion along Grant Street, the three figures presented a complete contrast, moving up the street at a rapid pace. The two officers accompanying Frost had no knowledge of the lurid plot unfolding about them but could sense the uncommon panic in Richard Frost's demeanor. Upon entering his dim candle-lit apartment at the Portofino Towers, Frost actually half- stumbled over the body of Michelle, lying face up on the floor, the top of her white robe soaked in red, her eyes open, her face and body frozen. Leaning down for a closer look, horrified, he screamed: "My God ... Michelle! Michelle!" The officers took a quick look and scrambled past Frost, pistols drawn searching the apartment. Frost placed his hands behind both her shoulders as to lift her, but then thought better—let one of the two officers decide what to do next. He must take the other Marine and get to the one place he believed his most familiar safe haven to be—his biochem lab at the university.

He laid Michelle back, closed her eyes with his fingers, and gently kissed her on the lips. "I'll be back, darling, rest." He did not want to believe what was happening all about him. He did not want to believe he had just seen his beloved wife lying murdered on the floor of their own home.

CHAPTER 19

"**G**eneral Armstrong must have left his office. I can hear sounds but he's not on the line," Ali said impatiently. It was near noon now. She hung up and called again. There was still no answer at General Armstrong's office at the Capitol. Michael was also growing impatient waiting for Ali's secure phone to connect again. The last call with General Ralston in Washington revealed little of the chaos that must be going on throughout the country. Michael's mind was racing: *Could it be possible that all power and all mobile phones are out everywhere? Maybe an EMP bomb did explode high over mid-America and could do this as General Ralston believes, but ... could this "dust" really be ubiquitous? How? How could it be delivered everywhere? If it's a chemical toxin, we would probably feel it by now burning skin, breathing. Could a live virus or bacterium really be attached to a chemical dispersant? Could this be bio-terrorism at its worst for America? For the world? Who? These Afghans? How? .... We have received no threats these last ten years.*

Michael understood the nation was ill equipped to deal with this situation. Contemplating foreign threats was unthinkable; American security measures had become lax as the nation had become isolationist. The only defensive feature in play was the secure fiber optics line across the military establishment and also into Denver, the temporary national capital. But even that effort was primarily installed to communicate about natural disasters, not about foreign invaders. And Michael understood that he himself was unprepared in the same way. He had been dealing with natural phenomena, not man-made. I must do *something*, he thought to himself. *But what?*

"Ali, I must go. I can't stay. This guy Farzam must be somewhere nearby in wait for you. He hasn't attempted to come up here, at least not yet ... we still don't know what's going on at the Capitol, but we do know with the Speaker and Richard there, there could be two assassins there too. I'll go there and be sure to call you on General Armstrong's phone to update you. Then I'll head to Rose at the MB lab. I'm worried about her. She's a target too. ... Ali, we have to find out quickly whether there really is a biological agent attached to this black dust, and if so, what in the world it is."

"Michael, assassins after us—this is unreal. No, crazy! Please be careful. I'll stay right here."

Downstairs, it was now Farzam who was growing increasingly impatient and frustrated. He was unaware that Alexis Graham, his target, had a secure communications line in her apartment office, and that Michael Reynolds had been there twice already. He was certain that the vice-president of the United States, knowing her power was still out, including her mobile phone, would eventually wander out and walk or drive to the president's mansion or to the Capitol in her dutiful curiosity. He had looked closely at the many other Beauvallon residents who had eventually come out of the front entrance—just to go somewhere in their frustration, but not her. Annoyed, he continued to pace in tiresome circles around the first floor doors and downstairs garage where her car was parked, but to no avail. Four hours now since detonation. The dark mist in the air was mostly now gone, but the settled black dust was visible everywhere. Good. The dispersion worked, and I, Farzam, am immune.

Maybe it's time to go up to her apartment.

CHAPTER 20

It had been four hours since the attack began. It was noon in Denver. Twelve thousand miles away in Dire, an already worried Antoine would have been even more disturbed if he knew where things stood in Denver. One assailant was dead—his name, Babur, and his intended target was alive—his name, Michael Reynolds. Just two of the other five targets were dead—the President of the United States, Paul Jennings, and the Speaker of the House of Representatives, Jeffrey Wilson. The two successful assailants—Amagan and Jaweed— had made it to their designated rendezvous in the tower building at Arapahoe Street and 16th Street Mall. The three other assailants—Farzam, Asa, and Fila— were becoming increasingly anxious, as they were ordered to finish their noble assignments before dark on the first day—9/11/21.

―――∾∽―――

Lacking knowledge that America was under foreign attack, there was no public panic in the downtown streets—only daunting curiosity. The blackened envelope above them was now a lighter, higher gray. Many believed smoke from a distant forest fire must have blown over the city leaving this fine ash spread all about them. Others believed the smoke was so black that it must have been from burning oil tanks or something similar. Without radio, television, or phones, the word had not yet spread of the president's assassination, or what might have caused the power outage, or that possibly a deadly pathogen was rapidly spreading among them, infecting them. Once again Michael was fortunate that Farzam had missed Michael's exit to the Volt parked by the garage of the Beauvallon. During their training, each assailant was required to learn the facial identities of all six targets in the event their paths were to cross. "Eliminate your target, but take out any of the others if the opportunity arises," were the explicit instructions.

Michael drove straight up Lincoln Street four of the five short blocks to the Capitol, and parked at East 13th. He jogged the last block to the basement entrance on the south side of the building and identified himself to three sullen-looking military guards now stationed at the locked door. Upon being quizzed, they knew nothing of the circumstances of why they were there, but recognizing Michael and knowing his stature, they let him through. He hustled up to General Armstrong's first floor office, and finding it empty, turned to leave when suddenly the general along with two Marines right behind him strode quickly into the room. Nodding to Michael and lifting one hand for Michael to wait, he punched the code buttons on his tabletop phone and without raising his voice: "General Ralston—hold. I'm getting the vice-president on the line." The phone went to speaker status as she answered:

"Yes, general …"

"Madam Vice-President … General Ralston, and also Michael Reynolds is right here with me …we have a tragic situation here. Upstairs in the House Chamber, Speaker Wilson, six senators and ten representatives have been shot dead. We have some fourteen more wounded. One man, one assailant, with an automatic rifle—he's gone. Without phones I have had to send my military out physically to get medical help here from the closest hospital … you were one hundred percent correct General, we *are* under attack."

"General Armstrong, you and Reynolds, you're out there tellin' me that the president is dead, the speaker is dead, that some strange toxin or bug may be in the air, and that some assassins are after you Reynolds and the vice-president too? God almighty! Get some military guards over to Vice-President Graham's immediately! I don't know the protocol for swearing her in, unless you can contact Chief Justice Jones, but she is now the civilian in charge."

Michael could stand to hear no more. He charged out of General Armstrong's office, headed back to the Volt, and off to the labs as fast as he could go.

CHAPTER 21

The appearance of the young woman fit right in with the others milling about the lobby of the Four Seasons. Her medium-length dark hair protruding from beneath a baseball cap, the bronze-colored skin tone of her flawless face, and her alert, penetrating, large green eyes all highlighted her perfectly matched strong features. She could freeze anyone's gaze. But others in the lobby were equally informal in their dress, and under the strange circumstances no one was noticing her and her outstanding beauty. Bathrobes, warm up suits, and long coats were all about as apartment dwellers grilled one another and the management staff about the annoying loss of electrical power and phone use. Fila's informal, long, dull-looking trench coat was not out of place.

But her hunch had been wrong. She had been waiting for two hours in the lobby with her weapons concealed beneath her trench coat—the AK-47, the Makarov pistol and the six-inch switchblade. She nervously made sure she did not bump into anyone that might suspect she was holding onto a hard object under her coat, but she had to be certain to closely inspect the face of each person entering the lobby. She had figured that Michael with his intuitive concerns would have driven off to the university fairly quickly and that Rose would be alone in the penthouse with her young child. But she thought for sure that Rose's curiosity would prod her to come down to the lobby to inquire why power was lost, as so many other residents had.

Changing strategy, she decided to leave the emergency-lit lobby a little after 10 o'clock to make her way up the stairwell to the penthouse, once there repeatedly knocking on Rose's door. With no response she sat down to just wait—frustrated but patient. By one o'clock, five hours after loss of power and the black dust onslaught, she knew Rose was not in the building and not coming back anytime soon. *Of course!* she thought, she must have gone with Michael the very first thing.

Down the back steps to the garage. Babur must have had it right. *Why am I so stupid?* After all, she had repeatedly listened at the couple's locked door. There were never any sounds inside. *They're both gone.* Her thoughts finally reasoned what must have occurred. She finally hit her mark—after all, the distance to the university was short, up 14th Street a block, left, and down Latimer Street a block. Across Cherry Creek and you are there. Rose was an engineer, but smart with the science too. She probably wanted to go with Michael to the microbiological and biochemistry laboratories to help figure out what this black mystery was. *Dummy! That's why I'm here—to stop them!* In order to avoid the soot, they would not want to walk to the lab with the baby. They drove! Fila felt annoyed with herself and hoped her comrades would never know of her wasted time. And she was supposed to be the smartest of the group!

So first, she continued to think to herself, let me check out the parking garage below. Maybe, just hopefully, Babur had done his job and Michael had been taken out as planned, and perhaps he got Rose too. *That would be something!* Moving quickly down the back steps to the garage, she suddenly remembered that during her time in the lobby earlier none of the residents or service staff meandering up and down the two stairwells or in the lobby had expressed concerns about any shootings in the garage—only their bewilderment about the power failure and the black fog.

Fila found nothing unusual in the garage, and yes she assumed that it was Michael's car that was gone from the first parking spot. Had Babur failed? Where was he? Maybe he didn't have a shot and had followed the car to the university campus. No way of knowing where her comrade could be since her own mobile phone was also inoperative. She began her own deliberate walk to the university labs.

Along the way, she began to think about how her own tangled involvement in this incredible plot came to pass. *How in the world am I here in America … walking through this sea of pathogens hunting for a woman to kill?* She recalled that after the American troops in Afghanistan vacated her nation, the Taliban retook control of the capital city, Kabul—a disaster for her and many other young women. Then 26 years old, her personal freedom and education had ended once again. Before the Americans came and after they left, young girls had no educational or career opportunities. Women were confined to the duties of the home. Even worse was the fact that if one violated in the least a canon of Islamic Shariah law as interpreted by the Taliban, harsh, often violent retribution would quickly follow. Strict obedience to God's will is a tenet in many religions and usually subject to wide interpretation, but never to be questioned by a young woman in Afghanistan.

Through a friend she had met in Kabul while in school there—an elderly man serving as a counselor who had traveled for many years as an overseas envoy—she heard stories of an offshore peace movement centered in a little island called Dire. It all seemed quite secretive, but after much prodding, her friend confided in her and made the necessary connections for her to meet with an undercover recruiter. Within a year of intensive interrogations about her personal motives, she received special passage on a small boat to transport her to the intriguing island. Joyfully in spirit, she very quickly acclimated to what seemed like a utopian life. She was soon introduced to Antoine and Aazim—both immediately impressing her with their sincere devotion calling for an end to worldwide violence, and she impressing them, partly perhaps because of her outstanding beauty, which could not have gone unnoticed by the dashing, vivacious Aazim.

Fila assimilated quite easily into the simple, peaceful farming society of the Dirists. But within just a few months, she accidentally overheard that a number of high-ranking Dirists led by Antoine and Aazim were advocating for a much broader cause than simply a *call* for ending violence—they were about *actually* ending it!

She learned that underground bunkers were being built; food and water rations were being stockpiled; volunteers were being recruited for secretive missions abroad. She began to think herself: *life is too simple now when so many others are suffering, so why not me too?* Why not volunteer for a nobler mission? An unofficial word was spreading around the island: the Dirists' leaders were going to use the threat of some very advanced weapons of mass destruction to bribe the whole world into giving up all of their arsenals. It wasn't until she decided to volunteer herself for the special force of 10,000 of the 100,000 residents that she learned the full story—the Master Plan. All the world's governments would be bribed with the threat of a deadly bacterium. "Disarm and receive the antidote, or else."

She later learned after some very rigorous interrogation as to whether she could maintain secrecy that the Master Plan excluded the United States. The planet's only true superpower, except during the few years of their catastrophic climate crisis, it was believed that America alone would be the one nation that would not submit to the bribery. "They must be taken out" was the phrase Aazim repeated. At first, the concept of spreading death through a highly contagious virus was repulsive to Fila, and the thought that an American president would be assassinated was not in line with the Dire precept of non-violence. But in time, after private audiences with Antoine and Aazim, the plan made more and more sense to Fila.

The ultimate advantage for the whole of mankind sounded so logical that she finally bought in completely. In fact, she so accepted it that she eventually volunteered to even be one of the assassins to be sent to America. Her transformation was complete—from submissiveness and witness to violence in Kabul, to peace and freedom in Dire, to a volunteer for the overseas bribery program, to a valiant peace fighter in America. Her determination, her intellect, her physical prowess had all paid off in her selection and training. Fila was physically fit, strong and smart, but perhaps her striking beauty also played a role in her appeal to Aazim.

She walked briskly on towards the labs, collecting her thoughts. *Lost time, but here I am—in America pursuing my prey. Move!*

CHAPTER 22

Before uniformed security on General Ralston's orders could reach Vice-President Graham's Beauvallon apartment, Farzam made his move. He decided to vacate his tiresome routine of walking circles, going from the parking garage below, around the lobby doors, and looking closely at every person in sight. Time to finally climb up the apartment's stairwell to the top floor—no more waiting. He already knew the number on the vice-president's door. The top floor hallway was empty. Moving quietly to her door, he slowly, silently tried the knob. Locked, as he suspected. He rang the bell. No response. *Just do it*, he thought, firmly resolved in his mission. He uncovered his AK-47 from his long coat and aimed it at the door latch. Without hesitating he began firing in rapid succession; then as quickly as he could, he shoved the door open with his shoulder and took his fateful steps inside. He couldn't believe for the world that the vice-president in any way could know she was the target of an assassin's bullets.

Michael had been right with his advice and warning. Ali should stay back in her office by the secure phone line while Tom should be ready with his pistol and station himself near the door entrance. It happened so fast. Farzam only caught a fleeting glance of what faced him head on as he broke through the door. His face lit up in complete surprise. He was not facing a woman in distress as he expected but staring at a man in a suit with a pistol pointed right at him. Tom fired only one shot—right to the middle of the forehead of the startled would-be assassin. The second of the six assailants was now dead. Thanks to Michael's warnings, Farzam the "worthy" one had failed miserably.

Alexis Graham was safe, for now.

CHAPTER 23

Asa too had been recruited from to Dire from Afghanistan after the Americans began to leave his native country at the start of the U.S. climate crisis in 2012. He was another enlistee from the Middle East and Far East weary of constant violence and who had heard from clandestine sources of the peace movement gaining in numbers on the island of Dire, 200 miles off the coast of India. It seemed Afghans were among the most recruited to populate the special 10,000 "volunteers" for the overseas "bribe" program conceived by the Dirist leadership. This targeted recruiting effort was perhaps fueled by the fact that the Afghan people were long unaccustomed to peaceful times, meaning that violence was a customary way of life, and that a certain number of them found such ongoing violence repulsive.

Born in a small village well south of Kabul, young Asa experienced the daily turmoil in his village as his family's tribal leader alternately and frustratingly played his hand to his advantage among the competing interests of the Taliban, his own villagers, the Americans, the reformers from Kabul, and the uncertain Afghan National Army. It was difficult to pick a winner. Because of his strong intellectual curiosity as a teenager, his father had been wise to send him to an international school in Kabul to escape the village turmoil. There, Asa learned and appreciated the values of the rule of law and the potential for prosperity for the many not just for the corrupt few—prosperity created by honesty, hard work, and free trade among peoples and nations. Like Fila and the other Afghans who were recruited to Dire and later sent to Denver in 2021, Asa found the return of the Taliban to near full control of the country repulsive to his newly learned concepts of peace and freedom.

A maturing Asa came to understand the Taliban was an Islamic fundamentalist political movement whose members believed in a very strict interpretation of Islamic Shariah law. Sharia, or "path", is the moral code of the religion of Islam, dedicating full obedience to God's word, and can be accepted by a very many Muslims. But Sharia can also be interpreted by some to mean that leaders set forth such extensive rules that every detailed aspect of daily life is subject to specific regulation. Contrasted with the majority of Islamic sects, this extreme version can then be seen to be repressive by most Muslims and certainly at odds with Western ideals of individual freedom supported by Judeo-Christian moral principles. Through his broader international studies, Asa developed a longing for personal freedom and an antipathy towards a lack of personal choice, understanding that *his* choices could not infringe upon the rights of others. He especially detested a system whereby the lack of personal choice was violently enforced by his religion's strictest adherents. He learned that both Judaism and Christianity had also suffered under such intolerance and violence many centuries before, and he found himself praying that someday Islam would also reach reconciliation among its many sects and factions.

Yes, he did learn that for a while, the Taliban had served a magnificent purpose. Asa remembered hearing about the Taliban military training in Pakistan to fight the Russian occupation of Afghanistan in the 1980's, foreign forces which were finally repealed from his home country in 1992. But after that war period, the movement became politically supported by hordes of students trained in religious schools in Pakistan; to such an extent that this factional group was actually able to take control of Kabul and much of the Afghan country by 1996. This situation lasted up until the Americans came looking for Osama bi-Laden after the infamous 9/11/2001 attack on America. The Taliban then went into partial retreat.

By 2014, after the completion of the American military evacuation, the Taliban movement once again took full political control of Afghanistan. But the force of one extreme movement always seems to breed an opposite other force. Those who taste personal freedom do not give it up easily. Through word of mouth the clandestine recruitment of opponents of sharia law had grown on the streets of Kabul. By 2017, Asa had grown weary of working for a Kabul merchant whose once prosperous business had soured under repressive government mandates. Making contacts with Dirist agents was not easy, as nothing about the movement was available in writing, and interrogations were secretive and extensive. No one on Dire except those among the highest circles had any electronic contact with the outside world. News of the peace movement was spread only by word of mouth. Once considered, one had to prove good intent and disprove any and all links to radical political associations, extreme religious movements, or existing government agencies. Once accepted, you were secretly on your way to Dire.

Even after arriving to the island, you were eventually grilled extensively about your support for the Dirist leadership in calling for a worldwide revolution to permanently end all violence caused by the human populations of the world. For those selected for further recruitment, it was at first about *"living"* in peace and *"calling"* for peace, but later it mushroomed into a commitment to conduct *"action"* as the way to achieve everlasting peace. The Master Plan for accomplishing this goal that was eventually revealed to the special recruits seemed ingenious. For who would not submit to a demand for disarmament in return for the only antidote to a ubiquitous, life-ending anthrax bacterium? Asa became so enthusiastic that he eventually volunteered for service in the special 10,000 person overseas contingent that would disperse the bio agent. After all, he was young, strong, determined, and would even be safely vaccinated in advance.

Asa's later transformation from an agent of bacterial bribery to a champion of viral lethality did not happen easily. Action to end violence with a *threat* of fatality is quite different than action causing a *certainty* of fatality. A year before the launch date of 9/11/21, he met Fila at an outdoor social gathering and was instantly drawn to her stunning good looks and pleasant personality. After sharing stories of their upbringing in native Afghanistan, they realized they had so much in common. Eyes gazing at one another on a warm romantic evening, they both felt an attachment and both inadvertently shared sketches of their missions with one another. Unwittingly, Fila let her assignment to America slip out, but not her role as an assassin. Antoine and Aazim never wanted the *details* of their Master Plan revealed to other than a very few in order to protect against leaks to the outside world.

But it did not take long for the enamored Asa to change his assignment from delivering the anthrax bacteria in Paris in order to bribe France to one of volunteering for the more dangerous assignment of becoming a dispersing agent sent to America to spread death. Pretending to set up a "chance" meeting with the proselytizing Aazim, and with his newly found love Fila always in mind, his volunteering for the American mission came easy, but the interrogation that followed was intense. He had to sound convincing that destroying the American society was a *good deed, not an evil one*. Moving to the final step of becoming one of the six assassins was even a bolder step. Falling deeply in love with Fila made that last hurdle much easier to cross.

And now, here he was—in America, fully committed.

Arriving from Richard Frost's apartment after murdering Frost's wife, Asa witnessed the obvious turmoil at the scene of the Capitol. He smiled as he thought that Jaweed must have down his job well by the looks and sounds of the military chaos outside the building. But his search for Richard Frost must continue. He thought of Frost's wife saying he must have gone to the Capitol or to the university. His persistent inquiries of the guards stationed outside finally paid off as one said he saw the president of the National University, Richard Frost, leave the building after the commotion inside. *I must go to the university.*

As he began his determined walk towards the university lab building, less than a mile away, he reasoned Frost would naturally go there eventually as it was the site of his prime technical responsibility, as opposed to his useless administrative office on Grant Street. *Of course! That's the exact reason why I am targeting him.* While walking briskly passing by dazed Denver residents, his thoughts turned back to how he graduated from a trip to Paris, France to spread the anthrax bacteria to becoming a disperser of the virus in America to now becoming an assassin in the midst of this deadly viral attack upon the United States—one where there was no antidote, except for the secret vaccine he was carrying in his own body. Beyond the assassinations, all on American soil would die, except him, his beloved Fila, and his other comrades, fortunate because they had been injected with a special vaccine that could only be produced in quantities sufficient for the 1000 volunteers who were to spread the virus throughout America. Or at least that is what they were told, and that is what they believed.

Yes, meeting Fila was life changing for Asa. He smiled to himself as he walked, remembering that after meeting and falling in love with Fila, he had it set up so that he would accidently bump into Aazim at a peace rally in early 2020 —Asa apologized, and then introduced himself as a special volunteer for the European mission. Aazim smilingly put his arm around his shoulders, pulling him aside. "Oh, young man, so you are in training for the mission to France. I know you will meet with complete success … Asa, Asa … a friend of Fila? Yes, she mentioned your name. I hear that you are uncommonly dedicated to our goals and to our mission, so I would like to let you in on a more dangerous, right, I mean to a bolder plan. Yes? … Good. You will keep this a secret. While we are all committed to a non-violent world, we also know that one country out there would probably not go for our anthrax bait. Right. The United States of America. They always thought as the great superpower they would be the ones to enforce world peace—the UN was dismal at that. But America failed worse.

Violence continued around the world. And they caused a lot of it—invading Iraq, Afghanistan, Libya … their CIA drones everywhere …

"I believe we should put an end to them, and you have obviously accepted the notion of complete peace. They, the Americans, are evil and they would rebel and rise. Yes, not a violent devastation kind of an end, but just a short sickness that closes their eyes forever. And we need an insurance policy to prevent against a small chance of success against us. Let me explain further, Asa…."

Those follow-on words of Aazim were not completely convincing on their own at first to Asa, but there was his Fila with her special assignment and after talking with her again and again and finally understanding her weaponized assignment, Asa recalled how he fell in line. The message about one act of violence in order to end all violence sounded so rational and sincere, but it was really his unrelenting attraction for Fila that moved him to the next and last stage of helping to prevent any quick American retaliation by taking out their leaders. He had become an assassin. All this background led him to a year and a half of intensive training for his path to Denver.

Asa had one more thought as he sped up his pace walking west on Colfax Avenue. *I will find and destroy this Richard Frost, before nightfall,* he demanded of himself.

Prior to its transformation into becoming the National University, the Auraria Campus in Denver was comprised of three collegiate academic centers. The five-story Science Building within the largest center, the University of Colorado at Denver, was located on the side adjacent to Speer Boulevard. With the desperate need to understand and seek technical knowledge regarding the country's climate crisis of 2012 to 2018, the nation's top scientists and engineers were brought to this campus. Next to the 7th Street garage in the middle of the campus had been a large parking lot known as "Holly". In 2013, the federal government designed and constructed a seven-story Advanced Science Building on the site, at 7th Street and Lawrence Way just across from the existing 7th Street garage and contiguous to the existing science building. The entire second floor of the new facility was the location of the ultramodern Advanced Microbiological Laboratory, capable of performing all the best protocols of the former Center for Disease Control and Prevention in Atlanta, Georgia.

Beyond serving as President of the National University, Richard Frost most enjoyed his secondary role as Dean of the new Biochemistry Laboratory, located on the entire third floor. He worked closely with the Dean of the Advanced Microbiological Laboratory, Jonathan Dean Ph.D. Dr. Dean had come to the National University from the University of California, Berkeley, and brought with him profound expertise in identifying and dealing with contagious diseases.

Asa crossed Cherry Creek and Speer Boulevard from Colfax and entered the campus at 7th Street. From there a short walk to the new lab building. There were students milling about while others were wandering aimlessly, looking somewhat dazed, wondering why their constant-companion cell phones were still not working. That had never happened before.

In the warm September air at mid-day, it would be peculiar to wear a long coat, but in the general confusion no one noticed the bulge that was Asa's AK-47 neatly hidden under his long trench coat. As he approached the building he paused for the first time and suddenly began to wonder what was the status of his fellow assailants and their targets. Did Babur take care of Michael Reynolds already … and my Fila of Rose Haines? If Richard Frost is here as I suspect, just exactly where would he be? Asa certainly knew that in addition to his target's uptown main administrative office, Frost also had an assigned office just outside the labs of his third floor Biochemistry Department. *He must be there.* He reasoned Frost wouldn't be in the second floor's Advanced Microbiological Laboratory because he would first want to know what our black dust chemical dispersant could possibly be … or, maybe MB scientists would already be there on the second floor beginning their biological detective work, which might mean Frost could also be there—curious.

Asa's mind was racing a mile a minute. His expression was one of momentary confusion as he frowned. Exactly where would Frost be? His office, his lab, the MB lab? His thoughts were that maybe the first thing he should do is cut the emergency power generator in the battery array behind the building, but then he might not be able to get into the electronically locked lab doors upstairs. Little did he suspect that in the second floor MB lab Michael Reynolds and Rose Haines were there together, right now. One significant flaw in the Master Plan was the failure of the six assassins to share information of their targeting methodology. Even with his closeness to Fila, he had little knowledge of her planned method of locating her target. He finally concluded that since he knew his own plan to target Frost outside his Portofino residence had failed, his best hope was that his mark had made his way to his third floor Biochemistry Laboratory, and that is where he would find him.

His one last thought about Fila—she must now be at the tower waiting for him. It did not cross his mind that at this same moment his true love Fila could be patrolling the unlocked first floor lobby of the lab building, contemplating her next move. Asa had assumed that she must have met with success at Rose Haines' Four Seasons residence and had proceeded to the assailants' tower rendezvous after experiencing glory in her mission.

He stopped thinking as began his move closer to the lab building.

CHAPTER 24

Right after World War II, the Center for Disease Control and Prevention, the CDC, was a new center, under a prior name, first funded as a federal agency with headquarters in Atlanta, Georgia. It was given the mission to improve and protect public health and to help prevent outbreaks by investigating contagious diseases. In 1951, it was also chartered to protect against biological warfare. By 1969, it had built and operated several airtight, high-containment advanced laboratories that could study such outbreaks as smallpox, Legionnaires disease, Ebola virus, influenza, West Nile virus, salmonella, SARS, HIV, and anthrax bacteria. Prior to the nation's climate crisis in 2012, it operated ten other locations outside Atlanta, employed 14,000 workers, and was funded to the extent of $11 billion per year. Upon the national move to Colorado, operations were suspended at all locations, and several hundred of the CDC's top scientists were redeployed to the Advanced Microbiological Laboratory at the National University in Denver.

This mile high site at the base of the scenic Rocky Mountains with its warm dry air had been most pleasing to those scientists these last few years, and by 9/11/21 the 25% who were asked to stay permanently couldn't have been more pleased. The prestigious Dr. Jonathan Dean relished his position as the head of the renowned laboratory in its serene surroundings.

———ɷ̃———

Prior to the appearances of Fila in the lobby of the laboratory building and then Asa outside, Michael had returned to the labs from his misadventures in town, especially those visits recalling his entrance into the president's mansion and then into the Capitol. Parking near the 7th Street garage just north of the lab building's front entrance and donning a hat and high-collared jacket from the Volt's trunk, Michael tried to look as unrecognizable as possible as he entered the lab building from the southwest side. He clearly understood there were more would-be assassins on the hunt.

The first floor entrance doors were customarily unlocked to allow students, scientists and technicians easy access to the administrative offices located on ground level. The stairwell door leading into the second floor opened into a bare, narrow hallway with a series of locked laboratory doors lining the hall. The high-risk containment lab was located through one of these MB labs, the one in the middle section of the building. Access from the hallway into the outer lab and then into the inner airtight lab was through a series of secure doors and could only be gained entrance by a few highly trained personnel who possessed the credentials. The point of all this security was to not allow any contagious diseases under study to escape from the inner lab.

"Rose!" Michael knocked and put his face to the small window in the door of the lab where he had left Rose and Alex. She opened the door quickly and stared at him speechless, starving for information.

"It's not good. This guy Jaweed, the one assigned to Speaker Wilson ... he not only got him at the Capitol, but a bunch of congressmen too."

"Oh my God. This is a nightmare, Michael. First the president, now the speaker ... and Ali? Is Ali —"

"She's okay," Michael broke in. "I was there again. I asked her to stay back and for Tom to stay armed near her door ... that an Afghan named Farzam was assigned to kill her. Ali has the full story, and with her secure fiber optics line to the Capitol and to the Pentagon, she at least has those communications. She's in full command now, Rose. She is our chief executive in—"

"In command of what, Michael?" Rose's voice signaled a clear sign of desperation. "There is no communication to the public. What can an army do anyway?" Half screaming, half crying, she was losing it after seemingly composed for so long. She went on. "Listen to me! I scrubbed myself and Alex, but I'm sure we have all inhaled it. Look Michael, I put this black dust we have been calling it … this so-called savior dust, under the electron microscope. There is definitely life, not a toxic chemical … could be bacteria, a virus? This dead guy here— Babur is his name? He was right. He called it 'black magic, savior dust, whatever'. It's alive! It must be pathogenic."

"*Calm*, Rose … look, how do we find out what it is?" Michael's voice tensed as he himself struggled to remain calm in front of an obviously distraught Rose.

"We have to get into the containment lab over there. I had the code for this lab here, but I'm not approved for that inner lab. If power is not restored, we only have about 48 hours for the batteries to start running out to supply power to our electronics. We have to get Dr. Dean in here."

Michael remembered that most electrical power for the whole university came from distant wind turbines and solar panel fields. Small backup solar panels were installed on top of several university buildings, but not these large science buildings. The lab backup system consisted of large electric storage batteries located alongside the back of the building, but they would discharge and shut down after two to three days of generating emergency electrical energy.

"Right," Michael replied trying to sound more optimistic. *No panic. Let's move ahead.* "Where would he be? This is his lab. He must be wondering why power and phones are off and what this dust—"

"We've been there, Michael. He lives on the top floor of the apartments just below the campus, remember, between Osage and Mariposa."

"Okay, okay, can you remember which unit exactly? I'll go –"

Just then a click at the door lock sounded. Michael and Rose leaned back, startled. The door swung open as Michael was reaching over to Rose's jacket pocket for the pistol he had taken from Babur, but there appeared none other than the MB department head—Dr. Jonathan Dean.

"Michael, Rose?" the tall, scholarly-looking, middle-aged professor said rather evenly. "Glad to see you! What in the world's going on out there?"

"Jonathan, you won't believe what's happened. Sit here … and listen. We have to work fast," Michael replied softly this time as he began to tell the whole incredible story all over again.

One flight above, a nervous, frightened Richard Frost sat solemnly at his desk. He was alone in his suite, except for the one Marine escort pacing at the outer door. He recounted over and over again the mental horror in his blurred memory—his wife had just been brutally murdered. He could not get the whole terrible picture out of his mind—the look of agony frozen on her face … assassins in the Capitol … no electrical power other than emergency backup … no mobile communications … Alexis Graham's and Michael Reynold's incredulous tale told in General Armstrong"s office…. *What do I do?* He was on automatic pilot. He had wiped that black dust off his arms and face. His first analysis was that the material was an extremely light chemical dispersant, very fine in texture, black in color when accumulated, but very free to blow and float through the air with ease. It had no earmarks of a toxic chemical, and he felt no ill effects from touching it or breathing it.

But Michael Reynolds had warned us of a deadly something. Yes, there could be a microscopic bug attached. And in addition Michael told me I'm also a target. *Why me?* His facial expression, his sagging shoulders, both gave away his look of desperation…. Finally, he ordered himself to recover and to follow his scientific instincts: *Maybe someone is downstairs in the Advanced Microbiological Laboratory trying to check this out.* "Young man, come with me," as he quickened his pace through the door.

CHAPTER 25

Before the federal government takeover of Denver in 2013, the 16th Street Mall had been a lovely pedestrian street, tree lined, red walking stones, and free electric buses to shuttle shoppers to its many stores and restaurants. During the congressionally approved Declaration of National Emergency, in effect from January 2012 through September 2018, the street had maintained its physical features, but functionally it had become a swanky haven for the suspended members of Congress. Over the last three years, with a reactivated Congress still in Denver, the street was still full of the liveliest bars and finest restaurants for those privileged few. The contrast was the huge Colorado Convention Center nearby at 14th and California Street—still empty and devoid of gatherings.

Nearby, at the top of the majestic tower structure at 16th and Arapahoe Streets sat the two successful assassins. "We have done our job well. We stay right up here, way up here, and wait for the others. We stick to our orders to stay in Denver for three days and observe our black magic working. Then we shall make the long journey home…. We have plenty of protein bars in our pockets…. Jaweed, did you hear me?"

"Yes, Amagan, I heard you. You know, I was thinking, until today

I never killed anyone. I was just reflecting how determined I was, and how I took out more than I was commanded ... but it was easy. I could do it again."

"You told me. I've heard that already. Of course, my friend Jaweed. We two are men of peace not violence, but when we have to, we do our job without remorse. I had no problem pulling the trigger on the President of the United States, not that I enjoyed doing it. It was my duty. America is a monster.... Jaweed, we are part of a noble historical mission."

"True, Amagan, true." Jaweed looked to the ceiling, and then he smiled, softly, content with himself.

The two proud successful assassins were holed up in a deserted room just below the clock tower with its 5000 pound bell in the Daniels and Fisher department store building. The whole tower structure was modeled after and looked exactly like the campanile at Saint Marks in Venice, Italy. Even the gold cupola serving as its crown matched San Marcos. The tower was located right on the corner of 16th Mall and Arapahoe, just three blocks northeast from the Four Seasons. Amazing to think this 1911 building was the tallest outside New York City until 1950—372 feet high with its flagpole. For stability and endurance, its foundation was dug 24 feet deep. Its structure consisted of steel-reinforced concrete, and its finish constructed with sandstone the first 40 feet up, while completed with brick all the way to the top. Even though it was close to the towering modern skyscrapers of downtown Denver, the scene still showed off in the year 2021 as a masterpiece.

"Amagan, you were here first. You know, I was thinking—what if the others need help?" Without pause, Jaweed continued to plead his case without awaiting a reply: "We were not instructed what we should do if all of us do not come together by the end of the first day. We were only told to concentrate on each of our assignments and finish our mission by the close of daylight the first day. The whole purpose is not to let America find a way to figure this out and save themselves or retaliate before the black dust does its job. Look, it's three o'clock already—it's dark in four more hours. Maybe we should—"

"Relax, my friend, oh noble Jaweed. You are the 'eternal' one. Have patience … you have learned to be too trigger happy," uttered Amagan softly as he slowly leaned back against the wall from his sitting position on the floor, smugly looking out a window at the confused populace below.

The two sat silently and waited, signs of pure confidence showing on their faces, but wondering inside just where the other four were right now, not suspecting in the least that Babur and Farzam were no longer breathing life on this earth.

CHAPTER 26

The door from the hallway into the MB lab hosting Michael, Rose, Alex, and the recently arrived Jonathan Dean swung wide open, and again Michael grabbed and raised Babur's now familiar pistol. It was a relieved Richard Frost who hurriedly entered, his Marine escort right behind.

"Richard!" Rose was quick to exclaim. "You're safe."

"Do you know—do you know what happened at the Capitol?" Frost stammered anxiously, not pausing in his excitement for a reply. "Michael, listen Michael, I overheard your conversation with Alexis and General Armstrong—something about six assassins, a toxic powder or bacteria or virus on this black dust—oh God, but my wife, my wife!.... She has been murdered, at home. Michelle ... she's dead!"

At first, all were speechless as Richard lowered his tear-filled eyes to the floor and then up to Michael's, begging for answers to this madness. "I'm so sorry, Richard," Michael finally replied coming closer to his trembling colleague. "But *you* were his target, not Michelle. He must have broken into your apartment thinking you were there when you were actually at the Capitol."

"Please Michael, please explain this whole rotten thing again," Richard implored. "I analyzed the dust upstairs in my lab. It's a very fine chemical dispersant with an exceptionally large surface area. It is not toxic, so this is not chemical warfare. It must have—"

"Right…. First, young man," Michael looking at the perplexed Marine: "Be sure this door is locked and stay close, your rifle ready. Anyone not looking like one of us breaking through or even entering with a stolen code and who looks armed, shoot first—in the legs if you can. We need more answers…. Everyone, please sit down." Michael recounted everything he knew to this point. Richard Frost, Jonathan Dean, and Rose looked on, half in fear and half in awe that Michael seemed to be calm, taking charge, a plan in mind. Baby Alex looked fast asleep. "Look. My assailant over there on the floor is out of their plan. As long as the others have only one target, I think I can go back and forth to Ali's since she is holed up there in her apartment with her security guard Tom. Only she and General Armstrong have communications at this point. She should have more guards there by now…. We have to find a way to take out the assailants who after you, Richard, and, and … Rose."

He looked at her momentarily in anguish but was distracted by his thoughts. "I'll get more guards over here…. Now Jonathan, can we get into the inner lab and find out what this stuff is? Rose has collected a good amount of it on this these plates and viewed it under the electron microscope. Richard, you confirmed it—it's not the dispersant. It's what's on it. It is alive."

"We need a couple of technicians to help. I can go get them. I can do the work, but I need help," Jonathan quietly answered. "We need to run lots of assays, tests to analyze, all at the same time. If this chemical dispersant you all described does have a living organism attached—as you said Rose—we have organic material on dishes we can grow it on and identify the bacterium, or if it is a virus we have frozen human tissue cells that we can grow it in by infecting them. We have lots of antibiotics and anti-viral agents in there…. It will take some time to get started suiting up … it's a clean containment room in there. Nothing microscopic gets in or out…. Wait! Of course, if we are already infected …"

His voice dropping off, Jonathan looked around, seeming to be puzzled. The group gathered in the MB outer lab was now a total of seven: a determined Michael, a flustered Rose, an innocent baby Alex, a perplexed-looking Jonathan Dean, a nervous Richard Frost, a startled young Marine officer listening to this preposterous story unfolding, and the dead Babur sprawled on the floor.

—���—

Collar pulled up, cap pulled down again to avoid recognition in the brightening afternoon, Michael was again out of the MB lab, down the back steps, and back in his Volt. As he approached the Beauvallon for this the third time, he saw the apartment building perimeter alive with police and military along with a curious crowd of civilians. Ali had already shared the news via the secure line with General Armstrong at the Capitol and General Ralston in Washington of her security agent killing her intended assailant. With the president dead, General Armstrong had his aides rouse the aged Chief Justice Jones from his apartment at the nearby Sheraton at 15th and Colfax, hustle him over to Ali's in an electric vehicle, slowly help him climb the steps to the top floor, and had her constitutionally sworn in as the 45th President of the United States.

Recognizing the well-known Michael Reynolds, the major in charge of the military team guarding the front entrance of the building told him the news of an assailant being killed inside the doorway to Vice President Graham's apartment and of her being sworn in as the new President of the United States. Granted quick permission to pass through, Michael journeyed up the emergency lit stairs, and upon opening the stairwell door to Ali's top floor, found himself face-to-face with several armed guards outside her closed door.

"Halt!" Uncomfortable in facing weapons raised towards his chest, especially after seeing Babur's pistol aimed and fired at him, Michael raised his hands high and quickly explained who he was. Upon recognition and an apology, he was granted speedy entrance into the new president's quarters. With all this new security here and

Ali's would be assailant dead, he shuddered momentarily thinking he was glad he had commanded Rose to keep Babur's pistol concealed in her vest pocket. *Thank God Ali is safe, but Richard and Rose's assailants are still out there!*

Moving into the apartment's living room, Michael observed several military personnel standing near a body on the floor, apparently pulled over to a corner. The room was much better lit now than his previous visits with the large windows letting in the hazy late afternoon sunshine. The black cloud was gone, the strange fog mostly lifted. Tom, looking dazed from his shooting of the intruder, was sitting on the sofa next to the assailant's body stretched out on the floor, the one Michal knew was named Farzam.

"Tom," Michael inquired. "Does he have any identification on him? Any documents?"

"Nothing. Not a thing in his pockets except about $1000 in cash with a rubber band around it."

"His name is Farzam," Michael said softly.

"Michael!" He heard his name called from behind him and knew it was Ali's voice. "Come back to my office." As he turned around, he instantly noticed a renewed glow on her cheeks, a new firmness in her voice, a new look of determination. True, she had been virtually an acting commander-in-chief these last three years while President Jennings had been hesitant and withdrawn in his leadership ability, but now—now she, Alexis Graham, Ali, was really the official President of the United States.

"Michael, we have work to do. General Ralston has no idea when the nation's power grid can be restored. Electrical junctions are physically destroyed from the EMP bomb. He believes it was a nuclear explosion high above Kansas that got the whole country, two to three hundred miles up. It had to be delivered by very powerful booster rockets. He says it could take months to restore electrical power. He says satellite communications should hopefully be on line much sooner, maybe just days if the solar power connections on the satellites weren't damaged, but cell towers for mobile phones are physically out. Fiber optic cables above ground are damaged at their sending and receiving points. There will be no internet communications via satellite for the same reasons. The general has no communications with overseas." Michael stood, stared and listened; his face blank as she went on non-stop. "My only way of communicating as president to the people is though the secure fiber optics line connected underground from the Pentagon to some fifteen military bases around the country, and from there by courier, like the days before electricity. Worse—*all* the bases reported a dark cloud dropping a black dust over them." She paused and looked him in the eye, as to pleading for a solution.

"Ali, if I may still call you that ... Madam President—"

"Ali, Michael, Ali."

"Right.... We don't know for sure what else this enemy, whoever it is, has out there completely, but they are powerful enough to have launched an atomic bomb to explode high over us. They put a live something they called "magic dust" on some type of dispersant and spread it everywhere. We do know from this Babur guy's dying words that it didn't matter that he didn't kill me because in three days it would get us. My hunch is that's it..."

"Go on," Ali injected after Michael's pause.

"I don't think there will be more attacks, Ali. They've done enough. They shut down our communications so this bug would do its thing while we're confused, and they plotted to kill the three in line to lead the country in a possible rapid retaliation and the three who maybe could find a quick answer to the pathogen. It can't be a big country behind this, like a Russia or China, although they have the means. They wouldn't attack us like this. We don't have a quarrel with them. It must be a small rogue state bent on destroying America, and who knows what other groups are involved helping them technically.... America has been out of the loop the last eight years. Whoever is responsible—they are advanced enough to be able to deliver one very big bomb while also developing, delivering, and spreading some type of organism, most likely contagious.... Bioterrorism in the extreme, Ali."

"But I am alive. I'm the president. I have to retaliate ... but how? I don't know who and where these people are. If you hadn't taken this guy Babur out, we wouldn't know anything ... Afghans—al Qaeda again?" Ali's composure suddenly changed from presidential to one of frustration.

"Maybe they thought if one of these six assailants were captured, we would torture him into revealing those answers and we'd send jets to nuke them," Michael mused. "How about if you do this: we have to find out what this organism is and how toxic, and if highly contagious, what the antidote or vaccine is. We've started on this already at the Advanced Microbiological Laboratory with Dr. Jonathan Dean, the department head, his staff, Richard Frost and Rose. You don't want to panic the public, Ali. Can you deliver a message through General Ralston to all the military bases around the country and have them multiply your message to the public through all the military personnel leaving the bases and delivering it verbally and asking the public to spread it like a chain to their neighbors? Your first message has to be to avoid the black dust—we don't know what it is yet but keep yourself clean of it—don't hint it might be a pathogen. Second, concentrate on a high air explosion of unknown origin that has temporarily knocked out power and communications, and that the federal government in Denver is working with the military and utilities to restore them as soon as possible, to stay calm and in their homes until the next notice."

"It's a start, Michael. It's a start. You're right—we have to seem in charge." Ali only sounded half convinced, but yes, Michael at least had a reasonable explanation for what's happened and a start on what to do next.

"And one more thing, Ali. Can you call General Armstrong and ask him to send military guards over to the National University, to the Advanced Science Building? Rose is there with Alex and Richard Frost—both are targets, and Doctor Dean is there now getting started on finding out what this bug is. No one should get into that building without clearance from us."

"Yes, right away, Michael, right away," she concurred wistfully, a look of bewilderment about the strange events suddenly surrounding her. She noticed the black dust on Michael's clothing, and then she saw even a little of it on her own arms and hands. It had gotten inside.

Little could they yet comprehend the awesome power of the "black magic", as Babur described it in his dying words.

CHAPTER 27

Walking unnoticed into the first floor lobby of the Science Building despite her long overcoat looking unfamiliar on a college campus in the warm month of September, Fila quickly found the directory for the exact location of the Advanced Microbiological Laboratory— that was just when the troops came into her view. Sighting several of them entering the front entrance, she crouched down behind the desk in front of the large directory on the wall. She heard one of them shout out to the four or five students milling about the large lobby, "vacate the building". It was going on lock down after they all left. Fila's thoughts became scrambled as she tried to concentrate on her mission. Her target, Rose Haines, was not at her home apartment tending to her young child as she originally thought, so she must be here, in that second floor lab. But now a complication with the arrival of these soldiers—*how do I get to her now?*

At the same time Fila continued to process her perplexing thoughts, Michael was back in his car debating what *he* should do next. *Follow the path of what's happened so far*: First, he would take the short drive from Ali's Beauvallon apartment a couple of blocks over to the former Governor's Mansion, now completely surrounded by military sentinels. Those poor guys, Michael thought. They must have no idea what's going on—a dead president inside, no power, black dust everywhere. Next, past the Capitol a few blocks up from the president's mansion, where he would witness the same scene—military guards completely surrounding the building, citizens on the lawns, the walks and the stairs all staring at the sentinels, questioning but getting no answers.

Turning the Volt westward, Michael suddenly recalled the folded paper in Babur's wallet. He had memorized the names and their targets. *Fila! Maybe our apartment!* Michael's thoughts raced in near panic: I'll go back to the Four Seasons. This Fila may be there now, stalking for Rose even though she is not there. Two assailants are dead. Their names—it was Babur and it was Farzam. They both failed. But two succeeded. It was Amagan and it was Jaweed. Where were they now? I remember the war in Afghanistan. These are all Afghan names. Could it be the Taliban Afghanistan attacking us? As Ali had questioned: could it be al Qaeda all over again—twenty years later? And where is Fila … and Asa?

Michael's mind continued to race as he accelerated his Volt west on Colfax then up 15th Street eleven blocks to a left on Larimer, one block to another left on 14th and one block down to the Four Seasons. Parking on the street, his collar pulled up again, his hat down, he cautiously made his way through some afternoon strangers strolling along the sidewalks appearing befuddled about their continuous loss of power. He looked carefully at each person located anywhere near the building. None seemed to be of Afghan appearance. None had a coat on or even a light jacket that could be possibly concealing a weapon, as the warm September sun was partially shining again. He walked through the nearly deserted lobby to the stairwell. No one looked suspicious. The emergency lights illuminating the steps were still operating. All the way up to the top floor. He opened the hallway door slowly. He wished he had Babur's pistol at this moment. He unlocked his apartment door, opening it slowly and quietly. He waited and listened a long time. No one—just as he and Rose had left it hours before—empty.

I have to get back to the lab—immediately!

⁓⁓⁓𝕸⁓⁓⁓

From the tall office skyscrapers just north of the Capitol complex to the twelve and fifteen story hotels and apartment buildings to the west to the five story campus buildings even further to the west, the scene in downtown Denver changes dramatically in less than a mile. Further out, always awesome, the mighty Rockies sprout up out of nowhere. After parking his Volt next to the Advanced Science Building, the ensuing events seemed to all happen in a rapid sequence, as Michael moved as fast as he could.

"Anything going on in there?" Michael anxiously asked the first soldier he approached after spouting out his name, worried that the remaining assailants may have tried to breach the labs.

"No sir. All is quiet—"

"Good," Michael said quickly, moving on and towards the entrance.

Knowing he was on the approved list, he hurriedly identified himself to the guards at the front doors of the lab building and was granted quick passage, but he failed to spot Fila slipping unnoticed from her hiding place into the stairwell a moment prior to Michael's entrance into the lobby. All the building lights were on in full power as the building's emergency generator system was working as programmed. Reaching the landing between the first and second floor, Fila suddenly heard the door below open and footsteps running up. She stopped, turned, and two faces expressed complete surprise as their eyes met just five feet apart on the landing. Fila already had her hand on the AK-47 trigger under her open long coat. In a flash, it was pointed right at Michael's chest as they both ended their momentary pause with her excited exclamation: "It's you—Michael Reynolds!" And without thinking, she automatically blurted: "Where is Babur?"

After leaving the security of the first floor entrance and lobby and heading into the stairwell, Michael, in his haste, had not thought it possible that this assassin could be inside. The building was under military guard! He was initially as surprised as she but quickly regained his train of thought that yes, *this* must be Fila, a female, the assassin assigned to kill Rose. His shoulders sagged, his heart pounded. He realized he had rushed to the lab to protect Rose only to be stupidly caught on the stairs a half floor from his destination. He shuttered, thinking Fila was going to finish what Babur had started. *What would a bullet in my chest feel like? Should I go for her rifle?*

Fila regained her composure. *Remember my training; be cool.* "Hands in the air! Take me to your wife. Where is she? In the MB Lab?"

"You don't want to do this. Why? America has done nothing to you," Michael said firmly as he also regained a small measure of composure. *She is not going to shoot!* She needs me to get to Rose, his mind flashed. *Go for her rifle*, but he felt frozen.

"Quiet! We are not here to debate. I have a job to do. Move up and open the next door."

"You are Fila. Your friend Babur gave up. He no longer has his weapons. If this dust, this black magic you call it, gets us, it also gets you. You are not going to succeed." Michael's tone was strong and nearly half convincing.

"How do you know who I am? Who Babur is?" Fila asked in astonishment. Michael simply stared at her coldly and did not respond as she paused, then continued: "No, we are immune; we are vaccinated ... American dominance will be no more. You are finished. Never again, Michael Reynolds. Now move up these steps and open that door. Keep your hands up." Two worlds apart, but it was obvious that Fila was shaken, that this Michael Reynolds knew not only her and Babur's names but already knew that this black magic contained something very deadly. Yet, that's exactly the reason why they were sent—that these Americans are smart and fast. They must be destroyed before they can react.... *But where is Babur?*

CHAPTER 28

Antoine, the one-time sophisticated, well-dressed European banker, puffed anxiously on his cigarette. Even in his shorts and unbuttoned short sleeve shirt, he was sweating profusely in the humid night air. He could not stop pacing the living room of the small beach house known as Dire's above ground headquarters. He had tried to sleep but it was useless. Middle- aged, once well groomed and handsome, he now appeared older than his years. His unshaven face and graying, disheveled hair both gave evidence of his intense anxiety from not knowing what was happening around the world at this moment and what the final outcome would be. The stress was taking its toll on the Parisian.

As planned, there would be no communications with any of the 10,000 Dirists sent to 125 of the most armed 195 United Nations countries around the world until the third day. At that time, captains piloting Dirist jets would return and give the answer from each nation: submission or death. Hundreds of millions of anthrax vaccination kits had been secretly planted in warehouses around the world. If the final word signaled willingness to submit to the bribe and to surrender their major weapons, the vaccines would be released. If not, the warehouses would be dynamited. Billions would die. Antoine had constantly worried whether there were enough vaccines; could they be distributed in time; would some of the national leaders submit to the bribe, distribute the vaccines, and then later renege on their promise? *Is this plan too ambitious? An impossible dream?*

And America: how could we in effect murder 300 million people just like that? He looked over at Aazim, sleeping comfortably on the sofa. He thought about Aazim always appearing calm, in control, confident—not a worry. *Does this man not have a conscience?* Antoine continued to pace and wonder how he would get through the silence of the night and all tomorrow. The only sound was the slight landing of soft waves on the nearby beach sand of this little island of Dire.

CHAPTER 29

The scene inside the Capitol was chaotic. Even with a dozen battery-powered emergency spotlights scattered about on each of three main floors, the spacious building seemed dimly lit, except close to areas where the hazy afternoon sun was shining though the fifty or so windows facing to the west. Uniformed police and military were at all the doors but puzzled as to what they were witnessing. They were ordered to allow uniformed ambulance and medical personnel in but no one else. To the dismay of all who came to help, the second floor House chamber where the massacre took place faced squarely to the western sun, and the window light clearly revealed the extent of the horror. The groans; the sorting out the dead from the wounded and moving them away from the seats of the chamber and onto the floor of the hallways; identifying the dead; getting the wounded to the hospital; the perplexity without working phones to notify family and aides of the fallen Congressmen—an appalling picture of despair.

Directly below that frightful scene, General Armstrong's spacious first floor office, also facing west and formerly the Governor's Office, was now a beehive of confusion. The general was trying to sort out the facts of the last six hours and think of what he could possibly do next. Michael Reynolds had revealed the attackers' plan to the general:

kill the president, the vice president, and the speaker while some type of what might be a deadly organism was being spread by a black dust.

At the same time, General Ralston in Washington had reported that an electromagnetic pulse bomb had knocked out all communications except for the secure underground fiber optics network from the Pentagon to the Capitol and to 15 military bases around the county. The only civilian connected was Alexis Graham, the new president. She had released a directive to all the bases instructing them to physically disseminate word to the public advising that the government was assiduously working to fix the power outage. Nothing was to be said about an EMP attack or the black dust released as a weapon. No need for the government to panic the public.

Next followed the request to send guards to the Advanced Science Building at the National University to keep everyone out while David Frost, Jonathan Dean and Rose Haines could figure out what the strange dust really could be. Ignoring the scurrying all around him, the white-haired, sixty-four year old general sat at his desk looking decidedly forlorn. His thoughts ranged from his decorations as a colonel serving in Afghanistan 15 years before, to the present where maybe, somehow—could I be strangely fighting al Qaeda all over again? How in the world could they ever get this powerful? *I'm the top military guy here, but what the hell am I supposed to do now?*

CHAPTER 30

In these situations of crisis, the mind races; the heart beats faster; adrenaline flows. Even his palms were in a sweat. Michael's mind flashed. He had only seen this scene in the movies—the good guy pushes the rifle barrel away and counters the attacker, but here *he* was—this time it was he with his hands up above his head, a rifle in his back, making the last few steps up to the second floor landing. He wished he had made his move for the rifle when he was facing her. Could he now really turn the tables on her physically? Somehow he needed to buy time. Think it out.

Fila instructed him to slowly open the hallway door and take one step inside and stop. She then peered around in both directions. The hall was empty. "To the MB Lab door where she is," she commanded. Michael hesitated. *Can I turn around quickly and disarm her?* If I take her into the lab, she will shoot Rose and probably him too. Fila's mind raced too. She read his mind. "Michael Reynolds. I'll pull this trigger now if you don't move. I'm not assigned to you. I will not shoot you if you cooperate." Michael took one step more and stopped again. He could not, he would not, lead an assassin to where she could kill the most beloved person in his life. Fila sensed his predicament, and without further thought raised the butt of her rifle and slammed it hard into the back of Michael's head. He went down fast, without a groan.

With Michael sprawled face down upon the floor, she looked at the several nearby doors. How simple after all. Each had a nameplate right below a small square window. She found the one with "Advanced Microbiological Laboratory—Disease Control". She peered through the small window. There she was—Rose Haines holding and bouncing a baby, the infant staring right back at her. There was David Frost— alive! *Allah, where is Asa?* There was one more person—a uniformed soldier with a rifle strapped to his shoulder standing close to the door. *It's now. Don't hesitate.* She turned the doorknob slowly and quietly. Locked. She remembered her training—how to shoot the door lock open, quickly turn the knob, push the door open, and hit the floor headfirst with your rifle in the ready-to-shoot position. It was the last part of this training that Farzam had forgotten upon his breaking through Alexis Graham's door.

She executed the move perfectly. The young inexperienced Marine was hit and down before he could even point his rifle at her down on the floor. Three shots—one to his shoulder hosting his rifle, two to both knees. She pulled his rifle way as he writhed in pain on the floor. The startled David Frost cowered backward, his face trembling in terror. Rose turned to the assailant now lifting herself up on one knee and pointing the rifle right at her. The child in her arms looked on in bewilderment with his eyes and mouth wide open. Strange that neither Asa just outside the building nor the military figures guarding the building entrances could hear or recognize the noise of the three loud shots echoing off the lab walls.

Fila stood up completely, square to Rose—face to face at last. Fila had studied dozens of photographs of Rose. She knew her target cold. Rose kept her steel eyes on Fila's but turned her baby to the side to shield him. What else could she do? Fila moved closer, her AK-47 raised and targeted on Rose's chest. The baby turned his head back over Rose's shoulder towards Fila, and to her he seemed to have a pleading look in his eyes, like he knew even as a one year old what was coming next, but yet appeared fearless. Fila glanced back and forth from the child's to Rose's eyes. They matched the baby's look of denunciation. It was not fear. It looked like courage, like daring. Fila hesitated. Not a word was spoken. David Frost was frozen. The stares continued; it was inexplicably silent.

This is the famous American—Rose Haines. This is the one who helped figure out what was going on during the American climate crisis, the one who helped save the American dream of freedom against the president's corrupt, tyrannical chief-of-staff. A heroine. But now— defenseless herself but unrelenting, here was a woman proudly holding and defending her baby. Fila lowered her rifle slightly. Conflicting thoughts suddenly flashed through her mind: *I am for peace, not violence. Somehow I became convinced that we must destroy Americans to achieve eternal peace. But can I achieve peace by being violent myself … against a helpless woman protecting her child? Something's wrong. This woman I face is to be admired not murdered.… Maybe it's my natural maternal instinct taking hold of me, overcoming me. How can I kill a defenseless mother holding her innocent child?*

I have to get over this. I have to fulfill my mission.

CHAPTER 31

Circulating among the curious onlookers skirting about outside the Advanced Science Building, all wondering why soldiers were guarding the doors to the building, was the assassin Asa. He was hoping that he did not look too conspicuous. His long olive green trench coat must have seemed odd in the warm late afternoon. Nothing wrong with his dark skin and black beard—there were always many like that around an ethnically diverse American academic center, but with the afternoon temperature at 75 degrees in the sunshine no one else had on a coat. He remembered and was thinking that he had been trained to face a situation where he would have to break into a building and through locked doors to get to his target—David Frost. But there were at least four armed guards at each entrance, and how could he be certain that Frost was up there in his third floor office, somewhere in his biochem lab, or maybe in the MB lab on the second floor?

And who was that that just gained entrance to the building in a white lab coat? Asa was not familiar with the looks of the MB lab chief, Jonathan Dean, who had returned after summoning the lab's best technician. Now becoming confused, Asa began to think that maybe he should retreat from his solitary mission at this point and go seek help. Others must be in the tower by now. Or, I could shoot my way into the building, rush up the stairs and burst into each possible location seeking David Frost. His thoughts continued. But what if there are more troops inside guarding each location? I might not have time to get them all—I could be *one* armed man doomed against *many* armed men. *That's suicide.*

And then, his thoughts turned to the matter of Fila. Asa was only twenty years old when he arrived in Dire in 2016. Unmarried, raised in a village near Kandahar raked with violent turmoil, he had little experience with members of the opposite sex. When he met Fila shortly after both had been selected for their missions overseas, it was for him love at first sight. At first, she enjoyed their romantic meeting but resisted his immature advances into her daily life. But as their training together progressed, so did their relationship. To Fila, Asa was warm, genuine, caring—qualities she dearly admired. Leading up to their departure to Denver, they unselfishly shared their minds, their bodies, and their spirits. Not once would they admit their trepidations to others, but to each other they secretly revealed their fears of ever being apart.

So where is Fila now? He questioned himself as he stared at the lab building. Did she fulfill her task at the Four Seasons and was waiting patiently for him at the tower rendezvous? He made his decision. I will get the others to help me. He turned away from the building, out of the campus and began his walk up Arapahoe four blocks to the 16h Street Mall. At least he was not the only one walking the streets in frustration, although he was the only one with a long coat on, and again that made him feel others were staring at him. The streets were full of people, walking aimlessly and wondering when power would be restored. They had not received word yet to stay indoors. In an age of instant computer and phone communications, it was very unnerving to learn only by word of mouth that some kind of malfunction must have knocked out the nation's power. And for those who came out early, what was this black soot on their arms, heads, and clothing?

But first a stop at the Four Seasons which was right on the way to the tower. He had to check on whether Fila was there, perhaps still waiting for her target, Rose Haines. He checked around the doors to the building and the parking garage below. No sign of her. Several persons were in the warm un-air conditioned lobby appearing quite annoyed at their inconveniences. The fact that no policemen or military were visible anywhere was a sign to him that nothing violent had taken place there. He found a uniformed young lady behind a desk and approached her uncomfortably. "Excuse me. I'm a bit confused by what's going on with the power loss, but can you tell me, have there been any troublesome acts here, like what might have brought medical help or police? I have friends here but I can't remember their apartment numbers—"

"No, no heart attacks or problems like that. We have accounted for all our residents in the building. They are all annoyed of course, but either getting by in their units, or must be out walking if we did not find them in. I'm sorry we cannot divulge unit numbers of our residents or their—"

"Right, okay," interrupted Asa. "I understand. Thank you. I can come back later."

As Asa continued his short walk to the tower, he wondered if his dearest Fila might have missed her opportunity at the Four Seasons and could possibly be—*at the lab? No, I would have seen her outside.* And those guards there were not aware of anything going on inside.

Asa slipped unnoticed into the tower's entrance door and made his way up the steps, a drenching sweat soaking his shirt. He took his trench coat off after the first ten steps, revealing his weapon, and proceeded to the meeting room near the top. He entered slowly and quietly, surprising Amagan and Jaweed who were sitting on the floor half dozing. Amagan started to reach for his AK-47 but realized who had entered. "Oh, Asa. It's you. You did it? Success?"

Asa searched the room for Fila, then dropped his eyes to the floor in disappointment. Barely audible, he mumbled: "No, no. I am not certain. I went to Frost's apartment. He was not there. I went to the Capitol. Maybe he's there. I don't know … " Asa voice trembled, revealing his confusion. "We were taught he would probably go to his lab. I went. It was heavily guarded. But guarded for him? For Rose Haines? For Michael Reynolds? I don't know... Can you help? Where is Fila?" Asa's voice dropped in dejection.

Amagan and Jaweed stared at him in silence for several moments. To this point in time the two had known Asa as relentless, dedicated, bold, but were now taken back at Asa's obvious hesitancy. "But Asa," Amagan finally retorted. "We were instructed to stick with each of our targets, to execute before nightfall. We have done our part. We are successful in our missions. We are going home soon.... We don't know where the others are." More silence followed. Amagan and Jaweed turned their eyes away and looked down at the floor. Asa felt almost embarrassed he had come asking for help from those who had succeeded. Maybe Amagan thought that after his own successful assignment, it would be suicide going to a heavily- guarded lab building. He wanted no parts.

But after a few more moments of silence, the ever-bold Jaweed finally spoke up, forcefully. He knew of Asa and Fila's romantic relationship and guessed that uncertainty now just might be the cause of Asa's emotional state. "My friends, I did my part, yes, but I also disobeyed instructions. I was to only target the Speaker of the House, Jeffrey Wilson, but I did more. I waited. I shot him, yes, but I got many more Congressmen in that House chamber. It was unbelievable. It was easy. Their Congress is destroyed ... Asa, I will help you, but we need a plan. I am not afraid." Amagan's jaw locked up, staring coldly at Jaweed's face and his show of overconfidence, his foolishness. This killing is mindlessly emboldening him, he thought to himself.

Asa's face turned up, eyes lighting up towards Jaweed's. "Thank you, Jaweed, thank you." His mind focused on Fila. Maybe she's waiting somewhere to attack, maybe she has done her job at the lab and the soldiers outside didn't know it, or maybe by now she's in trouble there. *I now have help!*

"I will go back with you to the lab," Jaweed continued. "I can start a deception at one end to attract the guards and give you a chance to break in to the other end. I remember now you being taught that if you couldn't get him at his residence, David Frost would try to get to his Biochemistry Lab because the magic dust would look suspicious and he would try to figure out what the dispersant is. After all, a virus is invisible so he wouldn't know about that. Our scientists did a great job to rapidly distribute the virus on a chemical dispersant to blow in the wind. It's visible, black. So, he will want to know what that chemical is. Let's go to his lab. I'm sure he is there."

Asa felt blessed. Jaweed did not *have* to help him. But now he was willing to put himself in jeopardy for Asa's sake, for the total mission's sake. Asa put his hand out to shake Jaweed's, a slight smile breaking on his face. Without showing an emotion, Jaweed nodded and stood up. "Let's go," he said firmly.

Amagan remained seated on the floor, his eyes down. He wasn't going anywhere.

CHAPTER 32

Fila, in her mind traveling to America fully trained and extremely dedicated to her mission, now found herself in a dreaded state of emotional confusion. She finally ended her hesitation and made her fateful decision. Dropping her voice into a low, mournful tone, she moved closer with her rifle raised and peered directly into Rose's once defiant but now terrified eyes. "Rose Haines, I cannot shoot you and your innocent child. I want America to ban its weapons, to disarm, but I do not want you to die like this … I don't want Americans to die. Your husband is in the hall, he's hurt, but not dead. I have wounded this soldier, but I'm glad I didn't shoot to kill him…. I must tell you this— this black dust you have seen—it is a chemical dispersant spreading the most contagious deadly form of Ebola virus. I am here to—"

"I know who you are Fila and why you are here," Rose broke in, regaining some measure of her composure, relieved to know she was not about to receive a bullet. "I know your name, I know your assignment. I know it is a deadly organism that is to do its work in three days. And so, a virus, the Ebola virus. Despite many attempts, none of them successfully completed, it's been incurable, for the most part untreatable in Africa. Do you know the antidote? Do you know a vaccine? How about you?"

Fila's mouth dropped. She lowered her weapon so it was now pointing at the floor. *How does she know so much?* How did Michael know her name? "No," she finally answered. "I do not know of any antidote, but there is a vaccine. I am inoculated with it, but I was not told what it is."

Rose now seemed suddenly in command of the situation. "Look over here, behind this bench, under the plastic wrap. It is your friend, Babur—that's his name, right?" The two moved to behind the lab bench. Richard Frost remained frozen, not believing what he was seeing and hearing. Fila's face dropped in shock. "Before he died, he told us of your plan. In his pocket was a list of your six targets and all six of your names, but we don't know who sent you. Who is behind a huge electromagnetic bomb going off and shutting down our communications, and who sent this virus?"

Fila looked distraught —*these Americans are too smart.* She was almost tempted to raise her AK-47 again. After a long pause, she looked up at the impatience growing on Rose's face. "Too long a story.... We only wanted to end a world of violence once and for all by eliminating America and bribing the rest world into disarming. We are people of peace." The two stood face to face, staring into each other's eyes, searching for some kind of understanding, both realizing the seeming incoherency in this plot—not an act of violence in self-defense but an act of consummate violence to end all violence? *Does it make sense?*

Perplexed, but continuing to take charge, Rose first placed Alex back into his blanketed lab sink, then turning to the other two: "Please. Fila, put your rifle down. Let's not harm each other. Help us.... Richard, help this poor Marine stop his bleeding.... And tell me about Michael.... Fila, where is he?"

"I'll pull him in," Fila said firmly, now almost mesmerized by Rose's composure, laying her rifle down and opening the lab door.

Thank goodness! Rose lit up as a groaning but non-bleeding Michael staggered through the lab door with Fila supporting him.

"Michael. Michael, you're in one piece. You okay?" Rose asked pleadingly.

Rubbing the back of his head, Michael looked bewildered, glancing at Rose unharmed and then at Fila propping him up without that rifle in her hands. "What happened? Rose, I was out there. She—"

"Shush—I know the story," Rose near whispered. "Fila is going to help us now. She is not going to harm us." Rose maintained an air of confidence in her voice lest Fila sense weakness and change her mind. "Michael, it's a deadly virus, the worst, the Ebola virus."

Before Michael could respond, in through the inner lab door appeared a startled Jonathan Dean and his assistant, expressing shocked disbelief at the bizarre scene. "What the hell?"

"It's okay, Jonathan," Rose answered quickly. "This woman, Fila is her name, is here to help us. The black dust all over—it's a chemical dispersant with the Ebola virus attached. She knows of no antidote but claims she is vaccinated against it. We have to find an antidote, an antiviral, or an instantly working vaccine –"

"But who is she? How did she get in here?' Jonathan interjected, staring at this strange young woman intruder dressed in a baseball cap and long trench coat, then to Richard tending to a wounded Marine stretched out on the floor.

"Doesn't matter now. We have to work fast. She was told it will be deadly within three days of contact," a determined looking Rose responded. "The five vials of the black dust I collected—Jonathan, have you also detected a live organism on it like I first viewed under the microscope? I'm just afraid a lot of it has gotten away already, released off the dust, and we probably have all inhaled it."

"Correct. The virus is alive, and we have either ingested the fine particles of dust into our lungs or the virus has been released for us to inhale," said Jonathan with the sound of certainty in his voice.

Regaining his composure, his head clearing, Michael interrupted: "Wait. Fila here is armed. I don't understand what just happened between you two, Rose, but she is armed, and she can change her thinking, whatever that is." He then gently grabbed her arm to be close by while he continued: "You have a pistol, Fila, and knife, like your friend Babur?"

Committed now to ending her deadly mission, Fila resigned her position of assassin and weakly submitted to Michael's interjection. "In my inner coat pocket, go ahead, take my pistol, and in my left boot is my knife." Michael without hurry or force removed both weapons and placed them next to her rifle now lying on top a lab bench.

"Richard, watch over these weapons," Michael commanded. Richard, instantly obeying, had yet to say a single word since Fila had entered. "And I hate to tell you—one more thing. A man named Asa is assigned to you, Richard. I'm so sorry he got to your wife at your condo and … I'm really sorry. He may be here now, stalking to get you. I'll reaffirm security around this building … Fila, how did you get in?"

When Fila heard Michael speak of her beloved Asa "getting to your wife", she recoiled, dropping her eyes and picturing the uncertainty of more tragedy just ahead. "I got into the lobby before the troops entered and was hiding," she mumbled softly, her mind turning to Asa. What would he think of her now, backing away from her commitment to assassinate Rose Haines. Distraught, she fought to hold off the tears she could feel coming.

"Jonathan," Michael continued "can we get a sample of Fila's blood to find out what this vaccine is in her, and can you hurry and get back into your inner lab to run tests on the strength of this virus? We have come up with a quick solution. We're all exposed and … " Michael hesitated as he thought for a moment why Jonathan Dean was not also on the hit list as he was the most knowledgeable in the country on anti-viral medicines.

"Right on," Jonathan replied. "Like I mentioned before, there's a lengthy procedure to go in again … well, forget it. Like we said before, we're all exposed already…. Rose, you stay here with your child and this woman after I take her blood sample. I'll take Richard and Josh in with me into the inner lab. Sounds ridiculous—the inner lab is our containment lab, but the virus is already everywhere in here. We have all breathed it in coming to the lab—it's everywhere outside. Anyway, in there, that's where our sophisticated equipment and antiviral chemicals are."

Michael nodded. "Okay, let's get started. I'll be right back. I'm going to check downstairs and make sure the military knows who to look for. I'll help carry this Marine out to the hall so his buddies can get him medical help. This Asa must be dark skinned and somehow hiding a rifle with him, probably under a trench coat like Babur's and Fila's. Am I right, Fila?"

The young woman now felt more torn than ever, her facial expression looking like a scared child, no longer holding back the tears. She had just learned that Babur was dead. Then in a matter of seconds, she had changed her own mission from killing Rose Haines to saving her and perhaps all Americans, then to learn her Asa was ready to make his move against Richard Frost after assaulting his wife. Now these armed Americans are waiting for him, knowing his mission. Looking up directly into Michael's eyes, she pleaded: "Yes, but perhaps you can talk to him. Tell him I'm here, safe, that we can stop this madness if...."

As Fila dropped her voice, Michael stared back a moment without replying. A beautiful young woman, now tormented, conflicted, eyes beginning to tear again. With no further words between the two, Michael turned away from her towards Rose. "Lock her rifle and knife in one of the lab benches and put her pistol in your other vest pocket."

As he labored to move the wounded Marine with his two shattered knees into the hallway then moving cautiously down the steps and into the open lobby, he heard the loud breaking glass explosion at one end of the large open- spaced first floor lobby. Jaweed had begun his diversion. From around the corner of the Facilities Management Building located just southwest of the 7th Street end of the Advanced Science Building, Jaweed fired 8 shots from his AK-47 into one of the large glass entrances. The noise of the shattering glass was awesome. He then withdrew and scrambled into a dark culvert on nearby 5th Street. He would stay hidden there until dark and then retreat back to the tower building. He hoped that guards at the Science Building would scramble to that end to protect and investigate while Asa would make his way into the northeast side of the building. That was the plan.

Asa heard the shots, heard the shattering glass, saw the nearby troops running towards the far end, and decided his fate. He moved quickly from behind a bench on the 9th Street walkway in mid-campus to the northwest entrance of the building. The door was unlocked. All the security guards there had rushed to the other end. He was in free from detection. So far the plan was perfect—until he bumped into Michael Reynolds just coming out of the stairwell. The dark skin, the black beard, the trench coat—Michael was on it in a flash—a diversion at the other end of the long hall; him coming into this end. *This has to be Asa!* Before the startled Asa could raise his rifle from under his unbuttoned trench coat, Michael tackled him hard and went for the rifle. He managed to kick it away in the ensuing brawl. It was over almost as suddenly as it began. In trying to pull his pistol from his inner coat pocket, Asa accidently pulled its trigger in the struggle, and one single bullet found its way straight into Asa's heart. With blood gushing from Asa onto Michael's shirt, an astonished Michael peered up as several of the guards came running back, surrounding the two lying on the lobby floor. Michael's mind was filled with only one thought now: *My God! That's three down with one upstairs. Two to go!*

⸻⟊⸻

Rose's eyes widened in horror as Michael reentered the lab. "You're shot! Are you—"

"It's okay. It's not *my* blood. It was Asa. He tried to break in. I was lucky. I guess I caught him by surprise. I knocked his rifle away ... in our tussle he accidentally shot himself. He's dead." Rose looked astonished. It happened so fast, sounded so simple. Michael stood tall, his deep blue eyes seeming to be set in steel as he stared down at Fila, now sitting on the floor against a lab bench. He had to get his thoughts together—he couldn't quite believe he had somehow managed to eliminate two heavily armed assailants himself. The experience at least served to firm his resolve to get them all.

Sitting up straight, Fila's expression turned from remorse to anger as she begged Michael. "No. No! You couldn't *talk* to him? Did you give him a chance? Are you sure it was Asa?"

"Fila, you say they are your friends. He came here to kill Richard Frost. Someone shot the glass at the other end of the lobby to create a diversion to get him inside. He was armed. And you want me to talk with him?" It was now Michael showing clear signs of anger.

Fila sat back, her ebbing tears beginning to flow again, rolling profusely down her cheeks. *My Asa, my dear Asa. What in the world is happening?* Conflicted again, she wondered if she should have kept her weapons when she had the advantage.

Can anyone really explain why one pulls the trigger versus why one drops the gun?

The late afternoon went into evening, the evening into late night. While Michael kept watch over Fila, Rose had gone to the first floor cafeteria and brought back a large supply of bottled water, protein bars, and dry cereal from the vending machines. She fed Alex and made him comfortable in the blanketed lab basin. The child slept peacefully. Occasionally, Jonathan or Richard would emerge from the inner containment lab to grab a snack and report on their progress, or lack thereof. Yes, the organism matched up with Ebola in most respects but did have some important distinguishing differences. It very well could have been modified and strengthened to spread more easily or to produce its deadly symptoms sooner, or both.

Michael understood the effects of sleep deprivation. As a young engineer working feverishly on the challenge of scaling up his ocean desalination technology, he had spent many near sleepless nights toiling at his tasks. The human mind and body become groggy at about 20 sleepless hours and will encounter involuntary sleep pauses by 40 hours. The solution was to set an alarm for 10 to 15 minutes duration and use it to pause from work for short "naps" about every six hours. While no external communications were possible, all their mobile phones were available for this purpose. He passed this knowledge on to Rose, Richard Frost, Jonathan Dean and his lab assistant, Josh. Fila spent most of the night dozing while sitting on the floor, her head leaning back against a lab bench. Her AK-47, pistol and knife were all controlled now by Rose, who was careful not to fall asleep while Michael napped.

During the night, hard to tell because of the bright lab lights, Rose engaged Fila into long conversations. Was she married? Did she have children? Where was she raised? "I don't understand this. I don't understand your mission. You say you are people of peace, but yet you came here to kill Americans, all Americans, and you—"

"I thought our leaders were right, that it was a brilliant plan. I had seen too much violence in my life. I escaped to the island of—I cannot tell you the name—where I was told it was peaceful, and then I learned of their plan. They became my dearest friends. I don't want to hurt them. I can't tell you who they are or where they are. They only want no more violence in this world. Their goal is noble. The Master Plan was simply to make people sick until they abandoned their weapons, then save them. Everywhere else, the anthrax bacteria, modified so that only we have the antibiotic–"

"Save *them*? But how about *us*—this virus! It's beyond sickness; it kills!" Rose pleaded. "Are your leaders not going to give us the antidote, the vaccine, even if we promise to disarm?"

Now even Michael picked up his ears for the answer as Fila paused in her reply. Fila finally answered in an almost remorseful whisper: "No. Here is where I now find the problem. I was convinced; no, I was told, that America was so powerful, that America had ruled the world ever since the end of the Cold War thirty years ago, that America was never going to give up its huge nuclear arsenal; that we had to take them out. That's what I was told. That meant we would spread a deadly virus that would kill everyone in three days time…. The biological technology was developed by our scientists. It would be dispersed in chemical clouds from huge canisters by one thousand of us here, spread out throughout the country.

"We are all vaccinated. We will all leave an America that is in ruins—can you imagine a mighty America with all its glorious cities standing intact but with no people in them, deserted ... and we, the thousand of us, will all return home to peace.... On our island I met Asa, the man you told me is dead. All my life I had never known love. One tribal faction against another ... foreign invaders. Nothing but violence, violence, violence ... the two of us, we fell in love. We were going to have a family after we returned, Asa and me...." She looked off into space as her voice trailed off.

"I understand Fila, but you six. Why were you six set up to try to kill six of us?" Rose begged.

"I was told you Americans are resourceful, that we had to take out the president and his line of succession in case somehow your leadership got word of us and could retaliate quickly, or in case there was a flaw in our technology."

"But me? My wife? The university president?" Michael interjected.

"As I mentioned Michael," Rose answered for her. "They must have thought we might be the ones to come up with an antidote, a vaccine ... the vaccine that you have ... the one you don't know what it is, Fila?"

"That's right. That's why you are the targets. The vaccine—they never told us what it is."

"So your change of heart, Fila. What changed?" Michael asked.

"I don't know. It doesn't make sense now. I shot that young soldier—he was armed. I didn't shoot to kill him. He was not my target ... but to shoot a defenseless woman holding her harmless baby ... do I murder the innocents in order to end violence? Somehow, somehow ... you two don't look like you are violent people ... but are your leaders?" her voice trailing off. With her Asa now gone, she wondered if she was asking herself the right questions. Distraught, nothing now made any sense to her.

"You made the right decision, Fila," Michael answered, "to try to stop this madness. And Jonathan Dean, the head of the infectious disease lab here, is he not on your list too?"

"I don't know the name. Not with the six of us trained for this mission. I don't know."

And so the conversation went on, intermittingly through the night. The ageless human instinct to be able to commit violence against another human for selfish gain or for self-defense up against the opposing basic human instinct for empathy and compassion.... Diverse human nature at war with itself.

DAY TWO

RACE AGAINST TIME

CHAPTER 33

The bright early morning sun shining on the hallway walls was evident, penetrating through the small window in the laboratory door. The black dust that was in the air the morning before was gone from view. It had settled. The virus it held had been released. It was everywhere, floating on minute dust particles, resting on objects, invisible. Awakening from his second mini-nap, Michael first wondered whether the prior day had just been a bad nightmare, but the aches in his body from being stretched out on the laboratory floor and then his sighting of Fila asleep nearby quickly ended that thought. He glanced around the room. Rose gave him a faint smile. She was feeding Alex cereal and some water. He wondered how she might have ever managed to change his diaper, but women are resourceful. The one year old seemed content. On the other side of the room lay the body of Babur, wrapped tightly in clear laboratory plastic sheeting. A gruesome reminder, Michael thought, of the seriousness of yesterday's events. The soldiers downstairs must have taken care of the wounded Marine and Asa's body.

With a serious look at Rose, he beckoned to her. "Look, keep Fila's pistol right there in your vest pocket. The other two, I memorized their names, Amagan and Jaweed, the president and the speaker …

they are still out there. I thought they may just stick to their targets, but now that they have succeeded, they may just try to go beyond their assignments. Someone helped Asa break in here yesterday. Hold onto that gun, and give me Babur's." Rose nodded and complied, dropping her smile.

The first report on conditions outside was ominous. There was a noise outside the lab door, and Michael raised Babur's pistol, the one he now considered his. Knowing Michael Reynolds was inside, it was a Marine passing on the latest news.

"Sir. One of our security personnel just returned from the big medical center over on Bannock after checking up on our wounded buddy—the one we got over there yesterday. It is filling up with young children and elderly persons who are quite sick. He said the doctors told him that black dust yesterday may have caused respiratory problems with the very young and very old … is that what you are working on here in the MB Lab, sir?"

The Denver Health Center at Bannock Street and West 7th Avenue is one of the largest hospitals in Denver with over 400 beds. It is just southwest of the Governor's mansion and not far from the university. It probably employs a strong emergency generating capacity, Michael thought, wondering what that source of temporary power might be.

"Well, yes, that's the idea. We have full backup power here for a few days from our emergency batteries outside. We have to find out what that black stuff was yesterday … but for you, with those terrible shootings at the president's and at the Capitol, and the incident with us here yesterday, we have to protect the university president who is here now. Just continue to keep your group posted at all the entrance and exit doors here. We know there are more assassins like the one downstairs who accidently shot himself yesterday in the scuffle with me. Don't let anyone in without contacting me first. We're still trying to find out what's going on.… Oh, and one more thing—send one of your men over to General Armstrong's office at the Capitol and request an update on the communications problem, both here and around the country, and also the world. Let me know as soon as you hear, okay?"

"Yes, sir, will do," instinctively replied the young Marine, with his eyes wide open, his jaw dropping, staring at Michael in amazement, not quite understanding all that he had just heard.

Sickness, young and old—already, Michael pondered. He glanced over at young Alex, doing fine, for now at least. He searched and soon discovered an "Infectious Diseases" manual in the nearby laboratory display case. Just what I am looking for, he nodded. Anthrax overseas, Fila had disclosed. Anthrax is *Baccillus anthracis*, a bacterium that can be modified to be effective in a narrow environmental range, like becoming very infectious and highly virulent in spring and autumn climates. He read on. It forms hardy spores—ideal for placing on dispersal aerosols. It can be fatal within three to seven days if left untreated. While there is no vaccine, antibiotics can be effective. Michael mused that these assailants must have modified it so that only they have the effective antibiotic.

Michael noted that biological warfare agents were outlawed by a 1972 Biological Weapons Convention, which was ratified by 165 countries. The treaty had its beginning back in Geneva in 1925 after Germany had tried anthrax with mixed results during World War I. Various biological weapons had been used many times long before, dating back many centuries. Later, in World War II, although Japan lacked efficient delivery systems for biological weapons, it did spread plague and cholera and death among hundreds of thousands of Chinese by deliberately distributing diseased foodstuffs. The United States responded to such threats by weaponizing anthrax and other pathogenic bacteria. Michael noted a reference to the possibility for a great loss of life from bio-weapons compared to other weapons because of their relatively small mass and low cost of development and storage. Such bio-weapons could have a great advantage over the skin-damaging, lung-impairment chemical weapons used in World War I because they could be easier to deliver and could be dispersed over a larger area.

Here, he found it—the section on the virus family: no or few treatments or vaccines for many of them; the simplest form of life;

147

they must invade a host organism to survive and multiply; they spread through the air, on particles, or in biting insects, or with human fluid contact; typically can cause joint and muscle aches, diarrhea, vomiting, the common cold, fever, respiratory infections, sore throat, pinkeye, conjunctivitis, pneumonia, bronchitis, gastroenteritis, and worse. The yellow fever, rubella, rabies, encephalitis, West Nile, Dengue fever, bird flu A, HIV, hepatitis, and here it is—the Ebola virus.

Ebola HF, Ebola hemorrhagic fever, was first recognized in 1976 and named after an African river in the Congo where it was first discovered. It remained restricted to that area although a large outbreak was recorded in three countries in West Africa in 2014. He read on. Looks like lots of studies on how this virus infects its hosts, but no mass-produced antiviral agents for its lethal infections have been discovered to date. Michael wondered how these assassins claim they are safe from its deadly effect. It's not known where the virus is tucked away in nature or how it is carried about. It seems to spread in humans through direct contact with infected bodily secretions. Seven out of ten infected with it have died on average, in some cases nine out of ten. It incubates in as little as two days. Symptoms begin abruptly as fever, headache, joint and muscle pain, sore throat, and weakness followed by nasal and internal bleeding, diarrhea, vomiting and stomach pain.

Here, here it is: Michael found the answer why the human body doesn't fight it and get rid of it sooner or later like it does other viruses. *It disarms the immune system thereby preventing an adaptive immune response.* Michael paused in his reading. These people bent on destroying us: they must have found a way to overcome this hurdle if they claim they are immune, and they must have found a way to spread it through inhalation not just through contact with bodily fluids. *Incredible!* These people, whoever they are, must have a scientific genius among them, he thought to himself.

Bumping Fila awake and speaking up so Rose could hear, Michael pursued these points. "Fila, you said you didn't know, but think. You said you received a vaccination against the virus? Was it an injection? A pill? ... A name?

"I was given a needle vaccination in my arm, two months ago."

"Did you not see or overhear what was in it?"

"No, I told you. I don't know. I was only told it would protect me from the spread of the virus attached to the black chemical. I could touch it; I could inhale it. It would not harm me."

"Did they tell you anything about your immune system?"

"Only that I am protected."

"So there is an antidote…. Jonathan has to discover what it is. Fila! Who are these people? Who vaccinated you? Who gave you these weapons? Who sent you here? Where did you come from?" Michael's questions now became more demanding as his frustration grew.

Fila stared momentarily at Michael, then at Rose and little Alex, then looked Michael squarely in the eyes. "Michael Reynolds, I feel remorse at what we are doing to you. I do want you to find what this vaccine is, but I do not want my people harmed. My friend Asa is already dead. I cannot, I will not, tell you the answers to your questions. But I *will* tell you we six are originally Afghan, as you know our names, but we did not come from Afghanistan to here. That country and its Taliban are not our people now. I told you—we come from an island, far away." She continued to stare directly at Michael, her face now resolute, coolly expressionless. Gone were yesterday's tears. She had changed from anger and crying the day before back to a warrior. She had to protect her sponsors, her dearest friends.

"Will you tell me where your friends are—your fellow assassins? You have two alive somewhere here—Amagan and Jaweed. Our President Jennings and our Speaker of the House Wilson are dead. You have shot a Marine. These are serious crimes. How did you expect to get out of here? Where are you to meet?"

"No! Michael Reynolds, I cannot tell you any of that either. As I said—they are my friends. Your job is to only find the antidote, for in three days the virus will kill you all."

"And you pray we live," Michael retorted. "And don't you think that an America that survives will extract its revenge on your little island? Have you not heard of Japan attacking us by surprise in nineteen forty-one or al Qaeda in two thousand one? You may have believed your purpose noble, but how would you ever rid the world of its hundreds of thousands of small weapons? The small weapons that kill thousands and thousands in tribal disputes, in civil wars, territorial disputes, ethnic cleansing, religious quarrels. So, even if all the nations you say you attacked gave up their weapons of mass destruction, you are not going to rid the world of violence."

"So maybe we are dreamers. You did not grow up in a childhood filled with constant violence, constant invaders, Michael Reynolds. We escaped to the island, a place of peace, a place where everyone took care of themselves and others, responsibly, without a gun, a sword, a whip over them." Fila's sincerity was obvious and overflowing emotionally as she continued on. " Our leaders became transformed—thinking they could pass on this ideal to the entire world—to end massive violence once and for all by removing weapons of mass destruction through action, not through the fruitless words heard over and over by those simply *calling* for peace … so yes, the problem of small weapons would remain. You're right, but the threat of mass killings would end, and—"

"Fila, the conditions you described from your youth were conditions of unresolved human nature and from the use of small weapons. You would only be solving part of the problem, and yes, all of us would love to see the destruction of WMD's…. The bribe, the anthrax threat around the world, but for us in America you are prescribing certain death. How does that solve anything? How can you call yourself a person of peace?"

She paused. "And so you have seen … I have given up my weapons. Have I not?'

Michael's questioning ended with a cold stare into the eyes of this mysterious young woman with striking green eyes, dark clear skin, long flowing black hair; beautiful, but potentially deadly. She stared back, expressionless. Understanding her and her mission was for later; now it was a race against time.

CHAPTER 34

Ali's residence was buzzing. Despite the lack of phones and internet service, the word had spread rapidly among government people of the president's assassination and the bloodbath at the Capitol. Surrounded by her closest advisors, it was as though Alexis Graham as the new president had called a Cabinet meeting. The difficulty for her and her circle though was how little she, or her central government, could do. In a society nearly totally dependent for communications on radio wave transmission through satellites, the attackers had found the key point of American vulnerability.

Frustratingly, the only long distance contact for Ali was the buried military fiber optics system connecting her, General Armstrong at the Capitol, General Ralston at the Pentagon in Washington, and fifteen widespread military bases countrywide. In contrast to the damaged commercial fiber optic systems with exposed transmission and reception connections, the military system was designed with secure connections. The news on the morning of the second day was not good: "General Ralston, you mean your military experts don't have any idea when satellite communications will be restored?" Ali's resolute tone of voice disguised her deep concern inside.

"No ma'am. We just don't know the magnitude of that explosion.

These electromagnetic pulse bombs have been tested before at different altitudes and at different strengths, but that was many years ago, out at sea. That took place long before we had so many interdependent satellite communications systems. Right now, all our calculations are theoretical. It could be days; it could be weeks.... Anyway, we are doubling our efforts to make sure our land-based connections are repaired and restored as soon as possible, but we just don't know when the air will clear and satellite transmissions can resume."

"Explain that General Ralston," Ali queried. "What do you mean?"

"Let's go through it. You and I are now speaking through an optical fiber, a thin tube made of glass, of silica, like the size of a human hair, which has light traveling through it. Varying refractions and reflections of light are contained inside the fibers, and so electromagnetic signals of voice and data can be transmitted through on these light beams. They are not subject to outside disturbances. And there is little loss of speed compared to electricity traveling through metal–"

"But don't you need electrical power to get the light signals started? And connectors?"

"Right," General Ralston calmly replied. "But our terminals are securely enclosed and power transmission starts using advanced batteries charged by photovoltaic cells, solar power, to provide electricity to the beginning and end points"

"And are we not connected overseas by fiber optics as well?"

"Yes. Fiber optic cables were submerged under the oceans way back in the 1980's, but we are not receiving any messages yet. Must be the cable terminals are not secure, just like our commercial systems here in the U.S. are not on line."

"Go on, general. I want to understand. Tell me more."

"Okay. So, first consider matter, or mass, and second energy, or movement of mass. So, our radio waves—theoretically they are both. Remember the electromagnetic spectrum, from the deadly short wave length of excited electrons, gamma rays, which are of very high frequency, high energy, all the way up the scale through x-rays, ultraviolet, visible light, infrared, microwave, and the oscillating radio waves, which are of long wave length and low frequency. Radio waves are of such low energy they do not harm our bodies, and their resonance can be transmitted and received through an electromagnetic wave with data attached, then amplified and decoded—our radios, TV's, computers, and phones…. Now, our communication satellites and cellular networks—here we transmit information by radio waves in the microwave portion of the spectrum using direct-line narrow beams and targeted antennas. Transmission power is derived from solar cells in the satellites, but just think, ma'am, the functional transmission of signals through the atmosphere assumes a fairly stable electromagnetic field surrounding the earth, to avoid constant interference…."

"Go on sir."

"Okay. As I mentioned yesterday, a large blast like that from a high altitude nuclear explosion upsets the stability of that field, and the system becomes jumbled from the interference. We have a suddenly fluctuating magnetic field above us. The bomb emits a sudden pulse of powerful gamma rays spreading out through space causing this. Even the solar cells on our communications satellites might be damaged. That depends on how high the bomb went off. At two hundred miles high, the solar panels on the satellites may not be damaged. With an explosion at three hundred miles high, the satellites could be destroyed…. Now, maybe, you know there is also technology for setting off an electromagnetic pulse bomb using non-nuclear activation. I think it's called 'magnetic flux compression' where the pulse is generated in the weapon … while a nuke generates the pulse outside the weapon … no, can't be because while those bombs may be more targeted, they are much weaker, and we have reports from our military bases that our whole country has been affected….

"You still listening, ma'am?"

"Keep going."

Back here on earth, the sudden electron power surge is what then damages connection points, transformers and other electrical equipment. You know commercial utilities generate and transmit electricity at very high voltages to be efficient and then use transformers to bring voltages down to usable currents…. You want more? This is technical."

"Yes, general, go on. Please."

"Now, back in 2001, Congress had authorized, and I quote: 'Commission to Assess the Threat to the United States from Electromagnetic Pulse [EMP] Attack'. The 2008 report indicated, and I quote again: 'Super EMP, particularly nuclear, can destroy even the best protected U.S. military and civilian electronic systems'. That's why, ma'am, we in the military installed this secure fiber optic system that we're talking on right now, but there's no national defense against the right kind of an EMP attack…. Right now we are seriously degraded throughout the spatial communications system, and we're uncertain when stability will return." The general paused again, the tone of his voice now revealing the gravity of the situation he had been describing, and waited for comment from the new president. It seemed as though a college professor was giving a lesson in physics to an English major and had finally talked himself out.

Ali's face turned somber, her voice now trembling. "Okay, general, enough said. I understand. I'll be sure to have General Armstrong stay on alert—we still have assassins here on the loose. Stay in touch with your bases and keep me informed … anything else beyond the technology enlightenment?"

"You should know," General Ralston replied soberly. "Reports we are getting from the commercial utility companies are that they have no idea when they will go back on line because all power is down, not like the normal shutdowns where selected damaged units are set up for mechanical and physical repair. In essence, they need power to restore power. Secondly, few utility companies keep back up transformers on hand … but worse, ma'am, we have reports from here in Washington and from all the bases that young kids and some very old folks are coming into hospitals quite sick. On that call yesterday with Michael Reynolds—he mentioned this black dust everywhere, that it might contain a pathogen. Could it be? Could it start working this fast? Can you—?"

"We're on it, general. We are analyzing it at the MB lab right now at the National University. We don't know yet. That's why my message yesterday out to the public through your personnel concerned only the downed power grid. We don't want panic–"

"But it's happening already. This wasn't just one hospital reporting—it's like a nationwide flu pandemic!" Ali didn't know how to respond to the general's exclamation. She held onto the phone in silence. "Ma'am, are you still there?"

"Yes, General Ralston. When I learn more from the lab, I'll call you immediately." Ali put the phone receiver down slowly, sat down at the desk in her office and stared out the window, aware of the swirl of nervous activity going on out in her living room among her bewildered staff. *How do I cope with this without setting off a larger panic?* Never in her life had she felt so helpless. Where was Michael?

CHAPTER 35

Michael paced the lab floor impatiently. He felt lost, hapless, while waiting for Richard and Jonathan to come out with something positive from the inner lab. Fila remained seated on the floor leaning back against a long lab bench. Her face looked cold, her eyes staring. Could he trust her? As a precaution, he had passed her rifle and knife from the lab cabinet to the Marines in the hallway downstairs, satisfied that her pistol was securely zippered into Rose's vest pocket. Michael noticed Rose was catering to Alex who was seemingly becoming agitated. Was it discomfort from sleeping and napping in a cloth-lined sink, or the unfamiliar cafeteria vending machine food, or *God forbid* could this be the beginning of the ill effects of the virus? The hours were dragging on. Then Richard Frost appeared from the inner lab where the sophisticated testing on the virus was being performed. He looked tired and distraught.

"Frustrating," he started. "Jonathan says it definitely is a genetically-modified Ebola virus, but enhanced, even more virulent than he could possibly imagine could be achievable. In Africa, it could only be transmitted by direct contact with the bodily fluid of an infected person or animal, but this one floats through the air on dust or tiny water droplets, like a cold virus. It will cause severe symptoms very quickly.... This woman here, you call her Fila, is right. In three days we can have death; sooner for the young, old, and immune impaired. The black dust that it's attached to is a very, very fine chemical dispersant. It will go right through the very slightest of seams in doors and windows, and be easily inhaled. And then the virus spreads secondarily by indirect human contact, like from breathing.... Like we said last night, we're all exposed already." Richard's expression soured as he turned his head down towards the floor and stood motionless.

"But her blood," Rose said almost demanding, "what about the vaccine?"

"Jonathan is running a complete analysis. He sees nothing yet."

"Take a break, Richard," Michael exhorted, frustrated with Richard's response. "Take a nap over there and get some rest. We *have* to find an antidote, something to stop it, kill it, or get our own immune system to attack it."

"Jonathan is trying, Michael. Jonathan is trying," he replied with fatigue in his voice. Michael, Rose, and Fila watched emotionless as Richard walked to the other side of the lab, sat down on the floor, and leaned his head back against a lab bench, his eyes already closed. Listening to the conversation with an expression of futility on her face, Fila closed her eyes too.

Rose looked towards Michael, silently questioning what they should do next. "Look, you've been awake for over thirty hours," he uttered softly, knowing Rose did not follow his nap recommendations of the day before. "We have to stay sharp. I was trained in this." Just for chance he interrupted himself and lifted the closest lab phone— dead. He tried his mobile phone—still no signal. "So, okay, learn to take mini-naps—ten to fifteen minutes at a time like I've been doing every six hours. Set your watch alarm. I'll stand watch. Then we'll wake Richard up. Both of you stay in touch with Jonathan. Teach him to rest.... I'm thinking—listen, I'll go back to Ali's—we have to know what's going on out there."

Michael's determined face turned downwards, suddenly looking dejected. His mind momentarily went blank. His thorough engineering training and all his successful practical experiences had served to overshadow his early doubts and insecurities about his abilities. He had turned in brilliant successes and greatly elevated his self-esteem during these past five years in Denver.

But none of that mix prepared him for this situation.

CHAPTER 36

Henri Bonaparte and Antoine met in Paris when both were in their early twenties. They became and remained the closest of friends even after Antoine joined forces with Aazim in 2008. Henri was the one person Antoine confided in as the plot unfolded to divert billions of dollars out of Swiss bank accounts and pyramid international investors in order for the two conspirators to purchase advanced weapons, to entice leading chemists and microbiologists to the remote island of Dire, and to secretly recruit tens of thousands more to their cause. For years, Henri thought his friend's grand plot was absolutely crazy, unworkable, and completely unachievable. But after each trip back and forth from Dire to visit his best friend, Henri began to feel awed by the growing reality that somehow Antoine and Aazim always seemed to be on target with the plan's detailed goals—goals that Antoine revealed each time they met.

Their private dinner conversations whenever they met in Paris began to seem less and less about an impossible dream and more and more about an unfolding reality. But the plan had risks. How could such a preposterous scheme ever be pulled off without some Swiss bankers or regulators finding out, or some Dire recruit accidently letting some uninvolved friends or relatives know about it? And while enough microscopic pathogens could be harvested, how could they ever be spread so widely in such a short time? And how could enough vaccines ever be produced in time? And how could it be possible to stage a rocket launch facility in Mexico undetected, and then place a stolen atomic bomb on top? And what if nations *did* agree to the bribe—how could such a massive number of weapons ever be controlled by so few Dirists in so short a time?

With each passing year, each passing month, and each passing day, the astonished Henri received rational answers to his valid questions, and he slowly came around to accepting the argument behind Antoine's excitement. *End violence by the threat of ending the lives of those who make violence.* Give up your government's weapons or your people die—the ultimate bribe. The one aspect of the plan Antoine did not reveal to his friend Henri was the pact Antoine and Aazim had made to actually let the infected Americans die—there would be no antidote for them. And only a select handful of the Dire scientists and Dire residents knew that significant fact as well. It was the one part of the plot over which Antoine suffered a great amount of lost sleep.

By 2018, Henri was divorced, had no children, and had lost both parents. His curiosity had peaked. He did not want to be alone in Paris in 2021 when this modified anthrax bug would be dispersed. "Antoine, I want to come. I want to come to Dire. I want to be the leader of the 1000 person force sent to America to disperse the anthrax. I want to see the Americans cringe and beg for the anti-bacterial agent." He never knew until close to the operation date why anthrax was going to be used worldwide except for the United States, which would face a genetically enhanced virus instead. When Antoine finally revealed that the bribe concept would not apply to the powerful Americans— that in fact they would all die without a choice—Henri's thinking had come so far towards total disarmament that he didn't even blink. He too had become completely transformed.

On the morning of September 11, 2021, at a mountain location just west of Denver, it was Henri Bonaparte who was in charge of the release of the modified Ebola virus, which was securely attached to a fine chemical dispersant hidden in hundreds of bound canisters. The virus could stay alive for many days without invading a host for life support. The dispersal technology was a marvel of biochemical engineering. The dispersant chemical was severely compressed inside the canisters—each canister holding many trillions of viral cells. Upon release the "dust" would rise, blow up into a huge cloud, flow with the wind, and eventually fall back to earth. Fortunately for Henri that morning, the wind speed and direction were just right for the dispersant to quickly blow right into the congested areas of eastern Colorado—right after the EMP boom overhead and the resultant power failure. The plan at that point was for Henri to lead his 50 person group back to Los Angeles in a solar powered, electric bus. There they would meet the other 950 members of the task force assigned to America, and then they would all transfer onto secret waiting vessels ready to transport them back to Dire. On board they would joyfully celebrate—hopefully a job well done—all of them safely vaccinated.

But Henri's unending curiosity, his complete devotion to the Master Plan, got the best of him. After the other 49 were all on the bus, Henri instructed them to leave without him; he would follow later as he had "just one more thing to do". He set out on foot for the one day walk to Denver. His mind was racing. *Did the dispersant get to downtown Denver? Were people there getting sick? Panicked? Were the six assassins successful? Were they gathered at their meeting place in the Tower? Was the temporary capital of America in turmoil?*

By noon the next day, slowly walking towards the Tower on the 16th Street Mall dressed like a disheveled hiker, but with his subcompact ten-round .45 caliber G36 Glock pistol tucked securely in his vest pocket, Henri discovered the answers to most of his questions. Despite the fatigue from his long hike and without sleep for 30 hours, he felt inspiringly rejuvenated.

The Master Plan was working.

CHAPTER 37

On his walk from the lab back to his Chevy Volt, Michael wondered if his little electric-powered car still had a battery charge. He knew the recharging stations in the parking lots were inoperative. He had felt relieved seeing some twenty uniformed police and military personnel surrounding the Advanced Science Building. The assassins assigned to him, Ali, and Richard Frost were all dead, and the one assigned to Rose was unarmed in the lab. But the two assigned to the president and the speaker of the house had hit their marks. *Where were they? Are they to pursue the other targets as well?* Just in case, he would make his way to Ali's, now President Alexis Graham, with caution. The Volt still had ample power. It was his fourth trip to Ali's in the last 30 hours.

He proceeded once again over West Colfax, down Speer Boulevard, left on 8th Street and left on Lincoln to the Beauvallon. But this time the scene was very different from the morning before and even the afternoon before. In an age of television, mobile phones, and instant internet access, the streets were clogged with curious people finding themselves out of their normal element, obvious in their state of frustration. Everyone seemed to be asking questions of one another. Worse, while news of a deadly virus in the air had not spread yet, Michael could sense that the people on the streets, despite their chatter, already seemed lethargic—sick. He was sure word was spreading that young children and the elderly were already filling the hospitals. And he was sure these people were not aware of the multiple assassinations.

"Michael, I'm glad you're back safely. What have you learned at the lab?" After the cautious parking, clearing security, and walking swiftly to the top floor, the out-of-breath Michael felt depressed that the first report he had to give the new president was not good.

"I'm sorry, Ali. Richard and Jonathan worked all night trying different anti-viral agents on the specimens we have growing at the MB lab … nothing so far." Forlorn, Michael softly continued: "We did confirm it is a more virulent form of the Ebola virus. The one from Africa apparently only spreads by contact with bodily fluids while this one has been genetically modified to act more like a cold virus. It can spread through the air, by simple contact and inhalation. It is attached to and staying alive on a very light chemical dispersant that is helping it spread everywhere—the black dust.…" Michael lowered his head as he paused. "Whoever these people are … they are very advanced. It's very sophisticated science. It must have taken years to develop by a group of unbelievably top engineers and scientists. The human body does not adapt an immune response to this virus—that's why it's so deadly." Michael looked up and regained his composure. "We have the female assassin assigned to Rose under control at the lab. She claims she has been vaccinated, doesn't know what it is, and so far Jonathan has not been able to identify anything different in her blood analysis. She is remorseful. She wants to see us find the antidote, but she won't tell us a thing about who or where her accomplices are, or where she came from, or who is behind this."

"Does it matter at this point, Michael? We have people getting sick right now. We have runners going back and forth with the hospitals … Denver Medical Center on Bannock, Presbyterion-St.Lukes on East 19th and Exempla St. Joseph's on Franklin. These sick people have no power at home, and they know the hospitals have backup power. So they are pouring in—suffering with extreme nausea, headaches, fever, weakness. Already we have nearly a hundred deaths among the very young and very old." Michael's immediate thoughts focused on little Alex. He seemed fussy at times but so far no fever, no vomiting, no diarrhea. "I feel helpless, Michael. General Ralston has no idea when power will be restored. What can *I* do? I'm the freaking president!" For the first time, Ali stared into Michael's eyes with a complete look of panic, of hopelessness.

His voice turning deeper, stronger and more resolute, Michael tried his best to reassure her. "You are doing everything right Ali. You have spread the word our power systems are out without creating panic about a deadly virus; you are staying put since we don't know what or who else is out there against us; you are in constant touch with the generals. Look, our best immediate hope is that our satellite communications are restored soon and that by tonight, tomorrow, we are able to find the anti-viral agent. I listened to the people on the streets out there. Right now their main concern is their lack of customary communications. Let's keep our hope up that we can get both—the antidote and a way to tell everyone."

"Michael, stay strong and be careful," Ali cried almost mournfully. "Please, go. Back to the lab. I'll be alright. Any news from the generals I'll send a Marine messenger over to the lab …. Go!"

"I'll go, Ali. I'll go, but…." Michael couldn't finish. From day one a few years' ago, from the first time he had met her, he knew he had a special affinity for and with Ali; not like the love he felt and shared with Rose, but an eye to eye empathy, like the two knew what the other was thinking, and that those thoughts were always on the same wavelength. They were connected.

Maybe what they both knew, what was left unsaid, as they stared at each other in momentary silence, was that each was already beginning to feel the effects of the virus—a little achy and feverish, slight headaches, somewhat nauseous.

CHAPTER 38

It was a restless night on Dire that first twenty-four hours after the multiple attacks around the world. Few of the 90,000 adherents to the action plan for peace slept well. The message among them for years had been one of optimism, of hope, of salvation for the human race. To a person who knew the anthrax part of the Master Plan, each was confident leaders of every nation would surely to accept the simple proposition to be offered by the Dirists: *give up your weapons of mass destruction in return for the right to life.*

Yet they worried—it was such an unbelievably bold plan. The genetically modified, enhanced version of the anthrax bacterium would surely not do its deadly work if common sense and the human instinct for survival prevailed. Anthrax was such a perfect weapon. Its strong virulence made it highly infectious; it was easy to deliver its hardy spores in dispersible aerosol form; it had no vaccine; it had a human death rate of 90% left untreated; and its susceptibility to known antibiotics was nullified by its genetic manipulation by the Dire scientists. Its use was for such a great noble cause. Around the island, only a select few knew of the more severe part of the Master Plan to wipe out all Americans without salvation using the enhanced Ebola virus.

The exception to the general feeling of anxiety was Aazim. As they would say, he "slept like a lamb" that first night, and in fact just like he slept every night. Born and raised from a staunch military family loyal to and protective of the religious leader of theocratic Iran, Aazim was indoctrinated at an early age to almost worship the act of mercilessly killing those who opposed the official teachings. The violent practices of protecting the doctrine of intolerance had expanded—the populaces of not only his native Iran, but also those of Libya, Egypt, Syria, Lebanon, Jordan, and Iraq, were now all in the grasp of theocratic governments. By 2021 in the Middle East, only the tenuous nuclear détente with democratic Israel prevented an outright Islamic war against the hated Jews, who ardently protected their Holy Land.

Earlier in his career development, somewhere along the way in the beginning of the 21st century, Aazim had a revelation, a transformation. Perhaps it was from his exposure to a combination of Western, Middle Eastern, and Asian ideologies in his role as Director of Foreign Intelligence for Iran's military. He began to think that maybe there was no one right way—no perfect ideology. Human philosophies and religions were all so variant with one another. It seemed man had a dual capacity for converse ends. He could easily kill another human in a competitive battle but he could just as easily show compassion and mutual respect for life.

Was the religion that regulated his daily life in Iran one of war, or one of peace? Some religious factions preached tolerance while others preached intolerance. He began to see that human conflict, suffering and death, all so normal events during his upbringing and early maturity, as something suddenly tragic. He discovered that it didn't matter what the religion or ideology or politics—man was still killing man. He thought to himself that if World War II killed 70 million people, then World War III with today's advancement in science and technology in weapons of mass destruction could kill 700 million. It was time for something new, something bold, something outlandish. His meeting with Antoine in Paris in June of 2008 was the set point. The scheme to end violence by threatening to *kill everyone* was hatched. For the next thirteen years he assiduously, calmly, energetically devoted every waking moment to that cause.

In the middle of the second day, September 12, 2021, Aazim could sense Antoine's continuing nervousness. "My friend, you Frenchmen cannot stand anxiety. Relax. It will be just another day from now, and we will surely then learn of our great success. You must have confidence, Antoine. Our execution of every last detail of our plan will be flawless. We shall be the eternal saviors."

"Like everyone else," Antoine muttered quietly back, "we have no communications. We know nothing. What if the rocket from Mexico failed, or was off in its trajectory, or the bomb didn't detonate properly, or the winds didn't disperse the chemical with the virus … or, my friend, what if it all *did* work perfectly? We are going to kill 300 million people without giving them a chance?" The sun was beating down brightly on the canvas half-covering the porch of their small rustic beachside house. With his neck bent forward, white tee shirt soaked in sweat, Antoine stared out blankly towards the Indian Ocean. He looked drained, emotionless, passive—older than his years.

"My friend, must I comfort you for the one hundredth time? I just told you—the weapons we obtained are the best. Our engineers are flawless. Our lab scientists have tested the bio agents—they are perfectly designed and packaged for delivery as planned … except for the vaccine for the Ebola virus." Aazim paused on that one exception but kept up his upbeat patter. His face looked jubilant. He didn't plan on or want to experience this one particular feeling, but it was an unavoidable consequence of the entire mission—that inner sense of **power**, that satisfying sense of superiority and control over others. Must just be another part of human nature, he mused. "Our planes and boats will soon return with the word. You will see my friend … Antoine the Frenchman. *Oui!* We shall be victorious." Aazim stood up and let out a big sigh as he confidently strolled along the porch, smiling broadly as he peered out to the blue waters of the calm sea.

"My friend, you want to see all the killing end, but you want to kill all the ugly Americans at the same time," Antoine replied somberly.

"Antoine!" Aazim raised his voice but kept his smile. "We have been over this a hundred times. The others are weak—America is powerful. We cannot end violence once and for all unless we kill those who commit the most violence. *Then!* That will be the end of it. You agreed to that."

"I agreed to the anthrax, thinking we would use that as an effective bribe, a threat no one could refuse. But this Ebola—"

"But you agreed our scientists created the greatest silent weapon ever devised with our modified Ebola virus, that without it we would always risk retaliation from the powerful Americans, that we couldn't take a chance on the Americans accepting the anthrax and its antidote, that ..." Aazim paused, his smile disappearing.

Antoine grimaced. "Okay, you're right, I did. But our own people. You know—the nine thousand at all the world capitals who have been successfully vaccinated against the enhanced anthrax bacteria—they will return here, assuming the bribe worked and they release the secret antibiotic ... but the thousand, the ones sent to America ... how can we let our own die? And worse, we let them believe they think they have a vaccine against the virus, but—"

"My friend, I understand your point," Aazim interrupted. We have one thousand comrades in the United States right now who will not return. They are paying the ultimate price to save the world. Each has one hundred canisters that they opened and spread—that's one hundred thousand releases of the black Savior dust. We shall honor their sacrifice. We shall say their vaccine wore off. They will be remembered as heroes.... My friend, we all die someday. They are dying a noble death."

Antoine appeared sullen, staring straight down, his voice dropping further. "And our good friends, the six assassins, the same fate for them? ... and my dearest friend, Henri. I deceived him.... Heaven forgive me."

"Yes, and also the same for our seventh secret assassin, our terminator … Tariq, our backup. I'm sorry for the deception to our friends, but we could take no chances. Tariq is the only one who knows among the thousand sent to America the vaccine is not perfected, that he too will die, but he is willing to do so for the cause. The crazy American imperialists are doomed!"

Antoine turned his gaze toward his colleague. His sad eyes spoke the words for him: *perhaps, just perhaps, maybe we two are the ones who are crazy.*

CHAPTER 39

ariq Badini was born in a small village in a rural western province of Pakistan. His father was originally related to distant tribal families in Iran. In a moment of self-discovery as a very intelligent restless teenager, he found himself longing to elevate himself above his tribal heritage. Through hard work in school he was able to garner a scholarship and attend university in cosmopolitan Islamabad, the ninth largest city in Pakistan and also its elite capital in the northwest. As a result of discussing his deep interest in governmental affairs with one of his influential professors, he was able to land a job after his graduation as an intelligence gatherer for the Pakistani ISI, the Inter-Services Intelligence. This was the Islamabad governmental agency with a checkered past of assisting the American government and the Afghan Taliban in the 1980's against Soviet Russia in Afghanistan while controversially continuing to support the Taliban in Afghanistan and Pakistan after the Soviets vacated.

By 2010, Tariq felt confused as to which side his agency really supported and was deeply conflicted with the ongoing violence involving his nation's Hindu enemy India, plus the Islamic Taliban of Afghanistan and Pakistan, and also Christian America. As a young Muslim, he was educated to despise Israel but at the same time could not appreciate Iran's declaration of the destruction of the Jewish nation. In 2014 he accidently overheard communications about a new group committed to world peace being organized on the tiny island of Dire. Through his intelligence gathering, he was able to identify the Iranian leader on Dire and make direct contact with Aazim. The two became close friends in a short period of time, and by 2015, Tariq relocated to Dire and unofficially became the behind-the-scenes number three group leader.

Antoine was puzzled by how quickly Tariq was transformed from a simple advocate of peace to becoming so committed to Aazim's plan to kill all the Americans. Antoine began to jokingly refer to him as the "Terminator." It became a much more serious commitment by 2020 when Tariq said he would gladly give up his life in return for mighty America to never again be able to wield its awesome military power. That's when Aazim brought him into his fold of confidentiality that the heroes to be sent to America would never return to Dire, even though they were led to believe they were inoculated against the deadly Ebola virus. That's when the "Terminator" title stuck in earnest—Tariq was designated as the secret seventh assassin. He would be trained to go to Denver early, stay behind the scenes, know everything that was transpiring during the mission, and if necessary be the final one to destroy any chance of the American elites finding a way out of their doomed fate. In addition to carrying two Makarov pistols, his vest was packed with powerful explosives for a suicide mission if needed. He was clean-shaven, of fairly light skin, and would not blend in with his Afghan comrades. Aazim informed him of every last detail of the locations and assignments of the designated six assassins.

By September 5, 2021 he was on location in Denver, learning every square block, every target's moves, and also ingesting every known immune supplement in order to prolong his strength as long as possible at the date the black Savior dust would arrive. By September 11, Tariq Badini was ready.

CHAPTER 40

By midday September 12, the blackness had fully lifted. The entire sky now appeared as just a light gray haze. Henri felt ecstatic that the scheme was working as planned. All electrical power along the city streets that he walked along seemed to be out except for the occasional hums of temporary generators working away. Cell phones were dead. People walking the streets seem dazed, confused, moving at a slow pace. They must already be feeling the ill effects of the virus, he mused.

Henri himself felt somewhat achy all over, but he attributed that to his tiring long walk into downtown Denver and lack of sleep. Locating the street intersection he was seeking, Henri gazed at the tower structure. Amazing, he thought. As a European he was very familiar with the structural beauty inspired by the early Venetian society. This clock tower in downtown Denver looked exactly like St Mark's Campanile in Piazza San Marco in Venice. A perfect replica built at the end of the days of America's Wild West. He wondered if all six assassins were up there at the top, each gallantly relating the success stories of their bold assignments. Or maybe they were already on their way to California to rendezvous for their journey home. Despite what seemed to be hundreds of weary-looking people wandering aimlessly along the 16th Street Mall, he entered the main entrance to the tower building without notice. The stairwell was dark, but he managed to slowly find his way up. He had to be careful upon reaching the top not to alarm his compatriots into thinking he was an intruder, so before opening the door at the top and moving into the light he shouted: "Dirists! It's me, Henri, Henri Bonaparte!"

Moving into the surprisingly quite bright tower room in the hazy afternoon sun, he found two Kalashnikov's pointed right at him out in front of two astonished faces that he recognized behind the barrels. "Amagan, Jaweed! It's me, Henri Bonaparte."

"What … what are you doing here?" A thoroughly surprised Amagan asked.

"The dispersant. It worked perfectly. The wind was just right. Denver and Eastern Colorado are in its spell. Sick people are now out there walking the streets not yet knowing what's in store for them tomorrow."

"But you are to return to Dire. Why did you come here?" Jaweed pursued.

"I was curious. The others in my force are on their way home. I had to know … wait, you are only two. Where are the others?"

The two assassins lowered their rifle barrels towards the floor and looked despairingly at one another. "We don't know," said Amagan. "I did my job—I got the president right at eight o'clock yesterday in his home … and Jaweed got the speaker at the Capitol yesterday morning. But the others.…"

"Maybe they are still lying in wait. Maybe something went wrong," Jaweed added, but I can tell you something of Asa. He came here yesterday asking for help. He was in wait at the President of the National University's apartment. He couldn't locate him there and thought … his name is Richard Frost … that he must have gone to his laboratory. I went there with him and created a diversion for him to get in. I don't know … he has not returned."

The three men paused and stared at each other uncomfortably.

"Okay, I have it," Henri finally spoke up with a tone of authority in his voice. "The word could be out. You Afghans all look alike …

and your long coats in this warm weather. I blend right in. I'll make the rounds and find out what's going on. I know exactly what each of your assignments were."

"Are you armed?" Amagan asked. "In case–"

"No concern. I have a pistol. I have a Denver map. I'm okay…. So first I'll go down a couple of blocks and check out the Four Seasons where this Michael and Rose live and look for Babur—"

Interjecting, Amagan added: "The theory with Babur was Reynolds and Haines would hurry to the Advanced Science Lab at the National University, being curious why the power was out and our black dust moving in. He was going to wait in the garage where Reynolds car is, but Reynolds could go out a door and walk to the lab too."

"And Fila? Where was she to be?" Henri asked.

"By the front lobby in case they walked down the main stairs," Jaweed added.

"Okay, I'll check both places. And Farzam? Farzam was to get the vice president at her residence at the Beauvallon. It's on the map—I know where that is."

Building confidence as he contemplated the importance of his new mission, Henri spoke evenly: "Got it. I'll check everything out. If we ran into trouble, let's finish the job. There's another day left, and we don't want any more miracles … like how these people managed to survive their climate catastrophe…."

The two assassins stared blankly at Henri, half wondering if their mission was partially failing and half wondering about the new mission of their surprise visitor and his confident tone, as if he was their new leader. "And us?" Amagan quizzed.

"You two stay right here and rest. I'll return as soon as I can … and again, I'll call out my name at the door."

———✲———

Back on the street, Henri was all ears listening as he walked southwest down Lawrence Street. People on the sidewalks and streets were mumbling about feeling feverish and getting stomach pains, joint aches, and headaches. "There must have been something in that dust making us sick, like the flu," was a theme, along with comments like: "Why isn't the power on yet? I can't even use my cell phone." Arriving at the lobby of the Four Seasons, he observed several residents demanding answers from the staff as to what was going on. Questions the staff could not answer. Finding a hassled, exhausted looking attendant by the door, Henri calmly quizzed the young man: "I know no one has any answers yet when the power is coming back on or why so many are feeling sick, but young man, tell me, since this all started have there been any incidents of violence here? Has anyone been hurt?"

Puzzled by the query but pleased that he finally had been asked a different question about something other than the power loss and the illness, the young man responded immediately. "No sir. No reports of any lootings, shootings, or any violence here. But we do have our security posted to make sure our residents are safe from any panic. Everyone seems so impatient."

"Thank you, young man. Keep up your good work." Henri's thoughts targeted in: Those two heroic Americans would not hole up in their apartment for almost two days with no power or communications. They must have gone to the labs. And if Babur and Fila had done their jobs not here but on the way to the labs, they would have been back at the tower. The Americans must have evaded them somehow, and *all of them are at the lab right now!* He left the lobby and continued towards the university. The modern Advanced Science Building was easy to spot and one of the first buildings in sight entering the campus from Lawrence Street, across the Cherry Creek bridge on Speer Boulevard, and down to Arapahoe Street into the campus interior.

Makes sense, he reasoned, this security I see does make sense. The building housing the Advanced Microbiology Laboratory and the Biochemistry Laboratory was surrounded by uniformed men—Army, Marines and police. His reasoning continued: this is where our targets must be working feverishly to find out what the black dust is, and they are being protected probably knowing that the President of the

United States and the Speaker of the House have been assassinated. It will be easy to find out for sure, he thought. Looking quite harmless dressed as a Colorado hiker, he approached the building entrance and the very first soldier he questioned was so obviously tired and sick that he didn't hesitate to respond after Henri began: "Excuse me. I notice all the security here–"

"Yes, that's right. No one is allowed past here into the building. How can I help you?" the soldier uttered in an extremely weak voice.

"I see that … I know there must be emergency generators working … so the big scientists in there must be trying to figure out what's going on."

"That's correct, and we are here to protect them from harm."

"Harm? What protection do they need to find out about the power outage and this black stuff all over?"

The young Army private, relocated from his normal station over at the military post located just a half mile away at the City & County Building, had been on duty here without sleep for some twenty-four hours. Still, he proudly showed this innocent-looking stranger some responsibility by shaking his gleaming M-16 rifle held out in front of his chest. "You haven't heard? It's more than communications out. The President of the United States was shot to death at his mansion yesterday morning, and the Speaker of the House and many members of Congress were shot at the Capitol right after."

"My God! That's terrible!" exclaimed Henri. "Who did it?"

"We don't know. They looked like foreign terrorists. Dark skinned, long dark hair, black beards—maybe Middle East, Afghanistan, Pakistan. I don't know, but you should know Vice President Graham has been sworn in as our new president. She is operating out of her home office at the Beauvallon."

"That's unbelievable … so, she is safe?"

After standing guard for so long and not feeling well, the young soldier was only too willing to unload his story. "Yes. An attempt was made on her life too, but they got the assassin as he broke into her apartment. Her security guy shot him dead."

Farzam! "My God … but why are you over *here*? Those harmed all are government people."

"Not sure," replied the soldier turning his head around and nodding upward, " but I hear the president of the university is up there with some scientists who had a run in with hit men. I think one of the guys got killed in a car chase over there," pointing towards Speer and Lawrence.

Trying to sound nonchalant, yet unavoidably feeling his heart beat accelerating, Henri asked: "Who got killed? The hit man or the scientist?" Henri tried hard to show his restraint in waiting for the response.

The soldier looked around and hesitated. Finally, he put the pieces together. "I remember. The story is a guy on a cycle shot at Michael Reynolds car—you know him, right? He's the guy everyone knows that did all that water engineering during the climate crisis … he's now the head of the environmental stuff here. Reynolds ran the bastard off the road and knocked him off into a wall. The guy's dead, but none of us here knows if they found out who he was."

Babur! Henri tried to hide his sudden horror and shocking disappointment. "Wow. That's amazing … so this Michael Reynolds guy is in there? Who with? With the university president?"

"Yeah, with other scientists and with his wife Rose Haines. She's pretty famous too. No one gets in unless Reynolds or, I think the president's name is Richard Frost, unless they come out and authorize the entrance…. Geez, I think that's all I know. Oh no, one more thing. A hit man did try to get in here yesterday, and I hear our Michael Reynolds was able to shoot him dead with the gun he had taken from the first guy, or something like that…. Amazing stuff, huh?"

Henri stepped back, hiding his astonishment. *Asa, too?* He had to readjust his thinking. "Thanks soldier. Do your job. Good luck." He turned and walked away, his mind racing, his heart pounding. This means two assassins are in the tower and three are dead. *Three are dead!* Babur, Farzam, Asa gone—his heart sank. The sixth? Fila. Where is she? Trying to collect his thoughts, he began the walk towards the

Capitol, almost a mile to the east. Further discomforting was that he began to feel his headache getting stronger and feeling more joint aches than he had felt just an hour before. Was it the shock of what he just learned from the young, all too talkative soldier, from his long walk from the mountains, from his lack of sleep, or was his vaccine against the virus not working as well as it should?

Damn! ... Babur, Farzam, Asa.

CHAPTER 41

Michael had experienced these mixed feelings before. Optimism and pessimism. Hope and despair. The family farm in central California had failed in a water crisis, and to young Michael back then his father seemed deflated, desperate. The family had done everything right—good education, hard work, and strong family values—yet their misfortune seemed overwhelming. His father's debt could not be repaid. He was forced to declare personal bankruptcy. Michael shared in the family feelings of depression. His dad nevertheless persevered and attended to Michael's future. "Strive your very best to achieve whatever you want to succeed in, Michael—let fate and the Lord do the rest. Life is not always fair, but give it a full shot," his father implored. He remembered how confident he had become after his exemplary high school grades earned him a full college scholarship. How joyous his father was when the university named him the 'top engineer' in his graduating class. "Never quit; do it right" were his dad's words which always stuck in his memory.

Later, he recalled the feelings of fright that he suffered when called upon to massively scale up the bench scale successes he had achieved with his novel ocean desalination methods—those combined with his unique wind and solar power inventions. Scaling up novel technology is always the tricky part. 'Highs and lows'—Michael recalled those feelings as he made his way south in his Volt from Ali's apartment. Before returning to the lab, he decided to stop at the large Denver Health Center on Bannock Street just below the university. He knew he had a strong internal constitution that normally helped him ward off illness, but he was already feeling somewhat achy and slightly feverish. Babur and Fila were not lying about the black dust. *I have to find out what's really happening to us.*

After he pulled into the hospital parking lot, he set his wristwatch alarm for ten minutes and quickly dozed off, overcoming his growing anxiety by catching a quick nap. He wanted to be as sharp as possible. At the front entrance of the hospital and all the way up to the front desk, he could not help but notice a long line of mothers holding babies and their horde of young children, along with several dozen confused-looking elderly waiting impatiently for admission and treatment. Michael spotted a tired looking nurse and politely interrupted her as she was trying to comfort a distraught mother. "The physician-in-chief, please— I'm from the university lab. I need to see him right away. Where can—"

Without even a glance at Michael, her weak voice responded: "Down the main hall—Room 115."

Without knocking, Michael opened the door displaying the doctor's name scrolled on the outside—'Clarence Durham, M.D. Physician-in-Chief'. He discerned a gray-haired man in a white physician's coat sitting perfectly still behind a large desk. He was looking straight down, holding his head between his hands. At first he did not notice Michael's entrance, but as Michael approached the desk the doctor looked up, stone faced. "Sir, Doctor Durham, I'm sorry, can I ask you some questions? I'm—"

"Michael Reynolds. Yes, I know who you are."

"Doctor Durham, we have a grave situation on our hands. I know you have sick people overwhelming your hospital, but do you know what's going on?"

"Please son, you tell me. A pandemic influenza virus? … No, it's not that," shaking his head. "It's much worse—they're *bleeding.*"

With that Michael told the whole story to the bewildered physician. "Doctor, until we can find the right antiviral agent, can you treat these people with something?"

"Michael, I have been through a lot in my long career. I have treated and saved many from chemical agents—arsine that attacks red blood cells, sarin that attacks the nerves, sulfur mustard that blisters, phosgene that chokes, BZ that attacks the brain. Then the bacteria family that we treat with antibiotics. And then the virus family, the adeno's and the retro's where we build up the patients' immune system to attack them ...but now I understand. I know the Ebola virus does not react to our known anti-viral agents, and in the infected there appears to be no natural human immune response. Perhaps the virus actually attacks our immune system as well. An impossible situation, and from what I know, you're telling me this strain of Ebola is much more virulent and its airborne.... The very young and very old are basically dead on arrival here, not days later as one would expect, and more alarming is that we are beginning to see normally healthy people who are getting sick in just a day or so. This is much graver, much more potent than the Ebola virus that is so devastating in the Congo and West Africa. How in the world did it get here? And why is it so contagious? We need answers." Dr. Durham looked up dejectedly, then hopefully at Michael, who was drawing a chair up next to the weary physician.

"Our best researcher at our simulated CDC lab, Dr. Jonathan Dean, and Richard Frost, head of the university who is also our best biochemist, are working on it right now. When I left there a little while ago, the antiviral agents Dr. Dean was trying were not killing it or retarding it. We are certain these people attacking us have genetically modified and enhanced the virus dramatically from the one at the Ebola River in Africa. By attaching it live to this fine chemical dispersant that is everywhere, this black dust you have seen, they have enabled the virus to be spread through inhalation, not just through bodily fluid contact ... Doctor, I came here because I have to know. What can relieve these symptoms in the sickest of all—the young and the old, anyone? We need to buy time. Have you found anything that has even begun to work towards alleviating its symptoms?" It was now Michael who was seeking answers.

"I'm sorry, Michael. No, nothing substantial. For our hard working staff, we simply have a fever relief med in limited supply giving temporary relief. We have tried all the known medicines for severe muscle aches, vomiting and diarrhea. The intravenous fluid systems are offering no relief either. This virus does it all—from fever, headache, joint and muscle pain, sore throat, weakness, diarrhea, vomiting, internal bleeding, and finally unbearable stomach pain and death…. Now a few years back, I recall there were efforts by some small biopharmaceutical companies to clone what are called monoclonal antibodies specific to the Ebola virus, but since the virus never came here beyond a few cases their financing dropped off. Yes—very difficult and very expensive. There were also attempts made to create a vaccine to help the Africans, but that effort also failed because the number of people infected couldn't justify the astronomical cost of production and distribution."

Dr. Durham paused as Michael sighed. "I didn't want to tell you, son. We are trying to avoid panic with our staff and patients, but our morgue is already about full with the very young and very old. Yet more people keep coming in, all ages. We have no beds. We are at the point of rejection, and you are telling me even the healthiest adults are already feeling symptoms … like you?" Michael sighed a deep breath as a sign of the affirmative, as Doctor Durham lowered his head and stared at his desktop. He looked broken. Michael glanced at the wall behind the doctor. It was full of diplomas, awards, and recognitions of a long illustrious career in medicine.

"Doctor, I'll head back to the lab. We have to quickly find the agent to stop this. You can't have a panic at your door outside. I'll ask the military to send guards over."

As Michael retreated back towards the door with his eyes still fixed on this renowned physician, Dr. Durham looked up at him hopefully, meeting his eyes, "God be with you, Michael."

CHAPTER 42

From the university campus, Henri walked briskly east over Colfax Street and then slowed to a crawl as he approached the Capitol area. He tried hard to ignore the miserable feeling in his achy body. Glancing at his small city map again, he would pass the U.S. Mint and enter the Capitol grounds at the large City & County Building on the western side and then straight through the lawns of Civic Center Park and Lincoln Park with the magnificent Capitol building straight ahead to the east.

As he walked, he noticed the array of high-rise, multi-colored office buildings to the north and the stately Art Museum and Public Library buildings to the south, but what he really wanted to tune into were the conversations of the slow moving pedestrians and the many military personnel surrounding the Capitol. He was amused at the buzz among the civilians about their power loss and the growing number of persons feeling flu-like symptoms, but amazed he heard nothing about the congressional shootings. The government must be keeping it mum, he thought. He tried the same casual approach he had used on the young soldier at the university with several of the military personnel who were assigned to keep anyone from entering the Capitol building. But the only replies were along the lines of the government attempting to track down the loss of electricity and mobile phone devices. Either the military outside did not know what had gone on at the president's residence and inside the Capitol building or they were under strict orders to maintain silence. They all repeated the line that they were simply keeping visitors out of the building so that the government could pursue the objective of restoring power without interference. None of the soldiers seemed to know anything about why people around the Capitol, including some among themselves, were beginning to feel flu-like symptoms.

Despite feeling feverish himself, Henri picked up his pace and found the beginning of the 16th Street Mall just north of Civic Center Park. It was about a ten block walk back to the Tower, and as he walked he found himself getting increasingly annoyed that he didn't seem much better than the straggling, complaining people he passed along the way. He struggled to find the energy to walk up the many steps leading to the top of the Tower. His earlier confident mood soured as he agonizingly approached the top. "Amagan, Jaweed! It's Henri." He pushed open the door and discovered the two staring up at him looking quite sleepy from their sprawled out positions on the floor. Impatiently, he snapped: "Are you still napping?"

The two didn't respond right away. Still breathing heavily from his struggle up the stairs, Henri continued to stare at them, curious and concerned now about their condition. Finally, Amagan replied. "Just a little groggy. I fell sound asleep…. What have you learned?"

"It's good. It's bad. The virus is working its magic. People everywhere are feeling the initial flu-like symptoms." *Even me….* "By late tomorrow, it gets very abrupt when nausea and bleeding take hold, and then poof, they're gone…. But our assassination plan has problems. Farzam was killed breaking in at the vice-president's residence. Shot by her security guard. Babur died hitting a wall chasing Michael Reynolds on his cycle. And that damn Reynolds shot Asa dead at the university lab—with Babur's gun no less." Henri had his facts slightly wrong, but it did not matter—three assassins were dead; Amagan and Jaweed both sat up looking mortified.

Amagan pleaded with Henri painfully: "With all our training, how could that happen? We did our assignments flawlessly. How—"

"We are dealing with clever people. I knew this wouldn't be easy," he sneered. "That's why I came here instead of heading home." Henri peered out the window into the late afternoon sun. "Let's finish the job tonight, before they get lucky and discover our vaccine, or some new anti-viral agent.... By the way, about our vaccine—how are you two feeling, other than sleepy?"

Despite awakening groggily from their naps, both Amagan and Jaweed had begun to feel slight headaches, general joint pain, and slightly feverish. But neither would yet admit those conditions to each other, nor especially to Henri, who seemed to them to be trying to take over their mission. "Yeah, I'm okay, but just how do you suppose to finish the mission, Messieur Henri?" Amagan baited.

"The vice president, the new president, Alexis Graham. She is holed up in her home office at the Beauvallon. She is being protected but she has no communications. She is helpless. Forget her. The other three are all at the Advanced Science Building at the university. They must be working nonstop to find an anti-viral agent. By now they must know exactly what that virus is.... Okay, so they will also feel the suddenly acute effects of the virus within the next 24 hours, but what if they stumble on something before then? We have to get in there ... or have them come out."

"I already tried that trying to help Asa," Jaweed said. "He must have been trapped in there, alone. We would have to go in together and blast them all."

Amagan looked on in silence. *Suicide!*

"Look. You two are executers, not planners," replied Henri. "We have to have a plan. The laboratory building has temporary generator power, probably from propane tanks located outside or from storage batteries or from roof solar panels. They don't like to put gas tanks in buildings or on the roof in case of accidental explosion.... Doesn't matter the source—they have power in there. Don't know how long that will last, but we could shut it down if we can't bait them out.

We could break in as it gets dark tonight. A security guard told me the university president or Michael Reynolds has to come out and authorize any new entrants. We could try that first."

"Henri Bonaparte," Jaweed chided. "You think you are so smart. Don't you know these Americans don't use fossil fuels anymore? Their emergency generator is probably running on solar panels on the roof."

"Like I said it doesn't matter the source. We have to shut it down or take the scientists out."

As Henri paused to try to get all his rapid thoughts in order, Amagan mused aloud. "To me, this sounds like a suicide mission."

"No, Amagan. He's right," Jaweed interjected calmly. "We came here to do a job for the good of mankind. We should pick up for our compatriots if they fall. This mission is bigger than anyone of us. Let's have Henri think out his plan. He is risking his life too … and he could have been on his way back to Dire by now."

Henri nodded in appreciation of Jaweed's support but felt he had to postpone his planning. "Right now, comrades, I have to sleep. I'm exhausted. Wake me by six. Then I'll have it."

Near dusk approaching seven, the plan was set. Amagan and Jaweed agreed to Henri's plot. They checked their weapons and began their descent from the tower close to sunset. None would admit his feeling feverish, but each began privately to wonder about the worth of his vaccine.

The walk to the university from the Tower in the cool dry air of early evening was uneventful. The three foreigners raised no suspicions on the crowded streets even though Amagan and Jaweed were hiding their AK-47 rifles under their long coats. With no power in their downtown apartments and condos, many people slowly walked the streets seeking some comfort from others in the same predicament. No one was obeying the rumor of a command by the military to stay indoors to avoid the black dust that was still occasionally blowing around. It was easy to overhear the complaints about some kind of contagious flu going around at the same time as the power loss, but it was alarming to the trio to realize that each of the three was feeling the same physical discomfort.

For Parisian Henri, it was eerie to notice in the dimming daylight that no lights were coming on in the downtown area of this big cosmopolitan city. The three crossed the bridge over Cherry Creek by Speer Boulevard on Latimer Street and turned left towards the rear of the nearby Advanced Science Building.

"You two stay here out of sight of the military guards, but position yourselves so that you can see me approaching the rear entrance." Henri commanded. "Let's go over it again. I'll ask for admittance to the Microbiological Laboratory as an expert in contagious diseases. If Reynolds or Frost comes down to verify, I'll take him out with my pistol. I have their pictures from your book; I'll recognize them. You two storm the guards and get inside. The University Guide Book I found shows the MB Lab on the second floor. We all get up there fast and take the rest out…. Escape out the back before the guards at the front entrances can get back there…. Okay, Plan B: if they let me proceed inside or to the lab to be identified, you cut the power lines you see over there at the backup generators. In the confusion, you force your way in and up to the lab. I only see three guards at the rear entrance. There were about twenty around the front main entrances. We still have enough daylight for another twenty minutes, and you both have flashlights when the lab goes dark … okay, I go."

"And we get out?" Amagan said seriously.

"Your rifles are fully loaded, right?" Henri replied. "You're trained killers. Do your job."

Amagan thought to himself, but at least without fear this time. *I was right —this is a suicide mission.*

As Henri approached the building, he recalled his early conversations with Antoine. How crazy an idea was it to steal billions of dollars out of Swiss bank accounts and from international investors in order to go and buy advanced weapons and even crazier to think that he and his brazen Iranian friend Aazim could end the world's violence by threatening death to those who didn't lay down their arms. Now, here *I am*—a complete convert walking into my own possible death. For what? To kill some American heroes who might possibly find the antiviral before they otherwise die themselves? Their chance of success is probably very unlikely. For the first time in many months he felt conflicted, but then thought maybe it's because he felt so sick and tired. His heart raced, and he felt chilled but all of a sudden reinvigorated in the cool of the September evening. Denver—one mile high. The symptoms of fatigue and fever that he had felt seconds before were banished by the sudden rush of adrenaline as he approached the armed guard.

The young uniformed soldier spoke with a weary voice: "Sorry, no one is allowed in the building. Some lab work going on in there, and they don't want to be disturbed."

"I know," replied Henri. "I understand they are trying to figure out why everyone seems to be getting the flu. Folks at the Capitol sent for me and told me to get over here. I'm Henri Bonaparte from Paris. See my passport…. I am an expert on influenza diseases. I was going to go on a hiking trip holiday, but stopped here in Denver first. I know your Richard Frost and Michael Reynolds. If they are in there, I need to go up and help them."

"Right, sir. Let me go up first. I'm under orders that if any scientists come, Dr. Frost or Mr. Reynolds will come down to verify. You must know of the assassinations at the Capitol, and the president just–"

"Yes, yes, yesterday. I know. Terrible. Sure, send them down. They may not remember my name at first, but this is urgent."

"Jason," the accepting soldier called to his nearby companion. "Stay with Mr. Bonaparte here while I go up to the lab to get verification. Yes, and check him over for weapons … sorry sir, routine sir," turning back to Henri.

Jason looked more alert than the young soldier who proceeded to slowly swing the rear entrance door open on his way to climb up the stairwell to the labs. Jason was wearing a similar uniform and was holding his rifle with his right arm. Before Henri could fully realize the intent, Jason did a quick body pat down with his left hand, feeling the shape and weight of something in Henri's right pants pocket. "Sir, I'll have to have you pull that out, just to check. We are under orders—no weapons inside."

Henri stood frozen. He had not planned on this. He could pull the weapon, shoot the soldier and the other one nearby, and call for Amagan and Jaweed to charge to get to the upstairs, but he had no training for this. He hesitated; he was not a killer. He was trained only to release the black dust. As Henri's trembling hand slowly reached for his pocket, Jason all too quickly assisted and succeeded in grasping control of the pistol, pulling it out. "I'm sorry, sir. I'm sure you're licensed to carry a concealed weapon, but I'll have to hold it for you while you're upstairs."

Henri's face went blank. He still stood rock firm and could only weakly mutter: "Yes, of course."

A short distance away: "They have his gun!" Amagan exclaimed and turned to Jaweed. "Now what?"

Standing unnoticed in the growing darkness behind a tree, only 100 feet away, the two looked at each other in confusion. Jaweed finally replied: "Let's go. There are only two guards. We take them out and get up to the labs. Forget the generators. We're better off with the lights on—we don't have much time."

At the same time as Amagan and Jaweed charged the building, the young soldier who had gone upstairs now reappeared with Michael right behind him. The startled Amagan, now less than 30 feet away, quickly pulled his AK-47 around to his front and fired right at the soldier's chest. The poor soldier gasped and fell instantly just outside the door. Michael reacted instinctively and fell to the ground behind him while grabbing the fallen soldier's rifle. Startled, Henri finally moved into action and grabbed his own pistol that Jason had by now dropped to the ground in order to get his own rifle into firing position. It was too late. Amagan and Jaweed blasted several rounds into Jason and the other startled guard before they had a chance to fire their weapons. Instead of turning towards the nearby Michael, Henri panicked in the clatter and with his pistol in hand began running the other way fleeing the scene.

But now the odds were with Michael—hidden from clear view in the approaching nightfall while lying flat behind the body of the fallen soldier. With the attention of Amagan and Jaweed focused on Jason and his two comrades, Michael took quick aim and fired the fallen soldier's M-3, hitting right into their chests, first of Amagan and then of Jaweed. *Crack, thump. Crack, thumb.* The contrast was surreal—from pandemonium and loud bursts to complete silence in the matter of seconds. Michael lay quietly and tried to fathom what had just happened. It seemed to him like an eternity, but within a few moments, hearing the gunshots, guards from the front of the building came running around the corner. They witnessed the scene in awe—a man scurrying away in the distance, three fallen soldiers on the ground, two dark-bearded men lifeless down on the grass nearby, and Michael Reynolds on his knees staring at the slaughter.

The Lord or good luck, or both, were again with Michael. Four times in harm's way and only a bump on the back of his head.

CHAPTER 43

Richard and Jonathan had reentered the front lab from the inner containment lab to converse with Rose about their status when a weary-looking Michael staggered through the door. "It was over in no time ... God! I can't believe it." The three waited anxiously for more. They had heard the multiple shots. Fila looked up quizzically from her sitting position on the lab floor nearby. "They killed three soldiers guarding the rear door. I was lucky. I was on the ground behind one of the fallen soldiers. I managed to get his rifle and fire before they could turn to me.... They're dead too."

All looked astonished as Michael paused.

"Who, Michael, who?" Rose anxiously asked.

Michael stared directly into Fila's eyes. "Your friends, Fila, your friends Amagan and Jaweed." Fila dropped her mouth, her eyes opening wide in disbelief. "That's the six of you, Fila, that's Babur's list of the six assassins. You're done girl, you're done!" Michael nearly screamed as Fila cowered. "They were coming after me, and I suppose all of us ... but there's one more—Henri Bonaparte. The guy is supposedly a disease expert who wanted admittance here to help us. I never heard of him. He ran away with a pistol in his hand.... Who is he Fila? Is he one of you?"

Fila's thinking was now more disturbed than ever. *Henri Bonaparte? What the hell is he doing here? He led the team to spread the dust over Colorado and was to return to Los Angeles.* Michael waited for an answer. Haltingly she replied: "You know it was Amagan and Jaweed? " Michael nodded. "Afghans. It's done. That's it!" Fila stared up at the ceiling, morally conflicted, wondering again whether she had done the right thing in trying to stop the madness, or now with all her friends dead should she herself have completed her mission and shot everyone in this room when she had the chance?

Rose, impatient with the pace of the dialogue, leered hard at Michael. "He may be legitimate. Maybe he got scared in the gunfire and fled."

"He has a pistol. He tried to come up here. I don't know any Henri Bonaparte."

"Nor do I," added Richard coming closer from the inner lab and entering the conversation.

"What did he look like? Like him?" Rose persisted, pointing towards the body bag of Babur, desperately looking for an answer from anyone who could actually help them in this dilemma.

"I'm not sure. It happened so fast, but no, no, he was different—not dark skinned or a beard," Michael replied.

"He is with us," Fila said calmly as she rose to a standing position. They all turned towards her voice in amazement. "He was the mission leader releasing the black dust over Colorado. He was to return. I don't know why he would have come here."

With that disappointing explanation, Rose's expression turned sour. *Oh no, another one.*

"Well, he has a gun, and he's on the loose," Michael said barely audible.

The room fell quiet. All this time, Jonathan Dean had been standing next to the bewildered-looking Richard Frost. Everyone in the room appeared forlorn, lost in thought. Finally, Jonathan broke the silence. "Look, we have isolated and identified this bug—a genetically-modified and enhanced strain of the Ebola virus. Like we said, it's a killer; it spreads in the air by this chemical dust and easily inhaled, but we have all the necessary tools available right here, equally as good as the CDC's best lab. We spent all last night and today searching but have not finished trying all of our anti-viral agents against it. Some take time, and there are more. And who knows about this three-day stuff that guy told you about, Michael. Maybe it's very slow acting; maybe even a vaccine—"

"Jonathan!" Michael vehemently interrupted. "You haven't found any vaccine in Fila's blood yet! I like your enthusiasm for a solution, but I already feel like I'm getting flu symptoms myself, and the situation at the Denver Health Center is drastic. The very young and the very old have overwhelmed it. The beds are full. Patients are being turned away at the door. No treatments are giving relief. The symptoms with the immune-impaired are advancing beyond simple flu symptoms like headaches, body aches and fever, the loss of body fluids through vomiting and diarrhea, to internal bleeding. Many have already died.... Even if we miraculously discovered an anti-viral vaccine today, there would never be time to manufacturer it and deliver it to the American population in time, especially without power. The military bases around the country are all reporting via their secure fiber optic system that the black dust is everywhere—"

"Okay, okay, right, no vaccine, that's impractical." Jonathan interrupted an impassioned but despondent Michael, "but an anti-viral agent that is common, not manufactured from scratch—one that we can get the word out and people can quickly get access to it. It's possible. Don't give up. We don't have them here, but there were some attempts a few years ago to develop man-made antibodies to the virus and also attempts to develop a vaccine. Let me try to pick up where they left off. Let's get back to it!"

"I'm achy all over right now too," Richard added haltingly, "but I'm ready to keep trying."

"Michael," Rose looked at him with a faint hint of encouragement. "They're right. It's not like you. Don't give up. This is our only chance."

"I don't want to give up, but you should see what's going on out there. I'm tired. I feel sick. We're praying for a miracle. I can't see it happening," he replied head down, barely audible.

A moment of absolute silence in the room followed, and then from little Alex crawling along the top of the lab bench came a sound, an "aaahhh!"

Michael looked over in his despair thinking his child too was now feeling the symptoms of the virus. But Alex was smiling, alert, eyes bright beckoning to his father. *What is going on?* Michael thought, staring at his son.

CHAPTER 44

It was now 7 p.m. and nearly pitch dark as Henri dragged himself back up Arapahoe Street towards the 16th Street Mall. In the very dim light remaining after the sunset to the west, it was eerie to see tall buildings in a major metropolis completely darkened with no lights, no neon signs on, nor street lights burning. Yet he thought this was only the first part of the Master Plan that was working perfectly—no electricity. As he walked on, the only noticeable lights he could clearly detect came from an occasional store or restaurant that still had their emergency generators working. And then he glanced at apartment buildings where he noticed an array of dim lights flickering—candles. The streets were now deserted. He thought about all those people inside. They must be terribly confused. Sick and getting worse, too sick to march in panic in the streets, sadly unaware they could all be dead in twenty four more hours. This was the second part of the Master Plan that was working perfectly—rapid illness. He tried his mobile satellite phone—no contact. This was the third part of the Master Plan that was working—no communications through space.

But why was *he* feeling sicker? Maybe it is just exhaustion, not sickness. He looked up and down the deserted Mall and then decided it best to climb to the safety of the Tower. His thoughts streamed unendingly in his head. The American military must be confused. Was he one of the assassins or was he the scientist sent to help at the lab and then innocently fled the shooting scene simply in horror and fear? *Play it safe.* Get some rest and then rethink what to do next. This was the fourth part of the Master Plan that was not working—the assassinations had not been completed. Most importantly, the persons who might just possibly stumble upon a quick antidote to the virus were probably at this very moment experimenting with a wide host of virus killing agents in one of the most advanced microbiological laboratories in the whole world.

But then, he thought, even if they discovered it and saved themselves, how could they ever get the word out, manufacture it, and deliver it to 300 million citizens around a huge country in such a short time? *Impossible!* Maybe Aazim and Antoine never had to attempt these assassinations in the first place. As he struggled in the dark up the steps of the tower to his sanctuary, he felt delirious, mixing his rational thoughts with wild emotions. *Why in the world did I ever come in here to the city? I could have been on my way home. I was going to help them, be a hero—now they're dead, and I ran. Am I a coward?*

As he collapsed exhausted on the floor of the room below the tower bell, he thought back to his joyful days in Paris as a boy and young man. Forget Antoine and his crazy ideas of ending violence around the world. Paris had been peaceful for eighty years, and even conquerors could never ever destroy its beauty.

I could have stayed right there, heaven on earth … and with those last tantalizing thoughts Henri dozed off into a deep sleep.

CHAPTER 45

It was time for Michael to take stock, probing deep into his mind to find a solution. Alex's smile an hour before gave him renewed hope. Richard, Jonathan and his assistant, Josh, had taken their agreed-upon 15-minute naps and were back in the inner lab, working to find the anti-viral agent that would stop the virus. First things first, Michael thought. The hurdles of solving this problem seemed insurmountable—finding a solution, getting it produced and then distributed were overwhelming. But on second thought, the only hope would be if they discovered something surprisingly simple which could be readily available—one that the military at the 15 communicating bases around the country could get hold of right away and distribute quickly. *Even then, is that possible?*

Michael abandoned his thoughts and glanced at Rose and Fila both asleep a yard apart. Strangely, the two looked peaceful, serene, after all the drama an hour before. The two were sitting on the floor with their heads leaning back against a lab bench. Above them, he peered closely at young Alex perched comfortably in a large sink atop the bench. Rose had padded the sink on all sides and it looked comfortable. Michael put his ear close to Alex's mouth and felt his head gently with the palm of his hand. Amazingly, the child had no fever and seemed to be breathing and sleeping quite normally. *How could that be?* Michael felt his own forehead—slightly warm. His flu-like symptoms of a slight headache and achy joints were now more noticeable. At least he felt no internal discomfort at this point—short of the point of vomiting or diarrhea, and no nose bleeding. *I have to get to Ali's again. We have to have a plan, just in case we do get that miracle.*

"Rose, wake up. You've slept your 15 minutes," Michael whispered softly, gently shaking Rose's shoulder. She opened her eyes slowly.

"Oh, I feel weak, Michael. My head hurts."

"Yes, me too." He put his hand on her forehead. "You're feverish too. We've got to fight through this…. Remember the dark days a few years ago, Rose. We got through. We persevered. We—"

"I know, but we felt strong, alive, alert … now … a while ago I was trying to pep you up not to give up, but now I—"

Outwardly, a mentally renewed Michael wouldn't give in. "Sit up on this chair. Watch Fila and Alex. He seems okay … somehow. I'm going to Ali's again. Through the military, she is the only way to communicate to the country. We have to have a plan if Richard and Jonathan come up with something. If they come out with any good news, have one of the soldiers downstairs run to the Beauvallon." He tried his best to sound convincing.

"Okay, Michael, okay. Be careful."

"And keep Fila's pistol in your vest pocket. Can we really trust her? And who knows who this Henri Bonaparte is…. Let me see her gun."

Rose slowly raised herself up and unzipped her vest pocket. She pulled out the confiscated 9mm Russian built Makarov and pulled out the pistol's magazine. "Ten rounds left, full. She fired three bullets from her rifle when she shot the Marine," she whispered to Michael, bowing her head to the floor. She had never used a gun before.

"Put the magazine back in. Put the gun back in your pocket."

"But I don't think I can—"

"You will do whatever you have to do to protect Alex, Rose. I'll be back soon."

Upon leaving the front door of lab building, Michael told the guarding soldiers where he was going—to Alexis Graham's office/residence for the fifth time in the last 36 hours. It was depressing for Michael to notice that they all appeared very tired or sick. He inquired what they had done with the bodies of their three slain comrades and the two intruders. They replied that with no transportation available, the bodies had been pulled into a small room inside and covered tightly with a tarp. They had sent one of the cooperating policemen back to the Capitol to report what had happened. Michael nodded and said: "No one is to enter this building until I return. Okay?"

When he reached his Volt inside the parking garage just one emergency spotlight was still shining. He hoped the car's battery still held power. But nothing. His 16.5 kilowatt hour lithium-ion battery was dead and so was his all electric-powered car. 'No problem.' he said to himself; 'it's only about a half-mile to walk'. The short journey down Speer Boulevard was strange beyond belief. Normally a busy four-lane highway in both directions, even after rush hours, the wide boulevard was empty. Michael could barely distinguish the tall, darkened office buildings standing against a nearly black sky to the northeast. Some faint lights could be discerned here and there in the smaller buildings nearby; maybe those are candles burning in apartment houses. Not easy to navigate, but once finding the Beauvallon at 9th and Lincoln, the scene changed dramatically. Lanterns were lined neatly along the sidewalks. The whole building seemed lit by candlelight. A horde of soldiers surrounded the side and front doors. This was the office and residence of the new President of the United States.

"I'm Michael Reynolds. I am authorized to see President Graham. Right away, please." The commanding officer who passed on him before was nowhere to be seen.

"Wait here, sir," replied the armed sentry at the main entrance. "Let me have your I.D. and we'll run it upstairs for verification. We have been ordered to be very careful."

"Understood, soldier, understood, but please hurry."

Five minutes later Michael was ushered into Ali's candlelit

apartment. The living room now looked as though it had been converted from an administrative hub into a command post, but strangely, the five or six weary-looking military personnel stationed there seemed to be *trying* to look busy. But it was obvious to Michael they in truth had nothing to do. Ali was sitting at one end of the couch, her feet stretched out on an ottoman, reading a book by candlelight. Looking up at an approaching Michael, she looked very tired, her normally bright eyes now showing fatigue. She managed a smile at seeing him. Despite his recurring visits bringing her no joy, Michael Reynolds was her rock.

"Ali, how are you feeling?"

"Michael, oh Michael, like everyone here," she replied in a hushed tone. We all feel like we have the flu, but I haven't divulged a thing to anyone, only to General Ralston and General Armstrong. They too are keeping the seriousness of this illness quiet. I wish I had never gotten hold of this book on viruses—the Ebola is deadly," she whispered. "But tell me—please, please—since this afternoon when you were here, what have you learned at the lab?" Her voice trailing off, she prayed Michael's presence would finally bring words of encouragement.

"I'm sorry, Ali," Michael replied in a dejected tone. "You must have received reports the hospitals are overloaded. It's affecting everyone, but the very young and very old are going fast…. Ali, according to Richard Frost and Jonathan Dean, like I told you before, this strain of Ebola has been genetically modified to travel through the air like a cold virus, and the black dust is a fine chemical dispersant to which it was first attached and is capable of spreading it virtually everywhere. The biggest problem is that it's the only known virus which will not set off the human body's own immune defense system. It shuts it down—"

"Michael! You've told me that already! I don't know if I want to hear that again," Ali cut in, now suddenly turning to the edge of becoming hysterical.

Michael expected as much and continued on calmly. "Richard and Jonathan are still continuing to work right now to find an anti-viral agent that will destroy it, stop its entry into human cells, or an antidote that will spark an immune response. Our MB lab at the university is the most advanced in the country. If it can be done the tools are there.

"But we need a follow-up plan", he continued. Michael could feel he was struggling to force himself to be more upbeat, masquerading to the new president that he is the eternal optimist. "Let's say by tomorrow morning Richard and Jonathan were to discover an effective anti-viral agent. I would run over here and inform you and then I'd go to our Denver hospitals. You'd get on the secure line to General Ralston in Washington and he'd get the word out to our military bases, and those people would have to spread the word, first to the medical community, and—"

"Michael, Michael!" Ali retorted with her voice raised as before— the first times in two days. "What are you talking about? The anti-viral—a drug?" The military in the room now could hear her and turned their attention to the two. "Is it in inventory at drug stores? All the known anti-virals must be prescription drugs at pharmaceutical warehouses and drugstores. How would there be enough? Are drugstores even open? The pharmacists are probably home sick themselves? What if it had to be manufactured? How would we get those plants running without electricity? How would we distribute it to three hundred million people spread over three thousand miles? How would we control a panic on the streets when there isn't enough? Michael, there isn't enough time!" Ali's eyes opened wide, a look of incredulity, searching for believability from Michael. It seemed for the first time in her three-year friendship with Michael that she suddenly doubted him. He had been wise beyond his years; always on target … but now.

Michael stared back, eyes firm. He prepared himself for this on his walk over from the lab, every question she raised. He knew the idea seemed preposterous that even if Jonathan found the anti-viral, how in the world could the agent be produced and distributed in time? But this was no time to give up on the new President of the United States.

"Ali, we have been assuming these assassins are correct. They are not scientists. They are only repeating what they have been told. Yes, the small outbreaks of Ebola in the past have always had a very high mortality rate, sometimes over ninety percent, but I checked—on average, seventy percent, sometimes as low as fifty percent. What if they only modified it so that it is transmitted through the air like a cold virus? What if they only strengthened it enough so only the very young, the very old, and the very immune-impaired face imminent death? That could mean the great majority of our population could survive well beyond three days, or forever, like the rest of us just get like a flu. It could die out.... Ali, yes, avoid panic using our military out in force but let's also get to the pharmaceutical companies now by courier and have them on stand-by.

"Dr. Durham at the Denver Medical Center told me there were genetically altered clones of antibodies experimentally produced few years ago that would attach to the Ebola virus and perhaps stop it, but the drug was apparently never produced in any quantities. What if our pharmaceutical companies still have the formula? The military has plenty of back-up generators to power places of manufacturing, and what if electricity, especially from wind and solar, is restored in just a few days, not weeks or months." Raising his voice, Michael pursued his main point. "Ali, we cannot take the risk of inaction in the event we *could* have done something—"

"Michael, it sounds farfetched to think anything could be scaled up in time, but I'm sorry. I don't think the way you do.... Okay, I'll call General Armstrong and General Ralston right away. Let's get the ball rolling. There must be thousands of emergency generators out there. You're right. I'm the president. I'm the leader. And I belong over at the Capitol with the grieving members of Congress and General Armstrong. The Army has moved portable generators over there and power is on. Wouldn't look right for me to just be sick up here in this apartment, crying the blues, waiting for me and my people to die an agonizing death with no hope." Ali stood up and looked closely at Michael, her face now softening with admiration in her eyes and voice. "What would I do without you, young man?"

Revealing a slight smile to show his approval of her sense of duty,

Michael completed his confidence-building strategy by reaching his arms around her and hugging her tightly. It seemed like a minute, as thoughts raced through his mind. *I exaggerated— she bought it. The young and old at the medical center were dying at an alarming rate for any kind of disease.* Even the strong were pouring in, and Dr. Durham had been left in despair.

Michael was growing weary. Another ten minute walk—three blocks west from Lincoln Street and the Beauvallon apartments, then several blocks south on Bannock Street. Michael felt his body aches more pronounced this time. In the past, on a couple of occasions when infected with a flu bug, his simple solution was to lie down for a day or two, rest, drink plenty of fluids, and let his body's immune response fight it out, knowing those powerful antibodies his body produced would soon wipe out the microscopic invaders.

Viruses—those simplest of living organisms could not even reproduce on their own like the one-celled bacteria do. They were little packages of DNA surrounded by a protein shell, and they needed a host organism to reproduce. How in this mysterious world did they ever become capable of entering a larger organism, find their way inside to bind to cells of its host, get inside the cell, take over its nuclear reproductive machinery, replicate itself, find its way out of the host's cell, invade the next cell, conduct a fight against its host's antibodies, and so and so on? But now Michael understood that this virus—the Ebola virus—does not provoke that human immune response which would otherwise eventually stop this chain of replication. Feelings short of panic, more of desperation, increasingly filled his heart physically with each aching step he took, but somehow his mind kept prodding him on, beckoning *let's not give up yet.* As he walked on in the near total darkness, he seemed oblivious to the streams of slow-moving people walking quietly past him in the opposite direction. They had been told at the hospital to go home and go to bed, that there were no meds. Michael expected to find panic as he approached the brightly lit medical center, but no one was in sight.

Moving down the hall to Dr. Durham's office he recounted the absence of the ghastly images that he expected to witness outside the hospital. Crowds of sick people should have been fighting for admittance to an already full hospital. Entering Dr. Durham's office, he found it empty. He spotted a nurse in the hall and shouted. "Dr. Durham! Can you tell me where I can find him?"

The very tired-looking young nurse turned to face him and weakly replied: "Yes, he is at the Convention Center. We have no room here. Every bed is occupied.... Please, tell me. What is this thing? Influenza? The very young, the very old, but why did so many young and middle-aged people come here so sick? And I have it already. Can you tell me?" Her weariness now turned to exasperation, asking this stranger for answers.

"I'm sorry. I don't know," Michael replied sheepishly, feeling her anguish. "That's why I want to speak with Dr. Durham. He is an expert in infectious disease.... Is there anything you are now giving, doing, for these people? Dr. Durham had nothing for them when I was here before."

"Like for me, the only help is lots of strong doses of the pain reliever, fever reducer acetaminophen, but we are running low on that. Dr. Durham had many carts of it wheeled over to the Convention Center. Our supplies of stronger pain medications are very limited, but we'll go into them next. Maybe they will help.... Who are you, anyway?"

Michael had already turned from her and was on his way to the Colorado Convention Center. From the bright lights of the hospital with its emergency generators still running, he was once again out in the dark of the cool evening. While September nights in Denver average over 47 degrees F, it felt very cold to Michael walking without a coat in the clear dry mile high air. Worse; his fever added to his shivers. Back up Bannock Street and left on Speer Boulevard for a quarter mile, there barely visible was the huge Convention Center building. As he approached the brightly lit entrance, Michael could see a crowd huddled in long lines outside waiting to get in. They seemed orderly, but he surmised that was only because they were feeling so ill. He wondered how long the center's emergency batteries would hold up. Just two uniformed policemen were manning the front entrance while several gallant soldiers were carrying folded cots through an adjacent open door. Others were carrying in cases of bottled water.

Walking to the front of the line, one of the two policemen waved a finger at Michael beckoning him to go to the back of the line. Instead Michael spoke up loudly for all nearby to hear: "I am Dr. Durham's assistant. He needs my help right away."

"Right. Come ahead. What's going on, anyway?" the drawn-faced policeman asked meekly.

"Yeah, everybody's catching this flu bug. We're trying to get a handle on it, but it's tough with all this power temporarily out," Michael tried to reply in a calm voice. As he and Ali had agreed, let's *avoid panic*. Moving inside to the spacious first floor, the open exhibit hall encompassing almost a huge 600,000 square feet of space, Michael soon learned the emergency batteries were only providing lighting to the first level. The meeting rooms on the second floor and the ballrooms on the third level were dark and empty. Water pressure in the restrooms was exceedingly low. The scene on the open first level looked like one from a disaster movie—cots lined up, people moving slowly, a very few uniformed nurses trying to make the reluctant inhabitants comfortable. Like the hospital, it was very quiet. People with a virus prefer to simply lie down, rest and doze.

Dr. Durham spotted Michael and slowly moved over towards him. He motioned Michael to step aside where no one could hear their conversation. "What have you learned, Michael, about the virus?" The distinguished doctor no longer looked even half as attentive as he had that afternoon at the hospital. He seemed far away, as though not expecting anything favorable from Michael, yet inside deeply longing desperately for some encouraging news.

"I'm sorry sir. The same situation as we discussed this afternoon. A genetically-modified Ebola virus enhanced to act rapidly and infecting through the air—after being spread by some type of fine chemical dispersant. It's airborne everywhere throughout the whole country, and worse, our military still has no idea when electric power and phone communications will be restored. Our lab people have no anti-viral agent against it yet, but they are still working at it. I have to know doctor—is it hitting hard at mostly the very young and very old in terms of mortality, and at everybody else just like a regular flu? ... I have to know whether we have a high percentage who will survive."

"Son, you can't see it from here what's really happening. And certainly you can smell it. With a contagious disease the protocol is to separate the infected and quickly dispose of their waste, but you can see we have no room or sufficient staff for that. You see us dispensing pain relievers, but we are also removing the deceased from the hospital and out of here through the back exits as quickly as we can. We are trying to avoid hysteria, but your answer is 'yes, no, and I don't know'—quicker death for the very young and very old but extreme sickness happening to everyone. We have some already dying who had said they are usually very healthy. So, we are well past an ordinary influenza epidemic and into a serious pandemic now that we have normally healthy people very sick, but I can't tell you how widespread or deadly that will be. The police, the soldiers—young and healthy—but sick too. I can't tell you how many of those responders may also succumb by tomorrow. Right now they are the ones filling the body bags outside."

The doctor let out a deep sigh as he paused. "I feel myself ... well ... fading ... and you?" The doctor looked defeated while searching Michael's face for an answer. But Michael now knew there could be no concrete answer to his questions. Maybe the assassins were right that in three days everyone dies. And that's just one day away, or maybe it will be like past episodes in Africa where some percentage of those infected somehow survive. Anyway, he thought, he did the right thing in getting the new president responsive to action and giving her some hope for survival.

"I feel exhausted doctor, achy all over. It would be too easy just to lie down under a warm blanket and—"

"Here, take these pain and fever pills every three hours and go back to the lab. It's the strongest I have. I only have enough for the medical staff to keep them going. Let's pray you all come up with something. I don't want to have to feel doom come tomorrow." The doctor pulled a packet out of his jacket pocket and handed it to Michael while pointing with his other hand to an unopened bottle of water on the floor.

Michael obeyed, his face showing obvious dejection, as he departed the tragic scene in this contrived hospital. The self-doubts and fears that had occasionally popped up in his formative years seemed insignificant to what he was facing now. Feverish, muscles and joints aching, headache—where does one find the will to go on in this seemingly impossible drama?

CHAPTER 46

Henri was oblivious to the footsteps coming up the tower stairwell. He was sound asleep until he felt something tugging vigorously on his jacket sleeve. "Henri, Henri, wake up." The intruder had placed a lantern on the floor illuminating their two faces.

"Tariq? Tariq Badini? What are you doing here?" Through half-opened eyes, Henri looked shocked as his mouth dropped wide open.

"May I ask the same of you, my friend? You released the canisters right on time. The magic dust arrived and worked, but you were to head for Los Angeles."

Still stunned, Henri paused and thought. "But I wanted to know if the Savior dust worked. I wanted to see the Americans suffer. And I wanted to know if our six assassins succeeded in their—"

"And they have not, have they?" Tariq's voice was very direct, very clear. "More failure than success."

"How do you know what's—"

"I know everything, my friend. I have been in Denver for some time. I know about the Americans' secure fiber optic line from the vice-president's residence to the military in the Capitol to the military in Washington to the fifteen military bases around the country. I slip in everywhere and overhear conversations. We have not one hundred percent knocked out all their communications. And I know about their experts working right now in their university lab trying to find an anti-viral. And I know we have only two targets dead but five assassins dead and maybe even the sixth, Fila, up in that lab. And I know that Michael Reynolds is destroying us. And I know when you came here, and I know when you went to the laboratory unsuccessfully and when you returned here, but I didn't know why you were here in Denver in the first place."

Henri stared in astonishment at the calm, solid look in Tariq's face. *How could he know so much?* But as he struggled to sit up to look eye to eye with the squatting Pakistani, he felt aches throughout his entire body and realized his head was throbbing too. "I have to wake up. I don't know why I'm feeling so awful. The vaccine should—"

"My dear comrade Henri Bonaparte," Tariq smiled. "You—that great friend of our banking genius Antoine, don't you know your vaccine is worthless. You have no defense against the virus. Like everyone else here, you are a dead man in three days."

"No, no everyone who came here has the vaccine. We are immune!" pleaded Henri.

"They told you so, yes, so that you one thousand would not think you were leaving Dire going to America on a suicide mission. Our illustrious scientists did everything perfectly the last ten years except for perfecting a vaccine to their wondrous improvement to the deadly Ebola virus. They never got the vaccine right ... nor did they ever find a truly successful anti-viral agent. You are doomed my friend."

With hope rapidly fleeting, Henri tried one last time. "No! I don't believe it. *You* have the vaccine. Your voice is strong. You don't seem to be in the least bit sick."

"It is I who willingly came on a suicide mission. I am the seventh assassin. I am the last resort to be certain the Americans cannot retaliate. I will die too, but if I seem strong it's because I have loaded myself with vitamins and minerals to stall the disease, and I have been taking powerful anti-fever, anti-pain medication ever since your dust arrived yesterday morning.... Here, my friend, take this pill with this water. You will temporarily feel better. You can help me."

Henri obeyed and swallowed the pill with the welcome water but sat silently while trying hard to absorb what he had just been told. Then he had to ask again. "I'm not just tired and feel a slight case of this terrible disease, but I'm going to die too?"

"Yes, my friend from Paris. You are going to die too. Just like the Americans, just like your comrades here, and just like me."

Have I been deceived by my only close friend, Antoine?

"Can I believe you, Tariq? I have come so far. Antoine's ideas seemed like madness at first. Then I came around. I followed him to Dire. I became a believer. I volunteered for—"

"Yes, Henri. Just like me … but you can believe me. I cannot answer for your Frenchman friend's deceit, but why would I lie to you now? Here's what we going to do … listen."

CHAPTER 47

No matter how bad he felt, Michael regained his self-determination stepping into the cool evening breeze outside the depressing scene inside the Convention Center. He changed his mind—he had one more base to cover before going back to the lab to see if Jonathan and Richard had yet found the miracle anti-viral. First President Graham, then Doctor Durham; now he felt the need to go to the Capitol and see General Armstrong. He prayed the general was strong enough physically to be in command. Another ten minute walk, this time east over West Colfax Street to the massive Capitol building between Lincoln, Sherman and Grant Streets. Great names, he thought. We need them now.

He wondered if there would be another great name arising out of this unfolding national chaos. The walk took longer than he expected. He caught a glimpse of a spotlight shining up through an American flag and onto the western façade of the building. The military must have proudly rigged up some kind of an emergency generator to a huge mobile spotlight. As he cut right and into Civic Center Park to get a better view, he slowed his pace. He seemed alone in the park, but it was the first time in two days he actually felt relief. Physically, the strong drug for pain and fever that Doctor Durham had handed him was already giving him temporary relief. Mentally, seeing the glimmering American flag waving proudly above gave him a moment of strong hope, even if fleeting.

As he approached the steps leading up to the building, he could make out an array of soldiers slowly walking the pathway surrounding the building. For some strange reason he stopped on the thirteenth step. This was the advertised, exact spot in Denver that is 5,280 feet above sea level—one mile in the mile-high metropolis. What did that matter now? After his brief pause, Michael felt tapping on his arm by a young soldier who had obviously grown quite weary.

"Sorry, you will have to turn around. No one is to enter the Capitol other than police, military or a member of Congress."

"I understand. I am an ambassador from President Graham to see General Armstrong. She may be here soon. Can you check my photo and take my driver's license here to him. Please hurry. Time is of the essence."

With a flashlight check of Michael's face and the license photo, the young soldier obediently moved away in the dark. It must have been a full five minutes before he returned, Michael's time spent by continuing to admire the flag waving above with the building façade behind it, the building architecture modeled after the national Capitol in Washington, D.C. It was a beautiful sight.

"Sir, follow me. I'll escort you to General Armstrong's office."

It was obvious no one inside the general's office had caught a wink of sleep in two days. The quietness seemed eerie, but no one was dozing. Cold coffee must have been keeping them awake as Michael noticed a number of empty and half-filled mugs on every desk as he walked by into the general's office.

"Michael, a surprise. President Graham told me you were just there." He continued anxiously: "Do you have news?" General Armstrong's tie was loosened, his medal studded jacket hanging on his chair behind. He struggled to get up to shake Michael's hand. He had not seen the American hero for at least six months. He was visibly exhausted and almost appeared apologetic.

"I'm sorry General. I have no news yet from the MB lab. We have not found an effective ant-viral yet. We're still trying. Please … sit. I want to discuss with you where I think we are and what we can do, and sir, I suggest to you that as soon as I leave, you set your watch alarm and take a fifteen-minute mini-nap. President Graham wants to come here at some point, but I beg not. It's still too dangerous."

General Armstrong broke a slight grin as he sat down again in his chair while Michael pulled up another chair for himself close to the general's desk. It was refreshing after the last two days of mayhem that someone sounded so authoritative. "Yes, Michael, go ahead."

"I'm sure you are up to speed on conditions at the city hospitals and now at the Convention Center. I was just there and spoke with Doctor Clarence Durham, the chief of infectious disease at the Denver Medical Center. We spoke about the fairly low incidence of the Ebola virus in Africa yet its high death rate. But the point is some ten to fifty percent of those infected do survive. Now these people from overseas, whoever they are, yes have brilliantly taken a deadly virus, one that does not spark a human immune response and can only be spread by bodily fluid contact, and modified it so it spreads through the air, like a common cold. As you now know, they have also brilliantly, from their point of view, been able to spread it quickly through our entire country by attaching it to a fine chemical dispersant. That you know.… But here's my point. Despite their belief, which I learned from two of the Afghans, the ones we call the assassins, that exposure means death to all in three days, we have no way yet to verify that. They are not the scientists."

"Go on, Michael." The general perked up.

"Sir, as Ali, President Graham, called you to set up a plan to have your military contact all the pharmaceutical companies, have them save their emergency generators and batteries, and have them ready if we discover the antidote, I have two more things. First, like I said, we should not just blindly accept the prophecy of doom for us all. Get your troops taking pain and fever relief like acetaminophen *before* they fall completely ill so they can respond if we can find the antidote. At the hospital, once the victims are down, there is nothing working to relieve them. Second, many of us might survive just fine if the virus does not attack us uniformly, or perhaps somehow some of us do miraculously create antibodies to this version of the virus. Let's use those people to help the weaker ones. Be ready to ask for volunteers to help the Red Cross."

"That sure would be easier if our radio communications get back on line soon," the general sighed.

"Right. And one more thing. Remember General Armstrong, I have the list of the six assassins. Five are dead, the sixth we have in custody at the lab. But there could be one more. He doesn't look like the others. Caucasian. He was with the two approaching the lab at sundown and pretended he was a scientist sent to help. But he ran away with a pistol in his hand. He is one of them. My wife thought it possible he may be innocent and just got scared in the shooting, but we learned he was the leader of a group who released the virus."

"So—"

"So we have to assume the worst. What would he do now? His comrades are all down. They succeeded in taking down the president but we have a new one. They succeeded in disrupting Congress and killing the third in line. We need a new Speaker elected immediately from the group upstairs. We need to further fortify the security around Ali, President Graham, and while she wants to come here as chief executive, I recommend keeping her there... So he sees that. Where does he go? The attempts on the lab have failed so far, but that MB lab is their fear. They want to make sure we don't quickly come up with an antidote, the anti-viral. You have put more troops around the lab building since the shootings and a larger detail surrounding the emergency batteries in the back. What would he do? He knows it will be difficult to get up to the second floor labs. His best option is to close down the building. Get it off our emergency power...."

"Yes, and how can he do that? He doesn't have a dive bomber," the general added.

"Not so fast. We have plenty of small single engine planes around our airfields that still fly on aviation fuel, not electric-battery powered. We are not yet a one hundred percent green economy despite what we think ... General Armstrong, can you get troops over there to those airfields if any of your vehicles are still running? This enemy is probably very capable of committing a suicide mission."

Wow! That sounded like good old military talk. From a civilian! "Okay, Michael, that could make sense. I can do it."

"Secondly, could he not find a truck that still has electric power left, or one of the real old ones running on gasoline, steal it and drive it at top speed off the curb, into the rear and right into our large battery station behind the building? General, I strongly suggest you send a runner over there as quickly as possible and use some of your troops to erect barriers around the exposed area and—"

"Michael, I'm with you! Finally, some action for an old military guy. I'll take care of it. Now get upstairs into the Congressional wing and see if you can get a Speaker elected. We have body bagged the deceased, and they have been carried to the basement. The wounded have been moved to the Supreme Court side. We must have over two hundred representatives up there now."

"We're on, General Armstrong, we're on," Michael countered as he departed. The weariness in the general's face had at least temporarily dissipated.

Michael walked down the dimly lit hallway outside General Armstrong's first floor office and up the 57 step marble grand staircase to the House chamber on the second floor. A sole Marine accompanied him to assure his admittance. The scene was devastating. The State of Colorado House of Representatives was a body of only 65. The U.S. House numbered 435 members, so the assembly room here had been squeezed and jam-packed for the last three years when Congress was again functional after it had suspended operations during the national emergency climate crisis of 2012 to 2018. The look of the room was nearly indescribable to Michael. Almost every U.S. Congressman had walked to the Capitol over the last two days after the prolonged failure to restore either their home electrical power or mobile phone use. Of course, the early arrivals like Speaker Wilson were the unfortunates gunned down by the assassin Jaweed. Many of the later arrivals brought their families, many of which were sprawled in sickness outside the chamber room. Inside, the scattered emergency lights appeared dim. Food trays and wrappers appeared on top of every desk—the cafeteria supply had made its way up here. Congressmen occupied every seat including all the portable chairs brought in for when the House was in session. It was a horror scene to Michael. It was so quiet. *These people are sick!* Almost no one was moving. Almost instantly, Michael retracted this part of his plan. Let's just keep Ali safe and forget the backup Speaker's role.

He quietly moved away, down the grand staircase, and headed out. He felt very tired, pushing himself, but back to the lab.

This medicine Dr. Durham gave me must be very powerful and very scarce, Michael thought as he picked up his pace walking back to the MB lab at the university. His fever was down slightly and his joints not quite as achy, just very fatigued now. Out of curiosity he cut a little bit northwest up to the 16th Street Mall, out to the landmark Tower, left on Arapahoe Street, and four blocks down to the lab. He wanted to see how things were going on this normally busiest of streets. He recalled television images from science fiction movies where stores would be looted, and panic would overtake the streets when some outside drastic element had broken down society. But here, in this reality, there was virtually complete silence, just the occasional slight hum of some emergency generators still running. No one was out on this commercial street. The stores were dark; no streetlights were on. Everyone must be crawling into his or her bed, he thought, too sick to even think of hunger and a restaurant.

Little did he know, as he passed the barely visible Tower, that his two remaining adversaries were right above him, plotting their next moves.

CHAPTER 48

"It will be getting light by six. I am setting my watch alarm for four. We will sleep until then … are you listening, Henri? Our first point of attack will be the connection site I discovered for their military's fiber optic line at the Capitol. The line is buried underground and comes into the basement on the building's south side, close to the entrance doors there. There are lines of soldiers right now outside all the doors. You will be the diversion. Your tactic will be to get them running to the west side. When I break in the south entrance, I'll have my two pistols ready if there are any guards inside. I will set a dynamite pack over the connection point to explode in one minute. We will knock out their only communications, and—"

"Wait, wait," an incredulous looking Henri cried out weakly. "What do you mean I will be the diversion?"

"Don't worry. You will be safe, Henri. We will meet at the bridge over Cherry Creek on Arapahoe Street right after. I have more dynamite for their laboratory power generators—the battery station they have right outside in the back. Listen to me—I have weapons, Henri. We have left nothing to chance. We will leave here together and set up together before I proceed to the Capitol. Right after firing, which I will teach you how, you will back up and get to the meeting spot. The firepower will be so loud and with flashes in the dark, their entire force of soldiers will rush to the scene to retaliate."

"Retaliate? All those soldiers against me?"

"No, no Henri—you will be gone."

Tariq paused and looked into Henri's eyes to see if he was grasping this turn of events and Tariq's boldness. Henri stared back, startled at such a seemingly impossible undertaking, but yet this man seemed so at ease, so confident, so assuring.

"What kind of weapons?" Henri finally asked softly.

"A new kind of machine gun your friend Antoine found for us. I smuggled four of them in. You set a dial on automatic, a timer on the interval for the elapsed time you want before it opens fire—we will set the four of them at different firing times and firing rates—pull the triggers and walk away. Once it begins, the slowest interval will keep it firing for five minutes.... On the west side of the Capitol are two parks. The closest to the building is Lincoln Park and further back the larger Civic Center Park. We will set the guns in the Civic Center Park, one by the Greek Amphitheatre on the south side, one by the McNichols Building on the north side, two in the middle—one by the cowboy statue and one by the Indian statue. All four will be lined up on the Capitol building. You pull the triggers and run. Each will have a delay before they fire. You will be long gone my friend.... It will be a real surprise for them, watching flashes coming from the dark and bullets flying at them. They will think it an army attacking." Tariq smiled with pride.

"Now close your eyes my friend—sleep."

CHAPTER 49

Approaching the lab, his walk back gruelingly labored and tiring, Michael's mood brightened as he could see that General Armstrong had acted quickly. A runner had obviously been dispatched immediately to follow the orders to buttress the emergency generating station behind the building. All kinds of materials were being pulled over to impede any kind of approaching vehicle. Around the front and sides of the building, there were more soldiers blocking the doorways than before; that was good. A few scattered lanterns revealed that over half of them were sitting against the building walls. They are sick too, Michael thought, but at least they are awake and armed. There were at least ten soldiers at the rear of the building.

The four emergency generators housing the huge batteries were each about fifteen feet square. The large electric storage batteries were kept fresh by being recharged through several small wind turbines located on the roof of the five-story building. Depending on wind speed variability, it was thought this system could operate for at least three days. Those same wind turbines were never intended to supplement the normal power coming from the large Denver wind and solar powered utilities. They were just there as backup support in the event of sudden power losses from storms. Almost the entire university electric power needs depended on the outside system, with no backup. One of the few exceptions was the Advanced Science Building, which had this small emergency battery system in order to keep cultures alive. In this fully green energy age, American power came from a combination of wind, solar, and hydro turbines, but now all were inoperable as the powerful electromagnetic pulse bomb had destroyed the capability of ground transformers. Battery operated emergency generators would soon lose power. The Dirists had done their job to perfection.

Michael entered the second floor MB lab and was surprised to see Rose sitting on a high stool bouncing little Alex on her lap. He was laughing. Michael felt thankful that his child still did not appear ill, but how so? Nearby, Fila was sitting on the floor, her eyes half open, looking very uncomfortable.

'What news?" Michael hurriedly inquired.

"Nothing yet. Jonathan wanted to explain it to you when you got back," as Rose's greeting smile turned to a serious tone of voice. She looked very tired. "And you?"

"It's bad, Rose, really bad. The hospitals are overwhelmed. They are now filling up the Convention Center with the sick. Fatalities are rising, not just with the very young and very old either. The streets are incredibly quiet. I think everyone is lying in bed sick, or they have dragged themselves off to medical facilities. I stopped by Ali's and the Capitol too … to encourage her and General Armstrong to follow up with a plan of action in case we come up with something. We have to have some hope…. Here, I have a couple more of these pills I was given. Supposed to last three hours. They must be very strong fever reducers and pain relievers. Take—"

"Michael, feel my forehead and Alex's. I obviously have a fever. I feel tired and achy, not real bad, but now feel his…. What do you think could—"

"Strange, Rose. I haven't met anyone yet this afternoon or tonight who isn't feeling terrible. Why is Alex … and what about Fila, Jonathan, Richard, Josh?"

"Whatever vaccine she thinks she was given surely is not working.

She has been feeling horrible. Jonathan has been out twice and hasn't complained at all like Richard and Josh have. I would just have to believe the virus just can't affect everyone the same way at the same time."

Michael again gazed down at Alex. *The very young. Why is he looking so lively? And no fever.* The inner door swung open and both Jonathan and Richard appeared, both looking frustrated. They both shook their heads negatively. Richard looked the worst. Maybe it was his age, Michael wondered, Richard being some twenty years older than Jonathan.

"You're back. What's happening out there, Michael?" Richard couldn't wait to ask.

Michael sat down on the lab bench stool next to Rose and put his head down. "It's bad—everyone is sick.... Who is behind this? These can't be just terrorists. They are brilliant. Their plan has been perfect, other than our luck against these six assassins. They somehow fire a strong electromagnetic pulse bomb high over America and knock out our ground power and air radio. They disperse a deadly virus ... and we don't have a response?"

"Michael! Snap out of it," Jonathan shouted. "I'm just telling you we have nothing *yet*.... We have to give these tests time. The antiviral drugs have to be proven out. They don't just reveal themselves as effective in a minute or an hour. The ones we tried yesterday—no go— but today's drugs are still being given a chance, and we have more to go. We'll know by tomorrow morning. We should all get some sleep."

"Take me in. Take me in to your inner lab where you do this work. I want to see—"

"Michael," Richard responded in a weak voice leaning against a bench. "Not your field—"

"No, fine. Follow me in," Jonathan interjected. "Protocol is wearing protective suits into a sterile environment, but we're all infected already. Come."

The secure inner laboratory was an even better model of the standard one in Atlanta, Georgia, home of the renowned Centers for

Disease Control and Prevention. It was equipped with the most up-to-date, sophisticated instrumentation in the country. And it contained all the tools necessary to thoroughly analyze every conceivable form of microscopic life.

"I understand, "Michael said, looking Jonathan in the eye. "I know you are doing your best. I just didn't realize what you have to do to get a reading on the anti-virals. Much more complicated than I thought. I guess like everyone else, I feel awful and have no patience."

"It's okay. Just give me a little more time. I was wrong—there is no record here of any of the work done a few years ago on producing monoclonal antibodies against the virus, and, well, we certainly don't have time for that kind of genetic engineering anyway. Maybe it will be some combination of our existing anti-virals. I'm still hopeful," Jonathan replied as Richard and Josh stared blankly at the famed microbiologist.

Michael again wondered why Jonathan was not on the list discovered in Babur's wallet. *Maybe there is a seventh assassin out there and Jonathan is his target.*

DAY THREE

TIME'S UP

CHAPTER 50

The alarm on Tariq's wristwatch beeped softly. It was 4 a.m.—time to move. He sat up, turned his battery-powered lantern back on and shook Henri by his shoulder. "My friend, it is time to go."

Henri groaned and struggled to move. "I feel so tired. My head hurts and—"

"No, you must help me. Get up," Tariq said, getting to his feet and pulling Henri up firmly by his arm. Once up, Tariq shook Henri by both shoulders and commanded: "Take this pill with this water.... Now follow me down. I have the weapons hidden at the second level." With lantern in hand, Tariq led the way down, stopping near the bottom. He opened a locked chest hidden behind a screen and pulled out six large zipped canvas bags—the four machine guns and the two explosives. "Put one on each shoulder and follow me." Tariq strapped the two explosive packs and two of the bags over each of his own shoulders and behind his back and then hoisted the remaining two machine gun bags over each of Henri's shoulders. Walking out into the pre-dawn darkness from the Tower building and east on the 16th Street Mall was haunting. The usually well-lit shopping area, even late at night after store closings, was completely dark and quiet. Their way was only navigable by the reflection of stars in the cool clear mountain air. Their loads were heavy and Henri moved ever so slowly.

When the two men reached Cleveland Place, it was only a half block south to the entrance to Civic Center Park. Tariq followed his plan exactly as he had described hours before. He had Henri set down his packages next to the park side of the McNichols Center, unload his own shoulder burdens, and unzip one of the bags. Setting the machine gun on its tripod, it was easy to point the barrel at the Capitol to the east because there it was—majestically symbolic to the Americans. By utilizing a giant battery-operated searchlight, the Americans were shining the light up to a huge American flag, waving gently in a modest breeze with the remaining light shining through and beyond to the massive Capitol dome beyond. Its golden top was glittering. Tariq set the timing mechanism on the trigger and the interval-firing mode. Then onto the same procedure at the grand statue of the cowboy, then at the Indian statue and lastly all the way south across the park to the inner park side of the Greek Amphitheatre. The four automatic firing machine guns were all set. It was 4:45 a.m.

"Now, Henri, listen closely. Give me exactly ten minutes to get in place on the south side of the Capitol where the entrance door to the basement is. Then pull this trigger. It is set for one minute. Go to the next and pull the trigger. It is set for forty five seconds. Then to the next and pull that trigger. It is set for thirty seconds. Go to the last and pull that trigger. It is set to fire in fifteen seconds. Then I want you to get out of here right away and move up 14th Street to Arapahoe Street. Go left and wait for me on the bridge over Cherry Creek…. Ready? Got it? Ten minutes."

Henri felt his muscles and joints aching more than ever, his head now splitting in pain, but in the shadowy light, he obediently found the strength to look up at this newly-arrived figure with the strong, confident voice, Tariq Badini, and admiringly mutter: "Yes sir. Got it. Ten minutes."

When the clatter of the four machine guns firing their bullets in Civic Center Park began to resonate through the smaller Lincoln Park and towards the steps up to the Capitol, the weary four soldiers who were sitting, but guarding the outside of the south basement entrance all snapped to attention and quickly scurried around to the west side of the building to see what the commotion was all about.

As I expected, Tariq smiled to himself. He was at the south door in a few seconds. He couldn't believe it was actually unlocked. He had thought he would have to bang on it to get the attention of the inside guards. Once inside it was completely dark and to his surprise, there were no guards visible. Turning on his flashlight, he quickly found the closet he had previously scouted out—the one containing the connection points to the Capitol's fiber optic communication system. This door was locked. He fired his pistol at the lock and he was inside within seconds. Removing one bomb satchel from his back and shoulder, he quickly set the timer to one minute and fled the scene as fast as he had come.

Around the east side, then hurrying north to the adjacent street Colfax, and then west towards the university to meet Henri. He moved on as though oblivious to the virus that was working its way deep into his lungs. He was running on adrenaline and his preparatory conditioning. He turned to look back and laughed out loud at this most amazing scene of sounds and sights as he made his way on West Colfax Avenue, walking past the northwest side of the Capitol and right alongside Lincoln Park and Civic Center Park. He had heard the muffled sound of the exploding bomb. *There goes the last of the American communications.* He heard the intermittent *bang, bang, bang, bang* of the four machineguns firing towards the Capitol. He heard the *clack, clack, clack* of the American soldiers firing their rifles back through the darkness, at what they did not know. What must be going through their minds, he mused. He could see the rapid flashes of light as the machine guns repeated their automatic commands. He could see the spot-lit Capitol dome, but the American flag was now unmoving, hanging down. Could the wind have stopped? *Not waving proudly at all now, is it?* he mused again.

But after turning right off Colfax and up Speer Boulevard, his mood changed during his near mile walk. He felt the abrupt hit of what seemed like a sudden onset of the flu. His brisk pace began to slow. Suddenly feeling weaker, a little tired, a headache coming on, slightly feverish, and now his nose was starting to bleed—a common symptom of the hemorrhagic Ebola virus—Tariq for the first time accepted the inevitable. He too would die soon. And poor Henri, a good man, he thought. There he was, he was also going to die an agonizing death, betrayed by his closest friend, his French countryman, Antoine.

But first, one more mission, the laboratory generators.

CHAPTER 51

Earlier—at 8 o'clock at night on the second day in Denver, it was 8 o'clock in the morning of the third day in Dire. Sleeping quite well after his pulsating, very satisfying sexual performance with his attractive young mistress the evening before, Aazim woke up with a happy smile, wonderful warm feelings all over, and a renewed lust for his lover. In his mind, he had convinced himself that abroad all must be going exactly according to plan despite the communications silence. In his heart, it was time for more pleasure. The early morning sun was shining softly against the half-closed curtains blowing gently in the breeze. The whole room seemed golden. Turning to her perfectly formed, unclothed body in his bed, he smiled fondly as he gazed longingly into her eyes: "Ah, you are even more beautiful in the morning light. Angel, I want you again—now."

Fifteen minutes later, rising to put on his shorts and tee shirt in the warm humid morning air of Dire, Aazim turned and whispered to her: "My angel, please, while I freshen up, put on your robe and go down to Antoine's room. He was so depressed last evening at dinner. I don't know whether he doesn't think our plans will work, or whether he is feeling … ah well, feeling remorse. I'm worried about him. Please darling, give him a big smile and tell him we shall enjoy a great breakfast together on the porch at nine." Without saying a word, the young beauty shook her head side to side with a slight smile and obediently put on her robe. She slowly meandered past a sitting room and kitchen and walked towards the other end of the seaside cottage where the other illustrious leader of the Dire nation resided. It was never clear to anyone whether this highly attractive, young, blond-haired, slightly golden-faced girl with the fair skin, maybe about 17 years old, was a convert to the cause or whether Aazim had simply recruited her from somewhere in northern Europe for his evening pleasure.

Strolling slowly down the next hallway, she stopped outside Antoine's closed door and knocked softly. Without a response in a few more moments, she knocked louder. Again with no response, she walked back to the sitting room and peered out the window towards the porch where the breakfast table was set. No Antoine. Back to his room, she knocked again. Maybe he had been in his bathroom. So, when there was no response again, she slowly tried the doorknob and casually pushed the unlocked door open.

Her loud screams echoed through the whole house. With her screeching seemingly continuous, Aazim stopped what he was doing and was there in a hurry. She stopped shrieking as she saw Aazim enter the room, her face turning in horror as she pointed. Aazim stood motionless as he stared in disbelief. Antoine's neck looked like it was broken sideways, his eyes open, his tongue out. With the sight of Antoine hanging on a rope from his bedroom's chandelier, a stool turned on its side on the floor below his bare feet, Aazim could not fathom why Antoine had decided to end it like this. He could only gaze in wonderment at his now gruesome-looking accomplice—the dear, brilliant friend who just could not reconcile their coming greatness with the bold plan calling for the termination of all Americans.

Maybe, perhaps, it was remorse for his betrayal of his very best friend, Henri Bonaparte.

CHAPTER 52

The world's religious and political balance changed dramatically after 2014. Similar to what the Christian Catholics and the Christian Protestants had accomplished 500 years earlier, the two main Muslim sects of the Sunnis and the Shiites had finally reconciled their 1400 year-old differences. By the year 2019, virtually all the Muslim nations had accepted the concept of sharia law—the infallible law of God as revealed to the prophet Muhammad—as political and economic law as well as personal religious law. The so-called "radical Islamists" had won the day over the moderate seculars, from Algeria to the West and Indonesia to the East—encompassing over a billion people. Only two exceptions to the victorious theologies remained. In the middle space, nuclear-armed Israel kept the Israelis and their Jewish religion intact while to the east, Hindu-dominated India also remained politically safe, protecting its democracy with its expanded nuclear force. Despite the Sunni/Shiite reconciliation, within the Islamic nations small rebellious forces yearning for individual freedom and democracy kept the state of affairs ripe with constant flare-ups of scattered violence. Never reconciled were the ongoing clashes between the followers of Christianity and the followers of Islam within the nations of Western Europe.

Such scenes of violence were also common further to the east and north with Russia continuing to expand its influence and territorial control as it attempted to rebuild its once dominant Soviet empire, repeatedly igniting ethnic clashes. It was all this continuing violence coincident with a growing number of nations armed with nuclear weapon capabilities that had motivated Aazim and Antoine to press on with their Master Plan.

In terms of historical significance, the story in China was very different. By 2019, political democracy, evolved through economic gains enjoyed by hundreds of millions of Chinese through free-market capitalism, became the victor over communism. Without the need to pay attention to its former rival, America—for years preoccupied with its climate crisis—China's primary military concern was keeping the radical Islamists from expanding up from Indonesia and into East Asia. One part of that endeavor was keeping an eye on the little island of Dire. Regular reconnaissance flights over the island revealed nothing suspicious, but word had leaked to Chinese intelligence that the inhabitants of Dire might be planning some type of warfare using weapons of mass destruction. To help ensure security for the Chinese people, the modern Chinese nuclear submarine, the Doo Sheng—short for 'victory'—was fully equipped with a full complement of nuclear tipped missiles and ordered to keep watch in the waters surrounding Dire.

China had never been a leader in submarine development. The nation went right to the 3rd and 4th generations starting in 1987 and to the latest by 2010. Going back to the time of World War II, it was Germany, Japan and the United States that had developed and produced vast numbers of diesel-electric submarines. Those subs were considered fast at a 10-knot speed submerged and a 20 knot speed surfaced, but they had to surface at night to use air to recharge their batteries. The first generation of nuclear subs developed by Russia and the U.S. were even faster submerged, could stay underwater for months, and had a 25-year life. The versatile nuclear plant on the sub made steam or electricity to drive the sub's propeller shaft, and also to purify the inside air, to distill seawater, and to provide power for all the sub's systems. Their only disadvantages were that the nuclear sub had to cool its reactor when not moving; the coolant pumps could be heard by sonar; and, the sub left a warm plume behind that could be detected by thermal imaging from above. Over the years, most accidents involving these nuclear submarines occurred due to leaks of this all-important reactor coolant.

In the early 21st century, China committed to building the most advanced and modern subs. By 2020, it had six of the latest nuclear submarines in the water, the Type 094 Jin-Class Ballistic Missile JL-2. Its submerged speed was 20 knots; structured with 6 torpedo tubes; it also contained 12 to 16 nuclear tipped ballistic missiles with a firing range of nearly 5000 miles; and was well more than a football field long at 133 meters. The Doo Sheng was one of these most modern of under-the-sea vessels.

The submarine routinely monitored the island of Dire from below depth observing the nature of all incoming and outgoing vessels while submerged and reporting information back to its home naval base near Hainan in southern China. It had arrived off the coast of Dire in the Indian Ocean as far back as 2017 and rotated back to Hainan once a year briefly for routine maintenance and food restocking before heading back to Dire. Its course took it into the South China Sea past the coastline of Vietnam, Malaysia, and Singapore; then thru the straits of the Java Sea of Indonesia into the Indian Ocean. Dire was some 200 miles off the coast of Sri Lanka at the southern tip of India, with the Bay of Bengal just to the northeast and the Arabian Sea just to the northwest. The sub's military mission was a nuclear missile launch against the entire island in the event a WMD attack ever took place against main land China.

The military thought it a very remote possibility, but just in case….

———∿∿∿———

On September 11, 2021 the captain of the Doo Sheng could not stop pacing back and forth past his radio operator, becoming increasingly more irritated that secure communications via satellite with headquarters in Hainan remained down for so long. Hours passed without a word. Captain Zhang An became even more upset when almost three days later his communications specialists still could not solve the problem. He was torn as to whether to return the sub to base to correct a possible technical defect on his vessel or whether because some catastrophe may have occurred to remain armed and in place. He struggled to keep his cursing under his breath.

Zhang is a very common family name in China. His parents gave him the given name of An, meaning 'peace'. He was proud to serve the cause of peace by protecting his homeland, but now he was growing increasingly confused. His mission order to come through the sub's radio, which was now frustratingly inoperative, would be a very simple command—*hui mie*, interpreted in English as "destroy". Captain Zhang dearly hoped that message would never come through on the sub's radio, which until now had been monitored night and day. He knew he was trained for warfare, but he preferred the hopeful thought that China's known military strength would always deter any potential attackers. Personally a devoted man of peace, he now knew that something must be drastically wrong.

And wrong it was. Little could Zhang An suspect that back in the Chinese capital of Beijing, the populace was already beginning to feel the effects of the spreading Anthrax bacteria. The pandemic was on, and the genetically-enhanced version of the bacterium could not be killed by known antibiotics. At the same time, all communications and electric power were at a standstill throughout China, shut down by the four non-nuclear electromagnetic pulse bombs that had been set off high above several scattered provinces. The Dirists in Beijing had been negotiating with the elected Chinese president for nearly three days. The Chinese leadership accepted the power failure around Beijing, as they could experience it, but they were very skeptical of the demands to dismantle their major arms and turn military base control over to the thousand Dirists already in the nation.

But by the third day, the Chinese president was receiving a massive number of messenger-delivered reports of a vast sickness spreading among the population; that physicians had isolated and identified the deadly bacteria, yet in their laboratories, no antibiotics had any impact on slowing the germ's growth and replication. The thought finally occurred to him that this must be the Master Plan behind the intercepted messages they overheard in Dire the last few years. Chinese intelligence had also heard of stolen weapons, rockets and launchers, including an atomic bomb missing from Pakistan, but their military intelligence could never put the full story together. Perhaps the Dirists could be stalled and fooled into releasing the contents of their so-called "antidote" while at the same time a message could somehow be delivered to the Doo Sheng to order it to attack and destroy the island of Dire with the submarine's nuclear missiles.

The former Communist Party president, Xi Jinping, who had by 2018 voluntarily transformed his nation into a multi-party democracy and was currently the country's duly elected popular leader, now faced the most difficult decision of his life—give in or fight.

CHAPTER 53

Ali could not sleep more than an hour at a time. Her joints and muscles ached, her headache throbbed, and she was beginning to feel more nauseous. She had been convinced by General Armstrong to stay put in her apartment. Early in the morning of the third day, she thought she heard a commotion nearby, like repeating gunshots. The rapid firing of the four machine guns taking place at Civic Center Park was only four short blocks due north of her Beauvallon apartment. Struggling out of bed, she moved slowly into her office containing the secure optic fiber phone line. She punched the code number for General Armstrong's office at the Capitol. Hearing nothing, she entered the code for General Ralston's phone in Washington. She wondered why the line was dead as she put down the phone. Back in her bedroom, she tried her satellite mobile phone on her night table. Nothing. Her thoughts went blank as she lay back down in her bed exhausted, sick.

———✖✖✖———

Reclining in his leather desk chair with his feet propped up on another chair, General Armstrong awoke startled by the repetitive sounds of gunfire outside his office on the west side of the Capitol building. He wanted to jump up but his body would not respond to his military instinct. He rolled to the floor feeling sick in his stomach just as several bullets shattered the glass window above him. He looked at his illuminated wristwatch—it was 5 a.m. His military training commanded him to act—the virus commanded him to lie still.

Dr. Durham mustered all the strength in his aching muscles that he could manage in order to slowly walk through the aisles and aisles of cots aligned on the massive floor of the Convention Center Exhibit Hall. The wailing and moaning of the day and night before had subsided. It was now the strong odor emanating from the sickest that was most oppressive. The next stages of the Ebola virus—vomiting, diarrhea and bleeding—were taking command. It was now horrific inside this large hall. These people are now so weak, he thought to himself, that all they want to do is to lie still, be quiet, and sleep—if they can. His mind flashed back to all the science fiction movies he had seen—panic in the streets with people running from alien attackers, buildings being destroyed, action and noise. This was different. The attackers were winning in silence. Sitting himself down at the foot of a cot holding a small child, he tried to recall his medical teachings of people suffering—from disease pandemics, from starvation in refugee camps or in prison camps—remembering that while many died some always survived. He put his hands together, and closing his eyes, he prayed.

CHAPTER 54

Michael's wristwatch alarm again awakened him. At first startled by the sound on his wrist, he finally glanced at it—it was 5:30 in the morning. The lights in the laboratory were still shining brightly. Despite suffering from his growing weakness and difficulty in breathing, Michael maintained his periodic ten to fifteen- minute mini naps. *Don't give up—there must be a way ... no, you're just giving yourself a pep talk. We're done. We're into the third day.* Confused in his waking thoughts, he stood up slowly from his reclining position against a lab bench and glanced around the room. Both Fila and Richard were stretched completely out on the floor—awake but obviously severely ill judging from hearing their weak groans. He noticed Richard holding a handkerchief to his nose. It was red from bleeding. He thought how bad it's going to get when the latter stage viral symptoms of vomiting and diarrhea begin.

At Michael's last pleading, Jonathan had gone back into the inner lab trying to come up with something humans could ingest that would fight the virus without being poisonous to them. Only an hour before, he had revealed to Michael that he knew Formalin had been used to kill the Ebola virus when skin tissue was sent from an African corpse to a lab for positive identification. But, like so many other disinfectants, such harsh chemicals are highly poisonous and if humans were to ingest them, it would only make their suffering worse and death inevitable.

"Poison the virus without poisoning us. Can't you swallow the Formalin and add something simple to ward off the poisonous effect?" Michael had asked him innocently, pleadingly.

"Not that simple," Jonathan had replied quietly. "In effect the antivirals do poison the virus without poisoning us. That's what they have been tested for in FDA trials. But I have more in there. There are dozens. Most antivirals inhibit growth of the virus. I have some viricides that destroy a particular virus, and I have tried them already. I tried the standard drugs for flu like oseltamivir and zanamivir, but of course they didn't work. I used a bunch of antivirals like amantadine and rimantadine, and then enzyme deactivators like acyclovir and zidovudine, some blocking antisense molecules like formivirsen and morpholino. So far, nothing ... I'll keep going. The other thought is finding something to spark an immediate immune response in the human body, but how in the world would we find it and test it. I don't know ... I'll keep trying Michael." But churning in Michael's increasingly blurred mind was this incomprehensible conversation with Jonathan as the microbiologist retreated into his inner lab. Their conversation had left little hope for a timely solution. In Michael's mind, it just seemed so easy to simply collapse when feeling this bad and so, so hard to keep going.

But, strange, Michael thought as he managed to turn his attention to Rose, who was wide awake while sitting on the floor, a slight smile on her face. She seemed weak but alert and calm, holding Alex on her lap, staring into his face. The ill effects were slower in affecting her. A mother's fortitude he thought. Somehow, remarkably, the child seemed to be dozing on and off peacefully, and when awake, he smiled back at his mother.

Michael's mind somehow became more lucid as he turned his attention back to the dying words of the young man, Babur, who tried to kill him two days ago— "You will die of misery in three days." It's now the beginning of the third day, Michael thought, as he sat down on a high chair against a lab bench, his whole body feeling weaker and achier, his headache now worsening. *What's next?* He recalled the hundreds at the Convention Center the evening before who progressed from experiencing total body aches to vomiting, diarrhea and bleeding, and some to dying. He remembered hearing the defeatism in Dr. Durham's voice. What *he* must be enduring right now.

He checked his pocket—four pills left that the doctor had given him. They had given him some strength the night before. He could take one himself, one for Rose, one for Richard, who was now really suffering the worst, and one for Jonathan. Jonathan has to find something soon. Jonathan Dean is a genius, Michael figured.

During those years when I was at Montecito University near Santa Barbara studying chemical engineering, Jonathan Dean had built a marvelous reputation at Cal-Berkeley developing anti-viral agents and vaccines against a host of flu diseases. Again he thought—why wasn't *he* on the assassin list? He is our most important asset. Must be because he was on sabbatical and not here this past year, and they missed him on their targeted list. I think he had gone abroad somewhere to do research. Or is there a seventh assassin out there? Michael's self-ramblings stopped as he turned towards Rose.

Before he spoke to her, he reviewed in his mind what she, Richard, and Jonathan had already accomplished. In the outer lab using an electron microscope, Rose had identified that a living organism was attached to the black dust that she had accumulated from his arms and face early that first morning. Its optical lenses beamed electrons to illuminate and magnify its target 10 million-times. In the inner containment lab, Richard and Jonathan had set up tests to analyze the organism's identity using human cells stored in freezers. Using an advanced centrifuge the assays showed a rapidly growing virus producing abnormal cell changes, definitely pathogenic. Confirming Fila's statement, they identified the virus as a genetically modified Ebola virus with antigens, or markers, that would not bind with human antibodies to destroy it as all other virus' do. They also investigated

Fila's blood sample and could find no weakened strain of the virus or any kind of specific antibody that could act as a vaccine. Nor did her blood contain any kind of a recognizable anti-viral agent. Michael's mind was now back on track.

"Rose, we need help," he said pleadingly. "Richard looks exhausted. *You* know the most chemistry, and some microbiology. Jonathan and Josh need help.... Try, try to stand up. You look stronger than any of us. I have some strong meds Doctor Durham gave me yesterday. It's temporary ... but take this one and give one to Jonathan. We have to find an anti-viral ... fast! I'll watch Alex." Rising to her feet slowly, Rose stared back at Michael sitting on the edge of the lab stool. She had never seen him like this before, his summer tan gone, his face pale, his look an hour before one of complete despair, but now his eyes were begging her to move, to act.

Michael had been aware of a man named Henri somewhere outside and his role through Fila's disclosure, the one who had run away with a pistol in his hand. But he was unaware that the attackers also had the ultimate failsafe weapon named Tariq Badini nearby. He suspected there could be more invaders involved than the list discovered in Babur's wallet, as perhaps someone assigned to kill Jonathan Dean, and he had warned General Armstrong there could be an attempt made on the lab's power. Looking up at the bright ceiling lights, Michael trusted the battery-powered generator station outside was now well protected.

Michael never thought the bridge where Babur had met his fate was now in play again.

CHAPTER 55

It was near dawn when Tariq arrived onto the Arapahoe Street bridge crossing over Cherry Creek. He could barely make out the solitary figure seated on the ground leaning against the guard wall. Looking closer, it was Henri, as planned. "Perfect," said Tariq. "Thank you, my friend. It could not have gone better. The show at the Capitol was spectacular, if not also amusing. Their communications are finished … now *we* finish." The light from the stars was not very bright. Tariq could barely see Henri's face, but he could detect blood glistening as it trickled from Henri's nose and ears. As he drew very close, he heard mumblings softly coming from this obviously very sick man.

"You go, Tariq—finish the job yourself…. This is where Babur died … right here. And my friend Antoine—yes, he is sitting in the sun on the beach now, joyous … ah, my best friend, my dearest friend Antoine." Turning his head in closer to listen to Henri's barely audible words, putting one hand behind Henri's neck to support the stricken man, Tariq did not notice in time that Henri had pulled his pistol from his jacket pocket. Suddenly, the barrel was deep into Henri's mouth.

The gun fired, the sound muffled. Tariq felt warm blood splash against his hand and neck. He jumped back, startled, as the dark blood poured out of both the front and back of Henri's head.

—⌇⌇—

Recovering his composure while contemplating and understanding Henri's plight, Tariq knew his final destination was only yards away from that bridge where Henri had just ended his misery. Tariq was now just a short distance from the rear of the Advanced Microbiology Laboratory where the emergency generators were located. But first he had to sit down on the hard pavement next to Henri's still body, now lifeless leaning over next to him, and determine his final strategy. The assassins had won the day against the president and speaker but failed in their mission to shut down the science laboratory. This poor friend of Antoine's had tried his best to help the mission. Now he too was gone. This is just what Aazim had been afraid of—this is exactly why Tariq volunteered to be the last resort—his suicidal mission to be sure the Americans couldn't solve the riddle of the deadly Ebola virus. *Now … it's up to me.*

It was still quite dark as the coming dawn approached, except for the bright glow of lights coming out through the windows of the Advanced Science Building. He knew their power source came from the lithium ion storage batteries outside, and that their size was designed to only generate full emergency power for three days, two of which were already gone. He must cut off the start of the third day. He wondered why the large solar and wind powered electric utility station near the campus was not supplemented by additional solar panels on the roofs of these buildings. They would keep the batteries recharged much more effectively than those very small wind turbines up there. Must be American arrogance that no power failure would ever exceed three days, he mused.

Leaving the bridge, approaching closer to the rear of the building, he immediately recognized what was happening. The illumination from several large lanterns along the ground revealed four or five soldiers dragging various heavy objects toward the generators, adding to the four to five foot barrier wall already built around them. *Yes, they're on to something. They are protecting the lab inside.* Tariq was beginning to feel weaker and sicker himself, especially after his experience with Henri, but knew this was his final act in the mission for which he had come to die. He now felt a keen sense of accomplishment overtaking his mind and body, brushing aside his growing illness. *This deed is not just for God, for Jehovah, for Allah*—this is for *world peace.* He wanted to repeat these two words to himself so strongly that he nearly shouted them out loud.

Pulling the last bag off his back and around his shoulder, he opened it, set the dynamite timer to 30 seconds, and reclosed the bag. Ten sticks of TNT bound together, tri-nitro-toluene—the four simple elements of carbon, nitrogen, oxygen and hydrogen—molecules so tightly and complexly bound that when suddenly decomposed by a detonator, the compound's chemical reaction releases tremendous explosive energy. Tariq saw the soldiers distracted by their tasks of adding to the barrier wall. *Perfect!* He saw a narrow opening in the wall and with all the strength he could muster in his weakening legs, he ran as fast as he could through the opening and into the generators, squeezing the backpack tightly against his chest, the timer with five seconds remaining.

The *boom* was loud and clear; the building shook violently for two or three seconds. The lab inside went dark. Rose, not yet into the inner lab to help Jonathan, screamed. Alex cried for a couple of brief seconds. Initially startled from the shaking and the noise, Michael knew almost immediately exactly what had happened. *Their fear—an anti-viral from our lab—knock the power out to shut down our research.* Just what he warned General Armstrong about, he thought quickly to himself. Michael remembered where a large battery-operated lantern was on top of the lab bench next to him and quickly groped in the dark to find and light it. Jonathan appeared through the door of the inner lab holding a second bright lantern in his hand. "What the hell just—"

"As we thought," said Michael. "Beyond Fila's friends, there are more of them out there, like that Henri Bonaparte. They want our lab power off.... Jonathan, anything, have you found anything?"

"No, no ... I'm sorry. Nothing will stop it. I've used everything we have in there," Jonathan replied in a firm, deep tone.

By the close light of the lantern that Jonathan was holding up, Michael could clearly see Jonathan's face. His look, too, like Alex's, seemed "peculiar", Michael thought to himself. He seemed to be moving easily and standing perfectly erect, his voice strong. Both men placed their lanterns atop lab benches, illuminating the entire room. With knowledge that the lab was now shut down, that there was no anti-viral solution yet found, that his body was telling him to lie down in his sickness and quit, Michael somehow called on his inner strength, blurting out almost unthinkingly:

"You ... you Jonathan ... and Alex," Michael asserted. "Look at Richard ... and Rose and Fila ... and I'm getting worse ... maybe ... am I seeing illusions? You two are looking okay ... you're not sick!"

"Michael," responded Jonathan calmly. "This virus attacks abruptly and then moves swiftly, but that is a generalization. We are all going to feel it hit at slightly different times and devastate us at different rates and—"

"No, no," Michael countered. "I have been with Dr. Durham twice, I have been to the Capitol, to Ali's ... everyone might feel its effects at different rates but everyone has it to some degree.... Rose! What do you feel? Stand Alex up." Michael was now frantic, or delusional, feeling himself wobbling.

"Michael. Sit down on the stool," Rose demanded of him as he struggled to get to his feet. "I *do* feel achy, sick," but she followed Michael's lead. She reached down and grabbed Alex under his two arms lifting him up. He smiled, giggled, and walked aggressively forward towards Michael holding his mother's hands.

Michael stood up straight and took Alex's stretched out hands. "Rose! For Alex—what have you done since we got here to the lab," Michael now demanded of her. "What has he eaten, and had to drink, or put on his skin?"

"Same snack bars and water like we've all had … except …yes, I have been putting these 'Immunity' lozenges into his water since we got here. I packed them in his diaper bag when we left the apartment. They are just mostly one thousand milligrams of Vitamin C, a couple a day for him, but—"

"Vitamin C!" Michael nearly screamed, finding the strength to raise Alex into his arms. "Ever so simple. Could it be? Like we learned about scurvy when sailors would die crossing the ocean … until they learned to eat limes for Vitamin C…. Linus Pauling. I remember my uncle heard him speak at a chemistry lecture at Stanford back in the 80's. He said almost all mammals synthesize Vitamin C except for humans who lost that ability many thousands of years ago. As he aged Pauling took eighteen thousand milligrams a day himself for his immune system and for his health, but he thought for the average person two thousand milligrams a day was optimal. It's too simple, but maybe it stimulates our immune system to attack this virus. Maybe this is not such a virulent virus after all. It just has the uncanny ability to shut down our immune system somehow, and Vitamin C restores it…. Jonathan, do you think that—"

Suddenly, Michael's mobile satellite phone in his shirt pocket hummed. He had kept its battery charged using the lab's power. To his immense surprise the phone had just come back on. Events were unfolding so fast Michael's inner shot of adrenaline revived him. He put down Alex and retrieved the phone from his pocket, unlocking it. The power bar was weak from some battery loss, but the phone was on. "Power!" Michael exclaimed. "The earth's electromagnetic field must be back to normal. We are getting radio waves from the satellites…. Jonathan, Rose, I'll call Ali and General Armstrong to get the word out—a couple thousand milligrams of Vitamin C—"

"Put the phone down, Michael!" Jonathan's strong voice came booming across the lab benches as he walked closer to Michael, who turned towards him in astonishment. Jonathan raised a pistol in his hand and was pointing it squarely at Michael's chest. "One chance in a billion you said, huh Rose, and by pure luck you found it. This boy

Alex. Yes, so simple—good old cheap ubiquitous Vitamin C. I take three thousand milligrams a day—more than enough. But that secret stays here."

"Jonathan, have you gone completely mad? What are you doing with that gun?" Richard Frost uttered weakly from the floor as he forced himself up to a sitting position.

"Ah, poor Richard.... Do you not remember last year I took a six month sabbatical? And the year before? Where do you think I went? Did you not know the brightest microbiologists in the world are on this little island of Dire off the coast of India? That's where our dear Fila is from, this poor girl who thinks she has been vaccinated. They are so very smart there, but not as smart as I am. I knew of their leaders' plot to destroy the people of the United States with a biological weapon of mass destruction. They never again want to see America make war, just as Fila here told us.... At first they were trying to make the deadly bird-flu viruses found in China, the H7N9 and the H5N1 strains, to be transmissible from human to human, but they failed. They then turned to the deadly but hard to spread Ebola virus. It was I who helped them, and after we brilliantly genetically modified the Ebola virus to spread through the air, we made it even more virulent, more deadly, to be easily absorbed through nasal passages and then to the lungs, raising the projected human fatality rate from seventy to ninety percent to one hundred percent, and in just three days after exposure.... Ah, then they tried but never could find a vaccine or an antiviral for it. I knew the answer was so simple, but they never looked to the obvious. I was the only one with the answer, but I didn't tell *them*. They believed I was in tune with their plot.... So my job? My assignment? To return here to this lab and be back up assurance that you did not somehow find the antidote that they themselves couldn't find. To be backup for their doomed assassins who were misled into thinking they had been given a vaccine. There is no vaccine. They foolishly believed I would go on a suicide mission for their cause. And whichever one of them bombed our generator outside is also doomed. Ha! How ignorant were they not knowing that now *I* shall be the sole survivor, and I will rebuild America my way—"

"You are mad, Jonathan," Richard repeated. "Your scheme, their scheme—all of you, it's crazy."

"Richard, you are a famed biochemist. Don't underestimate the power of scientists not only to do a great deal of good for the world, but also to do a great deal of evil, but one man's craziness may be another man's salvation…. Richard, I do have compassion. You are dying an agonizing death. It is better we end it quickly, like I did to Josh a few minutes ago in there." With that he turned the pistol away from Michael's chest, pointed it towards Richard's head and squeezed the trigger. *Crack!*—a direct hit into the middle of Richard's forehead, who fell back instantly onto the floor without a sound other than the *thump* as the back of his head hit the tile floor. Michael and Rose looked on in astonishment.

"And now you, my dear beautiful Fila. You and your Asa friend failed in your missions, you know, and you too are dying from this wonderful virus. They deceived you into thinking you were immune with their phony vaccine. I shall extend mercy to you and end your misery as well."

Fila struggled from her reclining position to up on her knees, squarely facing Jonathan, now *her* assailant. "I remember you now. Your look is different, but your voice … at Aazim's … he so admired you and—"

"Yes, my dear," Jonathan acknowledged. "Aazim, yes, and he admired you too—your beauty, your strength, and I know he would never had sent you had you not fallen for Asa. Just think, right now you could be back in Dire living the high life with your friend Aazim. You could—"

"No, that's not my take, you scum. You were arrogant then, like now," Fila replied as she valiantly attempted to raise herself and move towards Jonathan. The look of fear was gone from her expression.

With his attention on Fila's act of fortitude as she rose from the lab floor, Jonathan failed to detect Rose reaching into her vest pocket for

Fila's loaded pistol—the one Michael made her carry while he was gone from the lab. But Michael could sense that Rose, who was standing right next to Fila, was having a difficult time getting the pistol out and suddenly feared Jonathan would notice. Michael knowing he had to quickly distract Jonathan's attention away from the two women, raised his voice. "Jonathan Dean! Think again what you are doing. You have the chance to save America. There is no way you can rule it. Think, man!"

As Jonathan smiled sardonically, turning his head and eyes towards Michael, Fila grabbed the pistol from the struggling Rose. It all happened so fast. Before Jonathan could recover, Fila pointed the pistol at Jonathan and fired one, two, three, four shots at him, *bang, bang, bang, bang*, one bullet tearing directly through his arm, into his ribs, and into the middle of his heart. He fell in a heap. Michael stared dumbfounded at Jonathan lying on the floor motionless and then at Rose, who looked back at him—the two of them eyes wide open in astonishment, crying out to themselves *incredible!* They were both trying to mentally process these strange events, the attack, the growing agony—all they had witnessed over the last two days suddenly combined with this turn in fortune in just the last few minutes.

Fila dropped her pistol to the floor, grabbed the top of the lab bench for support, and began to weep. "Fila, are you okay?" Rose asked.

"Yes, yes, thank you dear Rose," Fila replied.

Rose, with her eyes gently pleading, said calmly to Michael: "Call, call her. Don't explain now—just tell her Vitamin C. Hurry!"

Michael opened his mobile phone to 'Favorites' and tapped Ali's number. The President of the United States answered as Michael was almost deliriously repeating "hello, hello ..."

"Michael! I can hear you," replied her voice anxiously ... hopefully. "Do you have news?"

EPILOGUE

At the same time as the sudden turn of events were unfolding in Denver, Zhang An, the dutiful captain of the Doo Sheng, the nuclear-fueled, nuclear missile-loaded pride of the Chinese navy, on September 13, 2021 gave the order to surface his submarine. He did so even though the sub was only twenty miles off the coast of Dire and could be easily spotted from shore. Zhang's growing frustration with lack of radio communications was eating at him. Despite protocols, he knew he had a better chance at satellite radio communications on the surface than below. But again, no signals, and as he was about to order his vessel to submerge, the fateful radio message suddenly came through. The solar-powered satellites' radio connections must not have been damaged. The earth's electromagnetic field had just restored itself to normal. He could clearly hear the call from Beijing.

"Hui mie! Hui mie!" In English: "Destroy! Destroy!"

Zhang had been extensively trained for this procedure. The words were precisely his order to fire his missiles. Beyond the simple surveillance of Dire, this was his ultimate mission if so commanded. But firing nuclear weapons, killing civilians, was not an easy command to follow, especially for a highly moral man who had never before witnessed the horrors of war. *It must be for the greater good.* He gave the order to submerge his vessel; he gave the order to place it in position pointing towards Dire; he gave the order to line up firing coordinates striking Dire on the left, in the middle, on the right, destroying all who were there. He then gave the order: *"Fire one, fire two, fire three."*

———ᴍ———

Satellite communications were restored on that third day as the earth's electromagnetic field settled down. Luckily most satellites were not physically damaged. Satellite-based mobile phones were back in common use. But ground communications took many weeks to restore. Most dreadfully, it took many months for most public utilities to repair transformers and return electrical currents anywhere close to normal power. During that period the American economy was in shambles, and the distribution of adequate food and water was a nightmare.

———ᴍ———

Within a week of that fateful day on September 11, 2021, some 20 million Americans died of the virus—mostly those who did not get the word in time or did not have timely access to the very abundant antidote no longer synthesized in our human bodies—the ubiquitous, simple Vitamin C. Out of a total population of 320 million Americans, that 6% fatality rate would have been much higher without the heroics of Michael Reynolds. American pharmaceutical companies never had the power or time to develop and distribute the experimental drugs that had been earlier designed but never extensively produced for fighting the Ebola virus. Fortunately, some 90 million Americans were never infected because they were out of reach of the "black dust". Also fortunately, the virus died out in its American isolation and never spread around the world.

In 1918, another viral attack, an influenza pandemic, killed 50 million people worldwide out of a world-wide population of 2 billion, or a 2.5% fatality rate, with another 200 million severe cases reported, 10% of the world's population. In America, with a population then of 105 million, 675,000 people died, or less than 1%, but the scene was devastating as cities virtually shut down, and many of the dead had to be buried in mass graves. The virus struck abruptly, causing panic. And it was gone completely in just seven weeks. It was later believed an influenza virus had mutated to an abnormal state of virulence for some unknown reason before settling back to its average state. In contrast to the Ebola virus, which does not provoke an immune response and kills its victims through massive viral cell replication, the 1918 virus attacked very quickly going deep into the lungs causing such a sudden, massive immune response that after a wide array of painful symptoms the resulting concentration of inflammation robbed the victims' lungs of oxygen. The infected literally killed themselves.

Alexis Graham exhibited great leadership through the national nightmare following September 11. She moved to Washington in early 2022 and became one of the most balanced, productive American presidents in history. She was a leader of *all* the people and united them through the most difficult of times. She served two terms—to 2030.

Michael Reynolds led the memorial service for Richard Frost and then was elected the new president of the National University. Despite suffering occasional inner doubts about his own capabilities and worries about his nation's future, manifested in periodic nightmares, he remained on balance the eternal optimist. Stable, competent Rose Haines was appointed to Dean of Advanced Scientific and Environmental Studies at the university. Their son Alex was forever given a daily dose of 2000 mg of Vitamin C and became a poster child for all of America to see.

There was no word on how other nations dealt with the worldwide Anthrax pandemic … or with the Dirists on their soil.

Fila was given an abundant supply of Vitamin C by Rose, regained her strength, and somehow mysteriously escaped to a remote area high in the Rocky Mountains. It was reported that she had been very resourceful in escaping capture and avoiding standing trial for the wounding of a U.S. Marine. Her beauty and her story became legendary in the early 2020's.

—⟨⟨⟨—

Ten years before this three-day event transpired, television news accounts carried stories of warnings about how indefensible the United States was against an attack by an EMP bomb. It finally happened on September 11, 2021. The worry continued about another attack on through the 2020's.

—⟨⟨⟨—

By whichever means or methods a deliberate viral or bacterial attack on citizens of the world could possibly occur, the threat of ongoing bioterrorism attacks on a massive scale continued to exist after the 2021 attack. The weapons are cheap and easy to produce and use. Just as the United States government effectively operated the sophisticated Center for Disease Control and Prevention, the CDC, to protect the American public from *natural* epidemics and pandemics, it remained imperative for the United States people to *be on guard* against *man-made* biological threats as well.

Congress eventually passed laws and a special tax to harden the American electrical grid to withstand shocks from an electromagnetic pulse bomb. Protection of satellite communications systems remained an enigma.

—⟨⟨⟨—

From the world of fiction to the world of reality, it is doubtful a simple antioxidant, immune system enhancer like ascorbic acid, Vitamin C, which in small quantities is essential to human life, could possibly combat the powerful Ebola virus. The enemy virus appears to be best combatted through advanced genetic engineering technology, such as targeted monoclonal antibodies—very difficult and very expensive. If the virus ever mutates to become airborne, if the fiction you have just read ever comes to pass, to survive a pandemic America must advance the science now.

AUTHOR'S NOTE

In my 2010 epic novel, *A Truthful Myth (ATM)*, I fantasized about an abrupt and catastrophic global warming event that decimated America. I also touched upon a wide range of other contentious issues pertinent to our times. The ATM story took place over a sixteen year period—from Hurricane Katrina in 2005 to the near return of normal by the year 2021. The main point I was striving to make, and still do in my public appearances and correspondence, is that **"science is never done"**, especially in the complex, constantly-evolving field of climate science. My other points, in the fields of sociology, economics and politics, centered around the need to better understand human nature and to strike an optimum **balance** in each field in order to achieve long term societal success.

In writing ATM, I certainly exaggerated to a great extent. Nevertheless, from my background research I found that the basic climate premises which I presented were sound—yes, **highly improbable, but possible.** I produced what climate scientists call an "abrupt warming" of America in 2010 due to a sudden melting of the huge organically-rich Arctic permafrost, rapidly releasing vast amounts of the powerful greenhouse gases methane and carbon dioxide to the atmosphere. As a result, enormous physical catastrophes despoiled the United States—widespread flooding along all our coastal cities, massive fires and droughts in the southwest, severe hurricanes and tornados everywhere else. The U.S. president and his advisors drew up a Master Plan in 2011 to move mostly all of our 300 million Americans to eastern Colorado—the only place of a benevolent climate left in the country. Overriding *fear* was the great motivating force for such drastic action. The Plan was approved by Congress in 2012 by means of the president's "Declaration of National Emergency". All powers of Congress, the Supreme Court, and the 50 governors were suspended. The move was completed by early 2016.

Meanwhile, two young chemical engineers meeting in 2011 had fallen in love at first sight, my protagonists Michael Reynolds, and Rose Haines. Michael had invented a more efficient system for desalinating Pacific Ocean waters and had brilliantly accomplished that feat using his own novel methods for more economically generating wind and solar power. He saved the day by successfully scaling up these processes and delivering essential water to eastern Colorado. Rose, an expert in climate change, later discovered the unique solar reasons behind the abrupt warming, then discerned and predicted its reversal in 2018. The National Emergency was cancelled that year and a Plan of Return initiated.

The mentally exhausted president, Paul Jennings, the benevolent Vice President Alexis Graham, and the again functioning Congress remained in downtown Denver until all Americans would securely return home.

All the while this saga progressed, my minor antagonists, Antoine, a French arms dealer/banker, and Aazim, a former Iranian Director of Foreign Intelligence, were scheming since meeting in 2008 to formulate and execute a fanatical plot to end the world's ongoing violence **once and for all**. Thus, in this sequel to ATM that begins on September 11, 2021, Michael is again the main protagonist while Antoine, Aazim, and their key henchmen become the main antagonists, especially the ambivalent Afghan beauty, Fila. The action now takes place in just three days at just two locations—the first at the small Indian Ocean island of Dire and the second within one square mile of downtown Denver, Colorado.

The third major threat against America in this trilogy will take place in the early 2030's. Michael Reynolds and Fila will be there.